# SMELLS LIKE DEATH

# STEVENSON MUKORO

# SMELLS LIKE DEATH

## ANOTHER SUSAN DAX ADVENTURE

ISBN 978-1-956001-75-4 (paperback)
ISBN 978-1-956001-76-1 (eBook)



Printed in the United States of America

# ALSO, BY STEVENSON MUKORO

## GUNS, DEATH and MR. KRAKAUER

In their latest adventure Susan Dax and Seymour Krakauer tangle with an old foe thought dead and a new one. Seymour Krakauer discovers when he saves a woman and her daughter on Baffin Island from hired killers that he has opened up a can of worms held by an old enemy.

Seymour Krakauer's undertaking plunges him into a slew of uncanny events drawing both him and Susan Dax into the inexplicable fluxes of political intrigue and corporate espionage. Seymour Krakauer must unravel the mystery of why the rescued damsel and her daughter is a target. What secret do they hold that is worth dying over?

Finding an uncanny gift, Susan Dax faces her foes in a terrifying death chase while Seymour Krakauer launches a deathly attack against an enemy he cannot defeat. The struggle against seemingly impossible odds is fought out to a desperate finale.

### The Doomsday Organism
Is a lethal organism that destroys petroleum at a molecular level in the most unusual manner.

### The Doomsday Organism
Becomes a paralysing threat to the world's oil producing nations in the hands of a grieving genius who developed it for America's germ warfare division.

### The Doomsday Organism
Leads Susan Dax to an international chase on the heels of an elite terrorist organisation whose sole purpose is see the west fall. A group she must seek and destroy before the release of the bacterium.

# SILENCING THE THUNDER

Susan Dax is coerced by the American Intelligence into not only aiding an unethical shady friend, who has been captured and imprisoned but also to look into the theft of an undisclosed weapon.

The developing plot takes her from the easy confines of Washington D.C. to Yemen, across the Middle East and the Mediterranean. Ending with her being double-crossed, captured and at the mercy of an extremist intent on poisoning and delving a crippling blow to the American public.

# COLD HEAT

Take six gruesome murders, one the former tutor to the wealthiest woman on the planet. Add a missing truck with a valuable secret. Stir in the activities of a mysterious crime lord who has made a fortune in various illegal endeavours and runs his operations with secrecy and ruthlessness. Jumble in the militia and a nervous government agent prickling the sensitivities of a diabolical authority and we have a little red pill with the inscription: Back off or Die.

Susan Dax heads to Moscow in the wake of her murdered mentor. No sooner than she starts to investigate, she discovers that she too has become a target of unseen hands. Could it be from the Russian mafia, the two professional assassins or the clandestine security force?

Together with her trusted confidant and guardian, Seymour Krakauer, Susan Dax must navigate her way through old memories, blood and dead bodies to find answers. Would she be able to find the person behind the mask and get to the truth before she is summarily disposed of?

# MY NAME IS SUSAN

Seymour Krakauer was the seventh to go missing and no one seemed to have any idea how him and other wealthy individuals were going unaccounted for. Susan Dax refuses to accept the obvious verdict of his disappearance.

To locate and free her guardian from the nightmare he finds himself in, she enlists the help of her aide and friend Daniel Anderton. But no sooner have they begun their investigation they tangle with a hellish assortment of villains in an effort to solve the list of clues they find.

Their voyage across the States invites danger froth with violence.

In their fierce and devious battle, Dax must outwit and shatter the illusions of those she's up against, including learning a terrible truth of her past.

# BEFORE THE "I DO's"
# & OTHER COMPENDIUMS.

*Every man deserves a woman and every woman deserves a partner worthy of her love and attention. However, nothing and no one is perfect, neither is any society. Hence, it is now of appropriate connotation to say that in the climate of political correctness and openness to say that every heart deserves a corresponding like-minded heart and vice versa.*

*No marriage is going to be perfect because unfortunately there is no "happily ever after". Fortunately, there is however a "happily after".*

*We all have expectations and yearnings that we cannot deny or fulfil but fortunately, there is also LOVE. We are feeling bubbling fleshy mass of erroneous and intricate emotions, us humans. We have the need to* analyse our doubts, give in to fear, pray to hope and lament in despair. Who could blame us?

This book is a relationship guideline for those percentages of us, the girlfriends or fiancées, the boyfriends or grooms who need to be at least fifty to ninety percent sure.

Take it to heart, but do not set your prayers by it. Your heart is the true gift you will ever need to be sure about that person standing next to you.

...

For that unknown
SOLDIER

The sobbing, rasping sound of the aged Indian man behind me breathing was beating against my ears. It was magnified in the tiny capillaries of the earthy cave. There seem to be no air in the cold air, while our hearts thudded in an effort to compensate.

The struggled crawl through the hard cavern was not only taxing his strength but also his nerves, even with me beside him. He claimed he was not claustrophobic, on the other hand the great mass of rock around us seemed to be pressing down on us. And even with my lack of claustrophobic tendencies I also was finding the cold, the struggle and the seeping blood down on my left side, bearing down on me.

I was genuinely pleased when we crawled through a narrow triangular passage which opened up just slightly until the walls suddenly fell away revealing a cathedral of fairy-like needles clothing a great rocky chamber. It had taken almost all night to crawl out of the cave.

The light from the head torch could not light up the quartz-like cavern. It was not too far now from the entrance, I could just make out reflected light down at the end of the rocky wall. I glanced back at the gritty but refined man who was staring almost drunkenly about him. I turned to aid him to his feet, nonetheless his legs did not seem to want to cooperate.

'You quitting on me?' I asked the man before me.

He shook his head, wheezing as he clutched at my arms 'My dear … that will be … the day. My wretched … body … won't collaborate. Give … me a moment'

I crouched, bracing him up and said 'Take it easy. Let's have a rest for a couple of minutes yeah. Breathe deeply and exhale …' I stopped. I had heard something. I tilted my head, staring at the narrow rift which we had just emerged from.

I set him down, moved away from him and creeped back through the mouth of the fissure and cupped a hand to my ear to have a real listen. The sound of a crag of rock grating against something hard was unmistakable. It was as if the whisper gallery was letting the faraway sound in through the rocky labyrinth. I could identify several faint cracklings of a boot on rock. The intervals between the cracklings told me that the person moving down the cavern was doing it with a certain speed that seemed implausible. It could only mean one person. Shit! My australopithecine friend was coming.

I could not exactly pinpoint how far the sound was, but it was still some distance away. It was close by, but not that close. I crawled away from the fissure and said in a flat voice 'It seems we have a guest'

The aged grey-haired Indian stuttered 'W-we what …?'

'I think it's our strangling acquaintance'

My uncertainty was for his benefit. That said I was utterly certain it was him.

He croaked the words 'Oh Shiva'

I was hardly listening. I was making a dozen calculations, knowing what inescapably route lay ahead of us. There was a boat that meant there was a river we would have to get to and cross. That wouldn't be a problem for our friend behind us. The best place to confront him would be on the far side of the river. Then again, perhaps laying in wait for him when he emerged from the cave was best. However, if he had a gun, he could easily shoot us down. That is if we could get out of this crystal cave in time.

I crouched before the man and said softly 'We have maybe three maybe four minutes, so I need one big push from you'

'You can count on me Susan'

'Good. Hang on to me'

With my arm about his waist and his arm across my shoulder we began to stumble up the step-like ridges of rock. It took us three minutes to reach the flat stretch at the brink of the cave. I ripped off the head torch from my head and surveyed our surroundings. I let the man sink to his knees and ran to the outcrop where Sameer must have hidden the boat. I found the canoe with a single motor engine under a camouflage tarp, from the wear and tear of the tarp it looked like it had been here for more than a week, which made me assume that Sameer had planned his escape long before I came on the scene. What the hell was he waiting for? Weapons were nowhere to be found. I contained my disappointment as I pulled at the canoe. There was no way we could get far enough away to avoid a confrontation. The aged man watched as I set it onto the water with hopelessness in his eyes. I echoed his feelings because I knew what he was thinking. He was coming and despite myself I knew it was almost a certainty that he would be our end.

Whether it was the anger I felt for knowing the certainty of it all or the hopelessness gripping at me, but I suddenly felt a camera bulb flash within my head.

The bulb flourished into fruition.

I had an idea.

I started stripping. My thoughts flying, I kicked off my loafers, hooked my thumbs through the top of my torn pants and ripped them off, the same I did for the blue and green Sari. With one fluid movement I stripped them off together.

I glanced at the gritty silver haired man as I stood naked in the morning sunshine. He stared at me somewhat bemused.

'Get over here old man' I asserted sharply as I tightly drew my black hair back and I ripped the sari into two and two.

He pulled himself together and came over to me as I started wrapping each piece round each of my hands.

'Open up the top' I told him, gesturing at the canoes' engine.

He flipped the two cover clips.

'Take the oil cap off' I said as I handed him part of the torn pants. 'I need you to lubricate me all over'

'What?' he asked, surprised by my request.

'Just do it' I snapped at him.

He pushed the torn cloth into the small oil tank and stood up and began to smear me with the oil. His cold hands moved over my firm flesh. I was grateful that they were little emotion, like embarrassment or carnal want, stirring within him. If I were to name the emotion I was seeing, it would be melancholy. First, he did my neck then my shoulders. When he started on my arms, I stopped him from oiling all the way. 'I need my elbows and knees dry'

When he began on my torso, from my neck to my groin, not avoiding the wax burn on my stomach, he said in a shaky whisper. 'You going to fight him' It wasn't a question.

'Huh huh'

'He's much bigger than you'

'I know'
'Will this help?' he asked indicating the oil he was now smearing on my legs.
'Yes. This is the place. A hard and uneven surface will be perfect. No surface for fancy kicks or chops. The oil will prevent him from getting full grip of me … an edge I would definitely need. He also would have lost some of his edge chasing us up here'
'He may be armed' he imparted, oiling my back.
'I think I can handle that'
The old man knelt behind me oiling my buttocks and calves.
A crackle of stone sounded from within the cave.
'All right. In the boat now and get going. Don't stop until you reach civilisation'
I crouched and held the canoe steady as he screwed back the oil cap, slammed on the engine cover and climbed into the canoe. The engine croaked tiredly as I pulled on the rope starter.
'Don't get wet' I said to him as I tossed in the rag pieces of my clothes.
'I-I …'
Looking at him with my face a few inches from his, I gave him a kiss on the cheek and smiled at him 'Don't worry old man' I proclaimed gently, giving him a little reassuring nod 'I'll catch you up beyond the stairway to nirvana, now go'
The man just investigated my face with an apprehensive look on his face.
'You better, my dear' he replied as I gave the boat a small push.
I stood up and turned my back on him and the boat. From that moment on, he didn't exist. I had shut him out. With my naked body and swaddled fists hanging by my sides, I stood waiting.
Yes. I stood waiting for the inevitable.

# ONE

I snuggled up against the man beside me, his hard, strong muscles which at this moment made me feel, utterly content. Except for Steven Duggan, my off and on lover, rarely had I been with a man like Sameer. The shadows of the night played over his coffee-stained skin and stubble beard and for a minute he looked like a man made from a wish of mine. The room was dark, the shades were drawn and thankfully the air-conditioned system was humming quietly against the sultry New Delhi night.

'You never say why' he whispered, his warm lips kissed me gently in the hollow of my neck and shoulder, my breasts caressing his hairy chest. I turned my face towards him and studied the line of his tightly held mouth. His brow was in a knot and he seemed precocious and somewhat unaccustomed to not getting his way. To my mind he was halfway between being a man and a full-blown man. All I knew about him was that he could play a mean sitar and seemed to be quite good considering the play of his fingers and the attention he received from the male and female staff and guests alike. Some guy even compared him to Ravi Shankar whoever that was. However, him being compared to someone told me he was better than just good.

'Why what, lover?' I asked my fingertips aimlessly tracing down his six packed stomach.

'Why you're here Miss Susan'

Despite my insistence, he persisted in calling me "Miss Susan".

I pulled myself away from him, propping my head up against the pillows. My black hair fanned out over the white linen like a black halo. His face on the other hand was sculptured with a seeming seethe of inner singular serenity and decisive gleefulness.

'I think I told you' I replied, trying to sound as patient and convincingly as possible 'My boss has me picking up pencils after him. He's negotiating a buy, you know fabrics, silk and the like'

Obviously, I was lying through my teeth. In any case he did not need to know why I was in the country. He did not need to know who I was, why

I was here, besides what difference would it make anyways. There was no reason to involve him, to break cover and inform him that I was Susan Dax, the seventh wealthiest woman on the planet and as a favour to MI6 I was here to more than take in the sights or pick up pencils.

Two days earlier, after I had checked my messages especially one from Barrister Robia Morrow, my off and on girlfriend who was mistaken for a defendant, twice in a law court by the staff because of her dark skin, I had arrived in the city, whose people think mostly about caste and creed, with the intention of aiding and coordinating the management structure of my newly acquired Telecommunications company INFLUX in response to the Delhi riots this past February and then taking in the sights of the city. The whole visit, according to Seymour who sent me here, should not last more than a couple of days. The last person I would expect to meet was someone like Sameer Kannauj or the aged official sent from the embassy to hand me a note to call the Director of MI6, Sir Conrad Steele.

The world has been in a loll for the past fortnight and the most important reports in the newspapers or the ten o'clock news were the meaning of Beckham's new tattoo, Lewis Hamilton's poll position for his first seasonal F1 race, the merging of the Kardashians with the Bradshaw clan, Liverpool's ten point clear bid for the premier league championship and the anti-Trump pickets in Orlando. Now the newspapers were filled with the several horrifying main stories of the week. A Jihadist group were making some crazy protests in the Philippines and a Nazi riot in Frankfurt involving thirty or more deaths. A religious riot in Mumbai and Bombay between Muslims and Hindi's causing multiple waves of bloodshed, property damage almost happening back to back. And another riotous clash in Greece by students against monetary restrictions. It seemed that in a matter of days the world was a few cups short of a tea service. How did that happen?

The adverse effects in India was causing displacement, violent outbursts of communal fighting and economic disasters. With corpses found stuffed in open drains, forced circumcisions and shooting of cops, it's no wonder that India was on the periphery of a full-scale genocide action. Causes stemming from sit-ins, hate speeches, protests of anti -Citizenship Amendment Act to religious nationalism. The papers made me feel very depressed, wishing if there was something more I could do and glad of the fact that I was only here for a few days.

The night life of New Delhi had undergone an amazing transformation in recent years. As the sun went down most of the people went home to cuddle before the TV, others, the most adventurous ones were prone to taking the night air and getting up to the mischievous activities the night had to offer.

It all starts innocently enough where a rich man's son will be the father of a rich son or a servants son will be destined to be a servant and with what the locals call a stroll before dinner, turns out to be more than a pleasant habit of touring the bars, open air dancing with regional cuisines or making their presence known to the criminal elements or the working ladies or guys of the night. But still in the slums, days turn to poison when the sun goes down. Places like Kitty Hu Club, Bhiro and the Blue Night bar are known for their top-level ambiance, sumptuous menu and privy or tabooed undertakings. Places where bottomless pits exist for the ignorant and the weak drown in.

I did not have much reason to enjoy the amenities of the night life New Delhi had to offer, even if I understood the language to get by, Oberoi Hotel had much to compensate me for that.

I had been sitting in the hotel's garden swimming pool after I had done a bit of "necessary shopping" with a blue sari draped over my head and shoulders when he had come over from a refreshing swim. A red and pale orange towel was draped over his wet muscular figure. The attraction was mutual. One word led to another and then a drink at a lavish sports bar and then he took me to an Italian restaurant at the Chanakyapuri oasis. It did not take much for me to allow him to seduce me and before we knew, it one thing naturally led to the other.

He had no idea that according to the account statement Seymour handed to me from a two-desk office in Brenner, Liechtenstein two months ago, my net worth was approximately thirty-four billion dollars, give or take several million. No more than six people know that fact, so there must be some other reason why I had ever considered him a threat or in danger or be a danger because of me. If my profile were ever to find its way into the public consciousness, I would be described differently and for me it would be unbelievably bad. Some might describe me as an illusion, maybe not a real person. They definitely will not believe that someone with such beauty, youth and ladylike refinement such as myself who possess an under thirty top Forbes type wealth was also, strong-willed, mercurial and in short, a badass.

All I could see for now was his eyes glowing in the dark, then again, the macho with dimples within his stubble said it all. Of course, there had been questions, flirting games, the cat and mouse stratagems of seduction but that was all more like innovative foreplay to this night of passion and lovemaking.

*    *    *    *

My conversation with Sir Steele earlier that day was less than productive hence the unlikely call for "necessary shopping" for items needed after Sir Steele's briefing. He informed me he didn't want to interfere with whatever I was doing in India nonetheless he wondered, that as long as I was here whether I could be on the look-out for a certain individual his agency had a vested interest in locating. I complained that I was not his personal watchdog and that I was no more useful than his agents or his crypto surveillance systems or face recognition programs.

All the same Sir Steele was adamant and impossible to reason with. He wanted a human touch, my touch, to handle whatever was brewing. 'Besides rumour is that even if he existed, he hasn't been sighted in years' I told him

'All the more reason I need you to feel around, keep an eye open and an ear close to the ground. You know the usual' Steele said with a dry sardonic laugh. 'Cultural clashes with armed weapons are a common occurrence in India these days. Calcutta is one hairs breath away from being a state of anarchy, Mumbai is not far off, New Delhi will follow in short order. We need to know whose providing these insurgents with weapons. In case you did not know they don't grow on trees, y'know' he joked

'Can't that be handled by their own domestic security?' I countered

'Of course, their intelligence deputy director Safi Dass maybe able to help diffuse any difficulties, he's already been making a name for himself quelling the potential hotspots but I already have a man there called

Anard Siddharth, having said that they aren't quite up to snuff yet,
besides a friend might be caught up in this'
I've always found Indian names more than a little odd.
'A friend?'
'My old Eton roommate Mahatma Bhave, a governor for one of the
state provinces whom I first heard about this. He on behalf of the
government ask that we investigate because he and they believe that the
Daayan sect is no laughing matter'
Considering India's almost third-world status and the recent riots it
was no surprise they asked for help. All the same asking from their old
colonial masters the British, was a surprise.
'Why is that, I wonder?'
'Well it seems the sect once ruled that part of India in the 1700's and it
was us that put an end to it. Now they feel obliged that the same should
apply here'
'An old witchy sect called Daayan from the eighteenth century has been
resurrected by an individual you think goes by the name Brahma and is
using the Cobra as his motif?' I could almost laugh at the absurdity.
'Yes, like the Thugee's of old they believe we are still up to task of
stopping them'
'Oh, and it has nothing to do with curses and hexes and such?' I asked.
'No … well … I … no … besides this Brahma has a knack for
ventriloquism'
'What does that mean?'
'Is your phone secure?'
'Do you want it to be?'
'Yes'
I tapped on an encryption App on my phone and informed him that it
was now secure. Within seconds a PDF folder marked TOP SECRET
was sent to my phone.
'This will shed a little light on our mystery man and why we think there
is more to our belief that he "does" exist'
It did not take me more than two minutes to speed read the report. Once
I read it, I understood Steele's resolute tenacity.
'Nasty wouldn't you agree?' he chuckled.
'You could say that. Cheeky also'

'Well the Russians aren't laughing neither are we or the Americans'

'Unorthodox'

'Yes, well there you have it, Susan. Our man maybe on the verge of smuggling tens of millions of pounds of heroin, or whatever into the UK, instigating riots all over the world not just India and that's the least of our problems. If it were just a matter of smuggling, I'd leave it to the Indians or send a team of consultants, but they hardly know what to look for. That's why I need you to poke about a bit. Let's be real, your contacts might be considerable in that part of the world'

'Not really' I replied

I only stayed in the refugee camp on the border of Kashmir, India for four months when I was 13 and apart from the language I picked up, India wasn't an ideal place for me. I was always on the lookout for rape gangs in the disputed region and food was rather scarce.

The PDF I had just read had come from 10 Downing Street. Nothing could get higher than that except for maybe the American's Oval Office. It concerned something I had read recently in the papers about an incident I would not have thought linked with this Brahma.

Apparently, someone had called the Russian embassy in London posing as the Prime Minister. It could have been a prank and nothing else except the accent and vocal imitation was flawless. It seemed the PM exchanged words with the ambassador that was less than conducive. There were threats of an incendiary nature which prompted the Ambassador to promptly leave for Moscow.

The hoax was cleared up and apologies gushed from Downing Street. It should have ended there, but it didn't. A couple of days later the First Secretary made use of his phone to call the United States President. With almost the identical dialogue as the one supposedly made by Boris Johnson. The tone of the exchange prompted the President to call for a meeting with the UN Security Council.

Once again, the deception was cleared up just in time. Since then, several rashes of incidents involving belligerent exchanges had occurred. Between Israel and Egypt, Mexico and Colombia, North Korea and Japan, prompting North Korea to enter a state of war footing and launching a nuclear test not already scheduled. There were other prank calls between competitive states. Most, except between India and Pakistan who have a much volatile state of affairs between them. In every instance a head of state or a diplomat's voice was perfectly simulated, triggering off a rash of angry threats and pointing of fingers. I wondered what would happen if this ventroquilism act was used on General's who had access to nuclear weapons. According to the techs on the case all they could figure out was that the calls were routed through numerous servers and VPN's.

After several analysts and computer specialists went through the calls, the signature of the call was linked to an old iconoclastic Sunni organisation called "Daayan" that hadn't been heard from in years and which most intelligence agency could not pin down but suspected it was located in Pakistan or India. I was betting dozens of agents had landed in country to seek out the leader of this organisation, a man only identified as Brahma. It did not seem so from my hotel room, but the world could easily slip from being on the brink of a nuclear war to being in one, especially with Donald Trump in the America's Presidential seat.

Someone was defiantly trying their damnedest to push them all over the edge.

'It is a little brazen to think that this Brahma could be the brains behind this, isn't it?'

'He may or may not be'

'Maybe this Brahma is an "it" not an "him"'

'Perhaps. We do not know if this Brahma exists or not, all the same we have rumours telling us this Daayan sect maybe back and they may be responsible for certain riots and drug trafficking operations, including making us all incredibly jittery'

My shoulders had a somewhat downward shrug, a sure sign that I did not have much faith in his theory.

'I have doubts that they exist … not after all these years'

'My nose itches and tells me that there may be more to this than a forgotten iconoclastic society'

'So, what, I'm supposed to poke around for someone who hasn't exactly been seen or a fictional organisation no one has heard from in three centuries, how the hell am I going to do that Sir C?'

'I've no idea but I have faith, besides you won't be grasping at straws alone for very long'

I wonder what he meant because it was not an answer I was hoping to hear, but hey, there are times you just cannot argue with the instincts of a man like Sir Steele. If he thought that my being here in the wild dry smelly yonder would aid him in his search for this Brahma or the organisation called Daayan, then who was I to argue. Though his words of "grasping for straws" sounded a bit ominous.
I did a quick rundown on the grisly alias Brahma. It was a pretty uncommon name in this part of the world, but more telling was its origins. It was the name of a god who created the cosmos, that said he was punished by Shiva the supreme Hindu god of destruction for going over and beyond his wishes. It was said that Brahma was always seeking to avenge his unjust punishment. Maybe that was why whoever was behind this took this name. That feeling of being unjustly persecuted is a powerful justification for creating anonymity. What this had to do with a eighteenth century sect founded in the village where the *Siddhartha*, otherwise known as the buddha, was courted as being a witch, was beyond me. A people who adopted a secret communication system and claim their hair as their most significant of their powers. A people who have all been hunted back in the day in the Bihar and Jharkhand provinces and had been all but eradicated.
Truth be told I had no idea where to begin. Where or how the hell would I begin to start following a non-existent trail that has not survived for years? If Brahma existed, it, he, she or them had covered their trail well or it was part of someone's lurid imaginative creation. Unlike the man beside me who was real, all right, fleshy, smooth, hard and wonderfully compliant to my touch.

*     *     *     *

Sameer was about to say something, but I slid over and stifled his next words by pressing my lips to his kissable pillow lips. His skin like mine was moist with a fine sheen of sweat and I rubbed my firm cream coloured breasts across his hard-stubbly chest, feeling myself become increasingly aroused by each passing second.
'Please don't. This is not a time for words' I whispered to him as he started to frame another barrage of questions we had not covered in our

brief liaison. 'I'm Susan, you're Sameer, the liliquor moonlit night is just what the doctor ordered and we both want to be here … at least for now' His long hard hand slid down my body and I gasped as his fingers reached between my thighs. I kicked the Madras throw covering us off the bed and snuggled up against him. I looked up at him, but his eyes seemed to be looking through me, fixed at something occurring across the room, in the direction of the door. In that moment I knew we were in trouble. The sound I heard that neither of us made was of something metallic as if it was rubbing itself against the electronic key-card knob. There was no doubt that someone was tampering with the lock. The raspy grating was undeniable. My old friend, my loaded Makarov was in the bottom drawer of the bedside table, but out of my arms reach. The scratching stopped followed by a muted beep and I knew I did not have time to get to it.

Instead, my nerves and muscles adjusted as if a switch had been thrown and I scrambled, twirling away from Sameer, just as the door burst open. Framed in the light streaming from the corridor were two bearded figures dressed in cream Kurtas and baggy pants. The favoured embroidered shirts and trousers that looked like pyjamas to us western folks. More important than their attire was the automatic pistol one of the turbaned individuals held in his unwavering hand. The pistol followed me as I leaped off the bed and there didn't seem to be anything, I could do about it. The gun with five lethal inches of a clipped-on suppressor was aimed at me and not at Sameer, which wasn't much of a surprise. Sameer had rolled out of the bed and was standing half crouched on the other side of the bed. For a formidable form he had, he was to my amazement, scared.

The door closed softly behind both our intruders and one of them flicked on the light switch, illuminating the bedroom in a stark bright light.

I blinked rapidly as my mind interchanged from a romantic ambience into fighting mode and started calculating. Part of my mind that was the analytical fighting computer started assessing a score of components from our two intruders, those known and those assumed. Who were they? Why were they here? Why were we being targeted? Did they know something we didn't? What the hell could that be?

Both our interlopers were hefty men, unshaven and bearish with grim-faced faces. Considering their untrimmed beards and methodically wrapped turbans, they were Hindis parading as Sikhs. They had curled lips with identical grins of sadistic cunning. Their teeth were stained red. I could be mistaken to say they were bloodied, then again, a second look confirmed that their mouths were stained crimson from chewing what I believed was *Paan*, a native healing herb.

'Evening, *mem-sahib*' The one without the gun said, a greeting which was followed by a lewd snicker seeing my naked exposed form. He glanced at Sameer's frightened vulnerable figure on the other side of the bed and his snigger widened.

My best ploy was to let them believe that I was who I was supposed to be. A businesswoman on business, taking in the sights like any businesswoman or tourist would. Stick to that persona until the situation changed or was unbelievable. I was very much considering an attack from my position and let the chips fall. However, wisely I chose the former and acted accordingly.

Assuming an offended tone, I shouted 'What the hell is this?' I made a move to the hotel phone, but my action was anticipated, and the unarmed Sikh snatched at the white telephone and tore it from its socket, wire and handset.

'That very unwise of you, girl' said the armed Sikh with a toothy grin 'We not give you permission to move. You too, *sahib*' he said pointing the pistol of savage and murderous intent at Sameer as he pulled a linen to cover his mid-section. The gunman nodded to his partner who promptly began searching our belongings.

'If this is a robbery, do you mind if I put something on'

The armed intruder smirked and gestured to the Madras throw on the floor. I snatched it up and wrapped it about me. His dark eyes never leaving me for a second.

'You're not going to find anything worth stealing' I told both of them 'Sameer, you got anything these gentlemen might think is worth their time?'

Sameer Kannauj nervously shook his head.

'Neither have I. All I've got are some Euros, no pounds, and no rupees' I don't think they were buying my act, not in the least.

'Check thah drawers Naveen' the armed intruder told his partner.

Even as he spoke, my body and my mind were preparing for that singularly violent fusion I knew was imminent.

The last time Seymour granted me a break from running my billion-pound empire, he insisted I forgo my usual rest and rehabilitation stint with my adopted daughters Bilquees and Nadia. In place of a well-earned vacation with them, he had me shipped to my old Korean sensei to perfect the rarer forms of self- defence. According to Seymour, I "was becoming too indulgent". It must have been true because I was finding a biochemical lecture for executives very forthcoming.

Though paralysed from the waist down, my Jiujutsu master *Kiyitsu* taught me old techniques that resembled in form of a Jedi self-hypnosis that was also comprised of a dash of autosuggestion. He also helped perfect my *Tae Kwon Do* and *Wing Chun* style of fighting. Including the internal mechanics of *Xing Yi Quán*, the art of striking. All helped with the concentration of power and momentum that can be achieved through the use of my entire body, my hips, my feet and in particular, my mind.

And so, even as one of the men began to rummage through my stuff, on the brink of finding my collection of fatal beauties in my armament, I was preparing my initial move. I imagined myself as a tightly wound asp, ready to spring. Capable of leaping over the bed and hurtling through space.

'We should kill thah boy you know. But it be pleasure to do job on you first mem-sahib Dax'

It wouldn't take a genius to imagine what kind of "job" he was referring to.

As I imagined, so I put into practice. With a sharp barking yell, a *Kiat-su* that put both men on the defensive, I threw the madras away at the unarmed intruder named Naveen and leaped over the bed, landing like a panther on the balls of my feet. A bullet whizzed ominously past my head just as I landed.

'Miss … don't' I heard Sameer scream out, imploring me not to put up a fight. It was too late.

Naveen and his armed partner did not exactly threaten Sameer, but me and me alone. I had no alternative to preclude that their hostile intentions were towards me and me only.

A *Tol Rio Cha Ki* round-house kick delivered by my left foot with every balance and strength I could muster knocked out the silenced gun from Naveen's partner. The gun whizzed through the air and bashed itself against the wall, clattering aimlessly onto the floor. Spinning around with my right foot snapping viciously to meet the vulnerable mark of Naveen's cheekbone. To say he flew across the room would be an exaggeration. He soared across the room smashing into the opposite wall. It startled me to see how much power I had put into that kick.

A nauseating gurgle from the gunman accompanied Naveen's startled groan as I followed my kick with a punch to the gunman's guts. His solar plexus to be exact. Air was knocked out of his lungs as he doubled over breathlessly to the floor, folding like a deck chair.

'I bet this isn't what you expected when you woke up this morning' I remarked, standing over him in my naked form as he lunged blindly at me, trying to grab for me. I was at least a fist cup away from him. It seems all the training from Kiyitsu was paying off in spades.

I raised my hand like a scythe, in a knife hand chop. My hand swished through the air to a point just behind his head to follow up with stiff fingers going down onto the bridge of his nose. I did not need medical training to know the man before me was dead before he hit the floor. I had somehow sent a shard of bone up into his brain. A spurt of blood flushed out of his inflamed nose and mouth.

A muffled rattling sound accompanied his sudden lurching collapse to the floor, limp as a rag doll. His jet-black lifeless marble eyes were fixed on me as they glazed over and close. I wondered if he knew how unlucky he was being killed by a naked woman.

I stood over him looking down at his grotesque face that almost resembled a bloody pulpy flesh of fruit.

The gunman was no longer a threat but a cadaver.

In the time it had taken me to finish him off, Naveen had recovered sufficiently to make another attempt to put me out of commission.

I heard him staggering presumptuously, dragging his winded body across the room. He was directly behind me, which did not give me much time to think twice. My elbow whipped round in a devastating *Pal-Kup Chi-Ki*, catching my attacker just under his chin. Naveen yelled miserably as I twisted around, just in time to see the cracked stumps of his formerly set of straight reddish teeth as he fell down to the floor.

Naveen's jaw hung down, limp and broken. Stream of blood was oozing, like puke out of his mouth, down his chin, down his neck and staining his cream flowing kurta. I had literally crushed the bottom part of his face into a dozen pieces. He was already suffering from a traumatised jawbone, sullied bruised eyes and cheekbones as he tried to speak. His voice came out unintelligible from his cracked mouth. However, before I could finish him off, his hand had somehow got grip of the butt of the silenced gun. I dashed sideways to the side of the bed as he squeezed the trigger of the gun at me. A heavy calibre bullet whined just mere millimetres from me and embedded itself in the opposite wall. The bullet sounded like one of those dumdum armoured-piercing bullets, capable of disembowelling a man like a freshly slaughtered goat ready for the cooking pot.

Naveen somehow scrambled to his feet and backed towards the door. I was already moving. zigzagging right and left before the Hindi could send another dumdum slug my way. Tackling a course which led me right up to him, but he had opened the door and slipped out so fast that he was gone by the time I had the opportunity to get close to him to wrestle the gun from his grip. I followed him swiftly out the door, but he was nowhere to be seen. I did however see the trail of blood and heard the clattering of heavy footfalls descending the fire-exit staircase close to me. I was about to follow it when I notice my nudeness.

Back in the room I drew on my red dress. Sameer was staring at me with wild panic -stricken eyes as I pulled it over my shoulders. 'Don't look at me!' I responded, 'Corporate espionage is a dangerous business'. His expression didn't slip one iota as I left him there with the bloodied mess that was once a human being.

I raced out of room. No one saw me chase after Naveen down the stairs. I had to catch up to him. With his partner dead, he and he alone had answers for me. I did not believe for one moment that they were common or garden variety robbers. They knew my name and they acted professionally, even if they hadn't any success. They had gone above the call of just petty thieves. They did not come to my room with the intention of profiting from some financial gain. There was something else that had brought them to me, and I was betting it had to do with Sir C's troubles. Otherwise how could they know about me and how this quickly?

Unless I caught up with Naveen and he provides me with answers, I would have a hell of a lot of unanswered questions rattling around in my head.

## TWO

The deserted lobby with the night concierge reading some pamphlet bore no heed to me as I raced through it. I caught a flurry of movement from behind the floor-to-ceiling long drapes that concealed the fibre glass walls and doors leading to the patio and gardens. With my ten bare toes, I rushed towards it and pulled them aside and dashed through into the darkened garden.

The grass in the garden was as expected, damp and cold beneath my exposed feet. The gibbous moon was concealed behind clouds crossing its swollen carroty face. Up ahead I could just make out clouds reflected in the hotel's swimming pool I had just enjoyed earlier. No more tinkle of glasses, or rhythm of *Pandura* type songs or the hawking cries of street vendors that permutated the air and the tranquil of the grassy compound.

Now there was just the rasping of my breath and the pulsation of my pulse. Cautiously, I crept forward, every sense straining to catch that hint of movement, that sudden tell-tale noise which would enable me to locate my quarry before he got onto me.

In my rush to go after him, I had forgotten to grab my gun. Which meant I had to depend on my wits and bare hands or feet. Though I had much faith in my abilities, a Chinese Makarov would have been a much more versatile weapon to be on hand.

Kiyitsu frustratingly had nicknamed me *Miseu Noji*, Korean for "Miss Nosey", for my persistent inability to keep my nose out of stuff. However now I wasn't feeling the opportunity to put my studies to their proper use. There was no stirring, only the gentle rustling of leaves from the banyan trees in the courtyard. Their gnarled trunks screening sections of whitewashed wall just to the left of where I was crouching. I crept forward.

I was searching for the Indian's hopefully bloodstained trail when I caught the abrupt glint of metal, a flash of steel followed by a low dipped hiss and buzz of a heated lead bullet. The high-powered dum-dum bullet grazed across my left lower arm making me wish I could scream out.

Instead I clamped down hard over my mouth to prevent my screaming out from the hellish burning smart.

I was lucky, I guess. The bullet had made a superficial wound. Unlucky though that the gunman had a bead on me. Gritting my teeth, I waited, feeling more vulnerable than I ought to be. The Indian I was betting was not about to make any chances or wait to see what I was going to do. A sudden trample of feet and I caught sight of him running to the nearby wall. He had apparently recovered enough from the beating I had given him to leap up and scramble up and over the wall with agility. I chased after him. I was not about to let him get away without a fight.

Despite my punishment he moved more like a cat than a man. The wall was stained with blood from his injuries as I in regardless of my wound was more so agile than him when I scaled the wall. I landed on the ground with my bare feet in a patch of sharp gravel. Another sound of what I believed was a slug leaving his barrel exploded in my ears. In a reflex I lurched forward to the ground. I should not have bothered. The sound was that of a scooter parked at the end of the wall's enclosure. The turbaned Indian had climbed on, started the faulty engine with a bang and took off without looking back.

I could have chased after him by hailing a pedicab, but I knew he would have no difficulty in disappearing in the winding alleyways of New Delhi's bazaars and slums.

So instead of continuing a futile chase, I turned back and holstered myself over the six-foot wall. Making it to the other side without much difficulty, I found the grass much more soothing to my bare feet than the harsh gravel on the other side. After rinsing my seared wound on my arm in the dazzling pool, I headed straight for the night managers desk. The night clerk sitting at an awkward level awoke at my arrival. Awaken from the nap that probably enabled my two guests to access my hotel room. I did not think of chewing him up for is ineptitude, they was a dead body in my room to contend with.

'Insomnia, mem-sahib?' he asked, struggling to control a yawn as he sluggishly got to his feet. He leaned over his desk to see the dishevelled look I was in. Maybe he noticed the raw crease of the Naveen's bullet or not, in any case he cast me a baleful and disapproving look. 'You need something, maybe glass of milk ... cocoa ...?'

'Thanks, but no. Where's your security room?' II asked.
He pointed to a door behind him.
As I made my way to it, he hurriedly stopped me, blocking my path.
'Sorry mem-sahib, no unauthorised person here'
'And the thief who stole my personal items is authorised?'
The shock on is face conveyed his surprise 'What?' he asked
'You didn't see him because you were fast asleep. What would your bosses say to that?'
'T-thief?'
'Yes, but if I can have his identity and you keep your mouth shut no one will ever know. That is ….?'
I left the question hanging.
'That is …?'
'That is, … unless you were in league with him'
'No no' he replied apologetic jumping out of the way and escorting me to the door.
It took two minutes to identify Naveen from the CCTV outside the garden and the night clerk to print out a photostat of him.
I thanked him and told him to forget about all this.
The less attention I drew to myself the better I liked it and the quicker I would be able to find the man Naveen.

*     *     *     *

Sameer was nowhere to be seen when I arrived back at my hotel room. Apparently, he had more than he bargained for when he met me. I bet he slipped out of the room and the hotel as fast and as silently as he could, without looking back, counting his stars on how lucky he was to be alive. The door was ajar, with no one lurking about. Apart from the stiffening corpse of Naveen's accomplice the room was deserted. His arms and legs were still sprawled out at a twisted angle with the thicken of his dark red blood under him.
The wrinkled bed sheets were a testimony of the fact that I and Sameer had spent much of the evening here. There was no way he could be trusted for one second to keep his trap shut. There was a strong

possibility he would be calling the New Delhi police and then I would be trapped for hours answering questions I wouldn't know how to answer. I went over to the corpse and began searching it. There was nothing of interest on his person until I turned him over and noticed something that made me start with surprise. One of his gauzy *Kurta* sleeves had rolled up displaying on his upper side forearm an indelible blue tattoo of a coiled King Cobra riding up his arm in a characteristic rearing stance. Its flaring wedge-shaped hood and flickering tongue was emblazoned on the man's cold flesh.

Could it be the Daayan existed?

Blue blustering barnacles! Sir Steele, he just might be right.

How is it possible? And why me? Could it be they sent Naveen and his cohort to make sure I wouldn't be around to see to their secret organisation's demise? How did they know who I was?

Nevertheless, this was score one for me. They had failed in their quest to kill me and I had proved that this subversive clandestine organisation of Sir C's might be real. The problem was, I did not yet know my adversary. The architect, behind a recent wave of global treachery perpetuated by the Daayan if they truly did exist.

But hey, it was early days yet.

Packing up the few items I had, I made a quick exit through the back. Scaling the wall, I disappeared into the night.

## THREE

The traffic in Nehru Park moved slowly with a dazzling operatic vista of circles. Beyond the light traffic of black and orange coloured cabbies, pedicabs, scooters and bicycles, there was the stark yellow pillars that once belonging to the Connaught Circus but was now an array of cheap low- cost houses. The smell of an old refuse pit still hung in the air, on the flip side, the buttery coloured pillars now bore witness, to the men in starched white trousers and plaid shirts, teenagers in the latest t-shirt get-up and dark-haired women in jeans and hajibs or saris who stride past it daily, like silent sentinels.

For all the dazzling sights, sounds and smell the town of early New Delhi could provide me there was only one thing that was on my mind and that was what none of the colourful exotic city could give me. Naveen.

I dialled my home in Green Park and listened to the automated message connected to Sir Galahad, my Interactive Artificial Intelligence Residential Automated Habitat smart house.

'Sir Galahad' I voiced into my cell phone.

There was a soft tone and before long Galahad's electronic voice that resembled Jerry MacDonald, a Canadian newscaster whose voice I loved hearing, came on. *'Please identify yourself'* it said.

'Rumpelstiltskin has a name' I answered.

The tone on the other end went quiet.

*'Hello Miss Susan; your last remote contact was Thursday … 12.24pm. How has your morning been?'*

'Just fine Galahad. Please re-initiate Apollo?'

*'Yes Miss, one moment'* there was a short pause *"Apollo priority command nexus located and contacted. Prepare for security identification"*

Another pause.

*"Miss Dax?"*

'Yes?'

*"Alpha is online"*

'Thank you, Galahad. Alpha, are you operational?'

*"Good Morning, this is Alpha secure server"* A different electronic synthetic voice came online not unlike Galahad's. This one was feminine and had a striking similarity to Vivian Leigh's voice.

*"Remote access confirmed"*

I spoke directly into the handset. 'Alpha this Cancer, confirm identity'

Without warning the cell phone flashed at me taking my picture and started running a facial and retinal identification program. It didn't take more than 3 seconds for it to identify me.

*"Identity challenge verified. Voiceprint ID authenticated. Facial scan authenticated. Retina scan authenticated. No indication of stress. Imprint scan required"*

A green flashing icon appeared on my smartphone. I pressed my thumb on it and it ceased flashing.

*"Fingerprint Identification confirmed. Password required"*

'Humpty Dumpty'

*"Challenge evaluated and authenticated. Retinal, facial, voiceprint and imprint scan verified. Identity assessed, established, and confirmed. Cancer authorised to remote access Alpha secure server system. Good morning, Miss Dax"*

'Alpha download photo taken 4.38am on phone'

*"Command acknowledged. Photograph downloaded"*

'Connect to the Indian Security Administration and identify individual'

*'Command acknowledged. Satellite tasking priority eminent. Running script … Running script … Running script… Running script …'*

There was a soft bleep and then for some reason Galahad came back on *'Miss Susan it would take some time for Alpha to connect to the Indian Central Bureau of Investigation'*

'Damn it' I groaned frustratingly 'Right notify me when you identify the individual'

What the hell do I do now, I wondered. I thought of calling Sir Steele's man Anard in the Indian Central Bureau of Investigation, then it hit me. As a rule, Seymour has instilled in me to make allies everywhere. Especially with enemies. Particularly those we considered undesirable, even if it was against our moral aptness. So, in a city where we have business but less influence, we have learnt to make contributions to the two foremost criminal organisations. In Turkey, it was the Grey Wolves and its Zaza branch in England, in Argentina, it was the Los Monos. In India, New Delhi, the two competing elements where within the Goa and Punjab Mafia's. As the name implies both mafia groups are involved in the small states of Goa and Punjab. With India being a transit point for Heroin from the Golden Crescent or as more popularly known the Golden Triangle, the mafia groups trade India's largest legal crop grower, opium with Europe and America.

The criminal group we donate to are the Bada Nair and D Company organisations. Headed up by two unscrupulous men, Dawood Salem and Imah Rajan.

Dawood Salem heads the Bada Nair organisation and is the fourth most dangerous gangster in the world. There is some speculation that he's Pakistani, at any rate those rumours are rarely mentioned. He is a master of extortion and other significant crimes, most notably drug smuggling, racketeering and murder. He is known to extort money from Bollywood celebrities and supply weapons to fanatics. It is alleged that he provided the logistics for the 2014 Mumbai Hotel attack.

As for Imah Rajan he grew up in a middle-class family in Chembur and was all about the money. His criminal life started when he scalped cinema tickets at his local theatre. Now he is boss of D Company after apprenticing for years with Dawood Salem. He disagreed with his boss's involvement in some bombings and especially the Mumbai attacks, hence his separation from the Bada Nair. Imah Rajan was first wanted for extortion, smuggling and murder by the age of fifteen. He was a risk taker and exceptionally good at it. There is a tale that he once aided a drugs and weapons smuggler get away from the Delhi police by driving his car recklessly over 100 km per hour.

If there was anyone who could aid me, it would be him. Though it wouldn't be cheap.

I put through a call to Imah Rajan leader of the D Company. After several false starts and one or two lieutenants intercepting, I was not surprised that he took my call. He suggested we meet at the Colonial Café in a village called Mundak on the outskirts of New Delhi.

I also put a call through to Safi Dass, the deputy director of India's Central Bureau of Security. His assistant named Makarand V Sanjit gave me a hard time before putting me through to him.

The deputy director didn't know the nature of my assignment, but he did know of my presence since Sir C had briefed him about me. I embellished

my mission by telling him that a multi-million-dollar shipment of Heroin
was in play and nothing about Sir C's voice imitator. I gave him as much
information as he would need including the dead body in my hotel room
and my proposed meeting with D Company's leader.
'Is that wise memsahib?' he asked
'No but I believe it's a place to start if you know what I mean'
'No, I do not Miss Dax' the man curtly replied 'I do not find it amusing
that you're meeting one of India's notorious drug dealers and I fail to
understand what this is all about. I doubt the British Government
would concern themselves with our drug problems'
'Look sir I didn't call you for an argument. You need my help even if
you don't think you do, and I need yours'
'Oh, how incompetent you must think we are'
'Will you arrange to have your man contact me this evening?' I asked
ignoring his statement about incompetence.
'You mean Anard?'
'Yes'
'Expect him around nine Miss Dax, he's equipped to handle even the
most difficult of situations. He has my complete trust'
'As I hope I do Mr Dass'
'And where are you now?'
'On my way to meet Imah Rajah at a Café in Mundak. Your man can
meet me at my hotel' I gave him the hotel's name and my room number.
'Well good luck with your meeting even if I disapprove of it'
I hung up the phone. It was a bit tough to hold down the sarcasm
threatening to invade my voice, but the man failed to hear the important
bits of our conversation.


*     *     *     *


Imah Rajan had a lean and hungry look about him as he sat behind the
café table. There was a set expression on his lips that told me he knew
the ropes and rules of the game. A man who would break them, no
matter how sordid. The scar that ran down the left side of his face did
much to comfort me.

'You know you a little of enigma you be Miss Dax. To me and my guys' Imah Rajan said to me as we sat across from each other in a small café on the outskirts of New Delhi where he insisted, we meet. He was surrounded by four of his heavy breathing minders in draping thug leather jackets and headphones in their ears, a less than sure firewall way to prevent them listening on our conversation.
'Is that a good thing?' I asked
'I not knowing … yet' he said with stern eyes.
'Then you better make up your mind quick'
'I hearing you serious fucker'
'Hey! That's no way to speak to a lady'
He sneered grimly 'I see you not be afraid of me or my men'
'Feed me strawberries and then I might force a tremble'
'You really not being afraid of me?'
'I doubt you could give me any reason to?'
'I could' he replied, his voice a little lower
'Yes, you could try, but it would be the last thing you do' I softly said without malice or intent.
He stared at me with a temptation in his eyes, a dare. I stared back holding no malevolence or objective in my eyes. I needed his help; I was not going to do anything to provoke a confrontation.
He continued to stare until suddenly his brown eyes softened.
'I be liking you'
'I bet you do'
I bet he wanted to tie me up tight and fuck me six ways from Sunday. He picked up the cup containing the milky mint tea we both had ordered and sipped on it 'So what you telling me is you hearing Daayan is back?' he asked in broken Indian accented English.
'I'm sure of it'
'How sure?' he asked with a troubled frown.
'Sixty-five … maybe sixty-two percent'
'In my grandfather's time, all he hears is Daayan. Those witchy thieves from Calcutta, Madras, Kashmir, Bombay he hears. We all hearing about Daayan. They making uprisings, insurgencies, unrest … always Daayan'
'And no one knows about their leader'

He chuckled. 'The man using Cobra? No not knowing him. Him new, but some say he always being here'. He said before leaning down and picking up a stone.

'What you see?' he asked showing me the stone rolling through his fingers.

'A stone'

'Good, stone as we say … specific, featureless blank slum stone'

I nodded.

'This you understand, this Brahma him featureless too, without identity, no face, no character' he said leaning over the table to fix me with a narrow glinting eye. 'A name him stealing from vengeful god. No, you stay away from this people'

'It also seems he has a hand in these riots I keep hearing about'

'I not surprised, I being telling you that already'

'You got any line on them?'

'No' he bluntly said, but I could detect a sense of uncertainty in his voice. It seems I was heading back to where I began empty handed.

'But …' he stopped.

It seemed he wanted to tell me something but wasn't sure whether it was the right thing.

'But what?' I asked softly

'Anurag Surte'

Another weird name.

'Who's that?'

'Why you want this people anyway?' Imah asked in a cautious low-pitched voice.

'An adversary of mine has a ten million pounds shipment of heroin headed for the US or UK and I want to prevent that' I lied

For the first time Imah Rajan smiled a cryptic smile 'Ah drugs. Most profitable business. Where is it?'

'That is what I want to know, all I know is that they are in league with the Daayan'

'Ah I see. What he do to you?'

'Whoever said it was he?'

'Ah' he smiled a knowing smile at me. This time a little eerier than the first time. 'So where this enemy of yours?'

'Don't know but I have a snapshot of one of their men'
I pulled out my phone and showed him the snapshot I had of Naveen
'Hmm' he mused over the photo 'Looks like Naveen' he remarked, unsure.
'Naveen?' I enquired, glad I got the name right.
'Use to be one of Didi's men'
'Didi?'
'Dawood'
'Your old boss?'
He did not answer. Instead he asked how important this information was to me 'What you do to prevent ….?'
I did not let him finish his question
'Why'd you ask such a nonsensical question?' I asked, fixing him with a stern look.
He stared at me for a long while, then grunted. 'It gone cost you'
'I know'
He made a move to get up from his seat. 'You'll be excusing me huh. I need to talk to few associates, see if they wan take risk'
'Of course,' I said as he pushed his chair aside and hurried across the café floor plied with tables with his men. I followed him with my eyes noticing him as he pulled out a mobile and tapped two points as he disappeared round the café. A speed-dialled associate, I surmised.
Sitting back in my chair I let my wander to the name Anurag Surte. There were many unknowns and loose ends that I think would require a lot of leg work before I could make a dent in making progress and now this Anurag Surte whoever was that. My eyes strayed across to the bazaar across the street.
'Two hundred rupees is all I gonna pay mate' said a familiar voice from across the street.
I whipped my head round with a start.
I could not believe my eyes.
Who the hell do I find standing there haggling with some street trader over a Pashmina Shawl but Sergeant Major Vincent Karl Briggs? A tough grim bastard and a former Sergeant Major of the 9th Special Air Command Dragoon division of the welsh brigade who had a fascination for Popeye. A man I was quite familiar with. The Sergeant stood about

six feet two with red Irish hair and a scruffy goatee of the same colour. He stood a good four to six inches above all other individuals.

Briggs conducted my paramilitary unit training during my sixteen weeks detached duty from the Navy. The old timer fucking believed in toughness of the body as well as mind, living with honour, the warrior's code. A code I thankfully can say he instilled in us trainees. He also encouraged us to volunteer for dangerous assignments because he believed whole-hearted that the warrior's he trained were invincible and if they weren't, they didn't deserve to be in his unit. His words of wisdom to us were, *"We are the pawns that make this blood-stained globe go round. If what we do is notable, then we are the most honourable pawns about"*

At one time, he truly hated my guts with a passion because I was, one a woman, two, a brat looking for jollies and worse still a mixed-raced kid with an attitude. He did his best to make me ring the bell and even volunteered me for missions no one had interest in. I in turn hated his honourable code to an unusual extent. That is until a chance mishap. After that mishap he loved me like a daughter and nicknamed me as his "Inspector", I had no idea why but as a result of that and based on his recommendation I was transferred to a combating unit within the SAS before I was "loaned" to the Russians as a Liaison Officer.

Presently he co-owns several multi-purpose garages which I financed as a silent partner. Apart from the field of soldiering he was a brilliant and discreet mechanic, fighter and procurer. One I could say was one of the finest specialists in England.

I rose and went over to him and tapped him on the shoulder.

His expression when he saw me was much more on par with mine.

'C- Commander … ma'am?'

'Briggs?'

'What the hell …?'

'That was going to be my question'

He reached into his pocket, produced a ticket and rolled his eyes

'Damn it, Ambrose you sly dog' he explained in his soft liquid Manchester accent.

'Ambrose?' I enquired

'I guess me all-expensive holiday was 'ust a sham'

I knew who exactly he was referring to. Mr Ambrose Wellington the personal assistant to the second-in- command of MI6, Sir Conrad Steele, and head of Special Executive Operations. He was a man of subtle tack, with an impressive operations record.

I guess now I knew what Sir Steele ominous words "besides, you won't be grasping at straws alone for very long" meant.

'Oh, that lordly despicable man. You too?'

'It would fucking seem so ma'am'

'Why you?'

'How woulda fuckin' know?'

'I am going to start loathing you again Briggs' I flippantly said, gesturing him to follow me.

'Sorry Commander'

Checking behind me to see if I was being followed or spotted I asked,

'You here with Margaret?'

'Yea'

'Which hotel?'

'The G-Gu-Guragon'

'The Gurgaon?'

'Yea'

'The Westin Gurgaon'

'Yea … it is something like that'

'The one in New Delhi yeah?'

'Yep'

'Fancy. Room?'

'214'

'Find Margaret and get back there now … if possible, change rooms or try a different hotel'

'What! Ah …'

He saw the expression on my face and knew better than to argue.

'Oh … don't be followed. If I can, I'll meet up with you soon, if not contact Sir C'

'Yes ma'am'

He disappeared quite quickly. I extricated myself from the bazaar and resumed my seat in the café, waiting on my host Imah to make his anticipated return.

I was still waiting four minutes later when a male attendant with a dark-complexioned face and starched red apron approached me. 'More tea' the waiter asked with his fixed eyes.

I nodded automatically 'Make it two' I stated pointing at Imah's empty cup.

'May I suggest some *pakoras* or some *samosa* ma'am while you wait memsahib?'

Again, I nodded absently. As he turned to go I caught sight of the bottom edge of his partially exposed arm. I could swear I spotted the bottom edge of a tattoo with the coiled end of a snake. It was not something I would easily forget.

I abruptly pushed back my chair as I hurriedly rose to my feet. Where was Imah? I thought to myself as I moved through the crush of tables. I was not worried for myself as I had been the night before. However, it seemed he was a tad longer than normal to get back from his phone call. Now I had my Chinese Makarov with Digital Imprint trigger snug against my appendix in its holster but Peko my stiletto that was usually snug in his sheath on my right forearm was back in my other luggage. We three had been in more capers than I can remember, him not being here felt like a black cloud over me. I shook his absence away.

'May I help you mem-sahib?' one of the attendants asked me as I pulled out my phone.

I did not answer.

I dialled Imah's number. It rang and rang, the echo of the ringing resounded some distance from the rear of the café.

I turned the café's corner where I last spotted the back of one of his bodyguard and headed in direction of the sound. Maybe I was over-reaching or being a tad anxious or nervous, then again when I saw there was no one around the corner, I was sure something untoward had happened.

Well there was one way to find out.

Slipping my hand into my jacket I put my hand around the familiar and reassuring butt of the Makarov and moved forward gently towards the soft vibrating sound of Imah's ringtone and the bushels surrounding the building housing the café. The branches swung back as it felt my touch.

'Imah?' I whispered.

I waited for an answer but was met with silence and the vibrating ringtone. All my senses were on alert as I called out again. No answer. I went forward sliding my old friend the Makarov out of my jacket. My finger resting lightly on the trigger that was sensitive to my touch. Both literally and figurately.

I set aside another clump of bushels to find the limp and motionless body of Imah Rajan and one of his guards lay face down in the dirt. His other guard was several feet away, the other was no were to be found. Holstering my Makarov and tucking my phone away, I reached forward and turned him over. His sightless eyes stared back at me with his black tongue sticking out from his mouth. There was also a whole section of the left side of his forehead missing, the same could be said of one of his man's head. They both had been killed with a bullet each to the back of their heads. A powerful luger silencer was obviously used. The third unrecognizable bodyguard seemed to have been garrotted. Even though Imah deserved his fate many times over, I couldn't help doing the responsible thing. Closing his eyelids and swearing under my breath. Fucking bastards!

I should have at least had one answer before they did him in, I thought to myself.

As I turned to leave, I noticed two puncture marks, less than an inch apart on his neck. They looked like they were administered fangs of a snake. Why? I thought to myself. I had done some study on herpetology, the study of reptiles. I know a snake bite when I see one. Imah Rajan had been bitten by a snake but that was not what killed him and his bodyguards. Why such an elaborate scheme to kill someone? A fear tactic, possibly. The puncture marks were obviously meant as a warning of a fetishist representation intending to warn off nosy parkers. I didn't intend to wait around and find out.

I stepped over their bodies and was heading away from the café when the voice sounded behind me.

'There be more practical ways to leave crime scene mem-sahib'

I froze any movement of mine. It was too late to reach for my Makarov, so I did the only logical thing. I turned my head to confront the armed olive-skinned smirking face of the waiter who took my order just seconds ago and, on whose forearm, I had noticed the tattoo edge of a coiled end of a snake.

Why was I still alive? Why had he not shot me like I assumed he did with Imah?

The silenced luger in his outstretched arm that was aimed between my eyes held no illusions whatsoever as to his intentions. I was familiar enough with a Colt luger to know how powerful they were at close range.

'Even for a smoke' I replied heartily

His grin instantly slithered from his face, not in the least amused by my hilarity. He unsteadily beckoned me to turn and raise my hands above my head. With his Luger still aimed at me, I followed his silent instructions. I could see from his eyes that he was tense, not a Pro and any deviation from his instructions would result in him pulling the trigger on his weapon.

'You tink you funny eh?' he said gesturing for me to walk backwards, towards the two dead bodies.

'No. You responsible for my friends' condition?' I asked jerking my head back to indicate Imah and his bodyguard's corpses

'Your friend was troublemaker as you be' he said as he attempted to snicker.

'So, I deserve their fate'

'So, they be telling us'

'You and who? The Daayan?'

'Me and my colleagues back at diner'

Though he didn't confirm it, he wasn't the only one here who was linked with the Daayan. It must be a very efficient organisation if they knew where to find Imah or me. Did they spot me with Briggs by any chance? I would have to say, yes. I needed to warn him.

'I thought you Indians were a colourful Bollywoodian people' I jovially proclaimed.

His shaky finger tightened on the trigger of his Luger 'Oh we are'

'Really?' I asked, making an effort to giggle at the same time 'Then you better tell the police officer behind you'

I had sized the waiter just right. He was not a pro. This was not his day job. He might have somehow killed Imah and his men in cold blood, but he was new at this type of work, inexperienced in killing, hence his tenseness and why he fell for the oldest trick in the book.

No sooner had I mentioned the words "police officer" than he whirled around to confront the imaginary interloper. In that split second, I reacted like an arrow springing from a bow.

I raced forward and with both hands slapped the Luger from his hand. The gun flew from his grasp and tumbled away onto the earth, disappearing in the undergrowth. His head swivelled back and before he could respond in any way, I punched him in the neck. He cried out as my other hand came down a scant inch above his collarbone then lashed out with a frontal kick with my left foot, up his groin.

His hands which grasped at his collarbone darted to clutch at his groin. He fell forward to his knees, whelping from the pain in his neck and groin. I did not feel satisfied that he was suffering. I made a *Gow Choy*, a hammer fist and rammed it viciously into his agonised face. The crack of broken teeth from the instant my fist came in contact was more than satisfying to my aching hand. The waiter slid first face down into the dirt. His luger lay inches away from his feet. I retrieved it and slid it into the small of my back. My blouse was loose enough to conceal the weapon stuck in my pants.

Grabbing a handful of the waiter's thick black hair I jerked his face up like a marionette and stared at his face.

'Oh friend … eating is gonna be hard for you from now on'

He gurgled something illegible before spitting out chips of yellow enamel, spittle, and blood

'Why didn't you kill me, like you did with Imah?' I asked 'You had every chance'

He spat again all down his red uniform. 'W-wom woman -different. No … not easy'

So, I had escaped with my life because of my sex. How blundering sexist that was, but I was also thankful that he at least had a conscience.

'*Khair iske liye Shiva ko dhanyavad*' I asserted in Hindi rather badly 'Now take me to your leader?'

I do not know how a dash of absurdity entered my conversation, but it did. The relevance was not lost on me but not my captive who stared at me with wild gluten eyes.

'Y-your ac-accent is for shit'
'Where is he?' I enquired again
'W-who me-memsahib'
'Brahma'
'*Vahan nahin … Bee-Brahma*' he whispered; his head hung limply from my grip.
Tightening my grip on his hair 'You lie' How could there be no Brahma.
'N-no no memsahib I no lie' He closed his eyes and coughed erratically. More sputum and blood sprayed out of his mouth.
'You better think fast and tell me where I can find him' My fingers formed a *Cum Nar* grip – a claw grasper and I thrust it deep onto his neck, choking the air through his throat. I could have ripped out his throat then and there and he'd be dead, but I needed answers. Not that I had any compulsion to avenge Imah's death but there was it.
He gasped filthily onto my hand choking spittle from his open mouth. I tightened my grip. Unbeknownst to me he had bit down hard against my grip, and before I knew it, I realised he had bitten down on a capsule, probably filled with cyanide. He convulsed a shudder. I loosened my grip as he then threw himself backward.
My captive, the waiter was in a sorry sight, his features turned all contorted. He was one rancid, foul smelling puddle of emotional fear. I had not tortured him long or hard enough to warrant the fear he was exhibiting or why he thought there was a reason that best resulted in ending his life.
I reached for his mouth and tried to pry it open with my fingers, but he suppressingly chomped down, keeping it firmly close. His eyes told me he wanted this.
I stepped away.
'*Am-mera parivar*' he choked when he saw that I was far away enough not to prevent his suicide.
'What?'
'N-nadir'
What did a foot have to do with this?
'What?'
'M-my name … N-Nadir'

'Oh goodie … now we know each other Nadir … tell me where Brahma is?'

'T-take care … Amira … *vah achchi ladki'*

'Who … your daughter?'

His eyes blinked a couple of times in response.

'Brahma, where is he?' I screamed at him

He moaned 'Jai …'

'Where?' I barked

His eyes slowly clouded over, and he slumped further back, escaping his physical torment and whatever emotional distraught that would require that he enter the painless oblivion.

I stood over him for a long second wondering what if it was Brahma, he was afraid of, maybe this Brahma and his Daayan organisation, if they were one and the same were actually something to be afraid of. To put a fear in someone to make them commit suicide is no easy feat even in a country were lives are cheap. No, I was not willing to believe that such a man or organisation had that much influence in this day and age of digital and educational aspirations.

His death did tell me one other thing. The cyanide. It was Russian inspired. Only a Russian or someone in their employ would implore such a contrivance. On the other hand, the Chinese are also known for copying Russian employed strategies, but I was willing to bet that none of the superpowers was behind the Daayan Cult.

I heard the rustling of leaves and crunching footsteps from behind me. Someone was heading to my position.

I took off silently.

'Nadir' said a questioning voice

Needless to say, Nadir was in no way able to respond.

I made it some distance away before I stopped to peek at the person seeking out Nadir.

The bushels were shoved violently aside and out stepped a man with a lazy, feline walk of a strolling Tiger. I snapshot the banal bearded face of the person gazing down at Nadir. It was the face of a stranger in a black blazer, someone I had never seen before but someone whom I had heard rumours about. This stranger did the oddest thing, he picked up Nadir's body with one hand as if it were a string of barleycorn and raised it above his head as he inspected it. He stared intensely at the body, hissed and then like a tissue, he tossed it aside. He looked about him, inspecting the bodies of Imah Rajan and his bodyguards before shrugging, turning and walking away.

A sliver of dread went up my spine. I could not believe that he was here and that I would be at some point be meeting him soon.

# FOUR

Sigrid "The Sin Eater" Eatherly was here. In New Delhi. I could not believe it. I knew him only by reputation. I did not know his full story, nor had I met the man, nevertheless over the years my Omega database has been trying to separate fact from fiction.

What I know about him is that he was born to Swedish parents. His father was a river pilot and his mother a nurse. It is rumoured that he was trained as an Accountant but never quite finished, instead he joined the army. His first trial by fire was the first Gulf war where he was nicknamed "the Sin Eater", partly because of his name but mostly because of his uncanny ruthlessness. After a long absence from the world he appeared back on the scene in the business of professional mercenary killing. From what I have heard he was someone you don't want in his crosshairs.

It is rumoured he is the greatest combat fighter in the world. Having studied with the greatest masters in Japan, Thailand, and China and summarily surpassed them all. A man who fetches a singular high price in killing. His victims, I hear he describes them as "models" to his art. His philosophy is derived from one of Fredrick Nietzsche's quotes *"you get more out of life by living dangerously"*

"What the hell was he doing here?" I asked myself

Since I was alone, with no other clue to go on, my only recourse was to trail him. I wasn't foolish to think that he may lead me directly to the mysterious figure behind the Daayan, then again, I knew once I was on his trail, eventually I might just get lucky. First though I had to device a way to get close without being spotted and that meant a disguise.

I had to make my disguise as simple as possible. The poor and incapacitated were common all over India and were mostly unseen by the masses. They puckered the earth in numbers totalling the populace of this outskirt village. So much so that one person joining their ranks would barely batter the eye of anyone watching. On my visit to Imah, I had worn a more than easy pleasant eastern type attire, a dark red *Shalwar* with matching *Kameez* pants. I would be spotted easily through them unless I downgraded my look. Fortunately, that was as easy as selling pie.

Spotting a woman with a bale of *Khameeri Roti*, a Muslim style of sourdough bread on her lap half hidden in a corner alley, I made a quick proposition and exchanged her clothes with mine and a bundle of Rupees, enough to buy her clothes and wares five times over. Her dirty brown *Sari* was a six yards long Indian petticoat that I quickly tied around my waist, knotted it at one end, then wrapped around my lower body and over the shoulder, her black heavily stained *choli* that ended up being part of a *Hajib* over my head.

Kicking off my skirt and passing them over her, I hid under the Hajib and the waddling dress, rubbed some dirt on my face, arms, chest and between my cleavage and hurried over to the cafe with the wares of my benefactor to stalk the nefarious squaddie.

I went with the flow. The disguise I wore made me aware of my own visibility. When a couple of passers -by intentionally avoided me, and a couple of bystanders clicked their tongue on how tall I was, an idea formed in me and I subsequently developed a false limp in one leg. I glanced at my reflection in a store window and I chuckled inwardly. The disguise I wore didn't exactly make me melt into the crowd, but it was well in the ballpark.

Refraining from patting myself on the back, I tracked my adversary. I peered from the corner of an internet café window, two blocks away from the café. No one had caught my hasty change of disguise or exit. No one had yet raised an alarm of discovery of Nadir, Imah and his bodyguard bodies. No ambulance or police vehicle on scene to disrupt the Sin Eater's deliberate mess. Tourists and businesspeople were all going about their business.

I caught sight of Sigrid's frame outfitted in slim pants and a rather generous sports coat. He was having words with an artistic looking Indian man whom I presume was the proprietor of the café I was in just twenty minutes prior. There was no doubt in my mind that the café proprietor knew his dead employee's side job, from the way they conversed.

Whatever the case may be, I intended to keep a close eye on the Sin Eater, until he departed.

Nadir had passed on before I could get anything concrete from him. "Jai …" he muttered with his dying breath wasn't exactly a post-sign.

As I watched, continuing to make the pretence of being a seller of roti, I lingered in the shadows trying to make myself as inconspicuous as possible. There were enough tourists and traders around that I didn't stick out like a sore thumb. The last thing I wanted was to draw attention to myself that would rouse the curiosity of anyone around.

In all my adult years I have learned that patience is indeed a virtue. Such was the case when twenty minutes later, a black Range Rover with tinted windows appeared and stopped in front of the café. I spotted the Sin Eater leaving the café. He came down the wide small steps, taking them slowly, two at a time. He was not alone. A man wearing white starch trousers and a dark shapeless buttoned shirt with a bandage rolled around his head followed him. Part of the dress uniform of the café, another waiter. Something metallic glittered from round his neck, catching the sun as he walked.

Stepping forward with the wares on my head, I kept my eyes glued to the big man and his cohort. He opened the back door of the Range Rover and disappeared into it. His cohort walked around to the driver's passenger side and got in. The time had just gone past five which meant rush hour. It would be a simple thing to tail them if I had a vehicle. Instead I did the next best thing. As soon as they were some distance away, I tossed aside my wares into the arms of a hawk-eyed girl selling Thali greens and hailed a black & orange pedicab. The young girl stared at me obviously unsure of her next move.

The pedicab cabbie was not all too pleased with my appearance when I jumped into the cramped battered narrow back. He couldn't frown away his feelings from the crinkling reddish rupees I peeled off from the bunch I had in my hand and held up to his face.

'Please follow my friend up aways'

If he was unsure of what to do when I told him to follow the Range Rover, I certainly was.

He snatched the notes from my fingers and quickly engaged the vehicle. He moved into the nearest traffic lane while I leaned back in the seat, keeping my eyes on the rear of the Ranger Rover which I hoped would lead me one step close to the tenuous and shadowy Brahma and the Daayan Cult.

The driver was smart enough to keep his cab back in a manner not noticeable to the Range Rover.

'Any idea where my friend is heading, *Bhaee*?' I asked the driver in his native tongue. Addressing him as brother really irked his view of me. From Mundak we had moved through the ring road of Connaught Place down half of the Faridabad Skyway before turning into one of the radial roads away from the financial and business centre of New Delhi.

'Old City' replied the driver he replied in familiar Hindi.

He glanced back at me through his overhead mirror

'Your friend *Bahan*, he owe you money?' he asked addressing me as a sister.

'No'

'He steal from you. If it be so I call police'

'No, bhaee nothing like that' I assured him. I leaned forward and whispered in his ear. 'He put my sister in family way'

The driver blushed under his copper complexion. 'Ah I see. You go make confrontation, yes?'

'Something like that' I grinned

'You watch out *bahan*' he cautioned 'Car look like it owned by man who not care much for anything. Not even your sister' he said flicking his thumb against his index finger several times in quick succession.

'Then you better keep eye on our friend then' I replied

While he drove blaring the sounds of Naezy the rap artist, I linked up with Galahad and inputted the name Anurag Surte.

It seemed Anurag Surte was an unknown organiser of sorts. He or she hired actors, players, fake protesters, all sorts to do whatever was needed. Fill up empty seats for organisers, promoters, casting extras for Bollywood movie projects and even rioters. According to the authorities the name Anurag Surte they were sure was a fake persona and that he maybe, a "student" or wealthy back bencher of the Indian parliament, because he didn't seem to be lacking in funds or information. It is rumoured he might not even be Muslim or Hindi or Sikh and that he might be a disgruntled wealthy Indian or expatriate. Though not confirmed like his ethnicity, it is said that he uses this medium to deliver seditious speeches directed at the country's contentious citizenship law, exhort people of a particular community to block highways, have sit-ins, burn mosques and vandalise Hindi and Muslim owned shops. This proved more than anything else that he was neutral and had no sides or agenda and that maybe he or she just wanted India to burn.

I had a thought that this was somehow, maybe a strategy from someone or a group of someone's with an alternate plan. Maybe to destabilise and capitalise on or done deliberately for some other darker purpose.

It was quite dark now and the traffic had thinned out considerably. We had left the dark red sandstones of monumental legacies left by Moghul Emperors far behind, by passed some bazaars and mosques. The Range Rover finally slowed and turned into a huge set of gates leading up to a red fort.

'Stop' I told my driver.

He obliged me as the Rover disappeared through the towering sandstone gates that were falling apart from centuries of weather and man-made use. As the driver wished me well, I slid off the seat and hurried over to the gates. The pedicab disappeared long before I reached the gates. A crooked sign-post flaying on one side of the gate named this area as the Shreyansh Fort. Glad now of the what the darkness afforded, subtlety I peeked through the gates.

The gateway was lined with knick-knack stands, print shops specializing in suggestive Moghul miniatures and the usual assortment of food hagglers.

I was not a tourist nor was I dressed as one and as such I had no time to linger over the wares being hawked on either side of the gate. I kept my distance and averted my eyes from the Rover up ahead that had stopped in front of a narrow wooden booth. The sign in front of it read that the *Son et Lumiere* show was about to begin.

Sigrid "The Sin Eater" Eatherly and his bandaged companion I noticed with him earlier exited the vehicle and without hesitation they walked straight into the booth without purchasing a ticket for the sound and light show. The Rover drove away and into what I believe to be a parking lot. I did not think twice about buying a ticket and joining them. The ticket vendor whose face looked like a bucket of mud found my smell and my facade nauseating but sold me a ticket anyway. I adjusted the hajib around the lower part of my face as I walked past her.

A smooth white gravel path led away from the ticket booth into the inner courtyard of the fort. There was a garden surrounded by marble type buildings and rows of folding chairs set out for the audience. A spotlight slid its blue-white beam over large marble pillars, and I could hear the taped narration of what seemed to be the famed Peacock Throne being pillaged by Persian hordes in the eighteen hundred's being broadcasted over the digital speaker system.

The lights went out and there was the dramatization of the events the organisers believed represented their truth. First was the clatter of the hooves of horses coming from afar, then the actors took the stage.

The show was a psychedelic history lesson. A "trip" without the benefit of a hallucinogenic enhanced drug.

I searched the dark for my targets, but I couldn't pinpoint them from the crowd though, from the hairs standing up on the back of my neck, I knew they were close and that I was being watched. I could not spot anyone, nevertheless I could feel the threat to my stomach. The feeling made me feel like a frog on a hot rock. I was still in the process of pinpointing them when I turned my head over my shoulder half expecting to spot them in the dim light, instead I found myself standing in the way of a slim and razor-sharp kukri knife.

How they spotted me or how they presumed who I was or figured out I was following them was beyond me, at any rate that did not matter now. All that was necessary was the fight and pray that I come out surviving. The blade was coming down for a sharp slicing cut. It would have accomplished its mission if ever so untimely. Without thinking I jerked a step backward, but it tore through the left arm of my Sari. I thrust out one hand in a *sohn -nul mak-ki*, a knife hand block but Sigrid's cohort wasn't around to try his luck a second time.

My assailant's white teeth flashed a sardonic grin through the white bandage around his head as the blade of his kukri hovered in the air. One of the spotlights from behind the stage caught him full in the face and for the first time I caught the appearance of his face. The spotlight light also luckily fleetingly blinded him. He threw himself sideways and began to run down the aisle between seats. Could it be? I asked myself. Naveen? From last night.

The audience, most of them, western tourists were blissfully unaware of the fleeing Indian and were truly gullible when they started clapping to his unintentional race through the aisles just as the sound of triumphant trumpeting blare coupled with the clattering hoofbeats resounding in the air to the wild barbarian war cry actions of the actors on the stage.

I was running, right after my assailant and like him I was inducted into the show's unintentional intrigues.

As I ran after him, I reached under the stained choli I was wearing and pulled out my Makarov. Not one tourist in the audience found our actions disconcerting even as the spotlight swept across the glint of black steel in my hand.

I found myself behind one of the pillars before the white spotlight could catch up to me. Narrowing my eyes, I strained to see through the shadows. The open walled fort reeked of age and earthly musk. My assailant was here, lurking waiting for my next move. For an instant I wondered what the Sin Eater would be up to since his presence was conspicuously absent.

I could have turned my back, hailed a pedicab and returned to my hotel. Forgetting the task Sir C had set me to, in any case I did not. I felt that I was on the verge of finding out whatever nefarious scheme this organisation whatever they're called. My assailant had to be found and I was going to do just that. However, I did wonder that if the Sin Eater was coordinating this little altercation my assailant was conducting, I might just think twice about going after him.

A dull thump complemented the first of my accoster's hassled footfalls. I heard him running toward the rear of the exposed building. Crouching down I went after him, relieved that he was getting farther away from the spectators and onlookers that would possibly be endangered by the vicious confrontation about to take place. Alert to every sound, it wasn't difficult not to hear a low pitch groan from over the drum rolls echoing from the acoustical system setup of the theatre. His white pants reflected in the shadows as I caught sight of him. It seemed in the darkness he had tripped over some accoutrement and sprawled half over on the floor. I squeezed my index finger on my digital imprint trigger and the Makarov barked once in the darkness. My gun shot flat out without aim and a spark.

The slug chipped off a marble stone near his feet, sending a puff of misty dust into the air. I missed my mark, in anger I hurried forward, but my assailant had already scrambled to his feet and was no longer in my sight. Hurrying over the low wide steps, I found myself emerging into a narrow dry path flanked with mudbrick walls on either side.

From behind me came a sharp intake of breath, I did not have a chance to put my Makarov to use. Instead I used my elbows to do my talking. I rammed both of them back and upwards, twisting my body at the same time, I caught him with a glancing blow to his shoulder.

His blade was much luckier. It sliced part of the top of my right arm, making me exclaim in pain as I sidestepped him. His second lunge was very unsuccessful as I slammed sideways into him with my shoulder ignoring the pain and stream of blood coursing out of my arm. Without pausing, I rammed my right leg into his groin and watched as he snatched at them with one hand before slithering down the wall. I noticed I still held onto my gun as he slinked down against the mud brick wall and pointed it at him.

'You done?' I asked him

'We be meeting again, memsahib 'he said with a coarse and feeble attempt at laughter. His words came out with considerable difficulty because part of his lower face was covered in cracked bruises.

'Naveen?'

'Yes' he sounded a bit too confident than when we met earlier, considering the situation he was in.

I moved closer to peer at his face in the darkness. It was the bloke whom I tussled with the night before. For some reason I did not know why I didn't recognise him earlier. The bandaged face should have been a big clue.

'Boy you do get around, don't you?'

'Yes memsahib' he replied with a scornful look.

The metallic glimmer that snatched my attention earlier was a metallic garrotting wire chain that was around Naveen's neck no doubt responsible for one of Imah Rajan's bodyguard.

'So what? Robbery wasn't enough, you want my life as well'

'Is no use memsahib. We know why you are being here. Kill me now and you still be knowing nothing'

'And if I don't?' I asked him

'It making no different'

'What is it about this …' I started to say, but in that split second, something thin and metallic flashed across my field of vision. I whirled around, squeezing the trigger of my gun. The bullet droned off through the dark air and then as if by magic it was simply literally plucked from my fingers. The muzzle in the grip of the man with the sunburnt smiley face and huge figure.

Sigrid "The Sin Eater" Eatherly emerged from the darkness like a streamer. Holding my gun with curious abandonment.

'Not so being clever as you think memsahib' Naveen gloated at me as he got to his feet disentangling the metallic wire from his neck.

'You've got to admire how small-minded these locals are, huh Miss Dax' Naveen's accomplice remarked with an amusing smirk.

I tried to move back but Naveen blocked my movement. The Sin Eater levelled the Makarov at my head, a more than sufficient warning to stop me dead in my tracks and not to try anything. I didn't have a clue on what I could have tried. A backward kick at Naveen would have been useless with The Sin Eater present. I was certain he would not hesitate to pop a bullet into my head.

'You know who I am?' I asked Sigrid Eatherly.

'I've heard of your reputation' he said with an Afrikaans accent. 'I never realised you were this pretty'

'Ah! So, what now?' I asked

'You will kindly raise your hands above your head' he ordered, grinning diabolical at my helplessness.

'Am I to be taken prisoner?' I asked

'Your choice. Death here or prisoner for some entertainment'

I raised my hands up as Naveen passed the garrotting wire through my shoulders and around my neck.

I stiffened my neck.

Naveen coiled the wire round my neck and tightened.

I was still facing the barrel of my Makarov in Simon Eatherly's hand. Suddenly my weapon of choice was no longer an old friend. It was devastatingly monstrous to look at. I had forgotten that because of the digital sensor in the trigger he could not use it even if he wanted to.

'You deserve plenty more memsahib plenty worse' Naveen hissed from behind me.

'See?' The Sin Eater chuckled

The wire cut into my skin and I could feel myself using up the last of my air supply. There was a point where I started gagging for air, Naveen behind me just snickered as did the Sin Eater before me.

'You be fool memsahib, Brahma know …. We be knowing all'

Trying to struggle and free myself I could swear his voice seem to be echoing from a darkened tunnel. Try as I might, I could not get a grip of him not trying to strangle me. I could hear myself moaning and groaning dropping forward, struggling for breath. At the last moment, the Sin Eater let go of the trigger on my Makarov and brought the butt down across my forehead.

A black pool opened up beneath my feet and I dove in. It had no bottom, but I felt rather good, like an amputated leg sinking.

# FIVE

I returned to the surface smoothly.

Or so I thought.

It was a persuasive, dreamlessness stir of blackness that was both comforting and consoling. That was until I neared the light. A protected film of dark moisture came to me making me smile. But the higher I rose the higher it began to itch and ache at me, like shards from broken glass. I tried to shrink away from it but the more I shied away the more it pressed on me, trying to flay me alive. In response, I charged at it as if I were rising from the bottomless sea like the Kraken. Too bad I was not the Kraken because the higher I got the more pain and confusion I felt. 'No … I will not' I heard from someone far away only to realise that I was the one speaking.

I heard myself repeating it over and over, louder and louder as I scratched at the pain pressing down across my eyelids. It took me a while before I could flutter them open and I found myself staring through a film of moisture something dun-coloured, ochre moving back and forth in front of me pulsating in and out of space.

I blinked my eyes rapidly for a couple of seconds at the same time polling myself forward from the pain encroaching in my head, my neck and my arm and vibrating all over. The vibration suddenly stopped, and I sank down too dazed and queasy to move.

I do not know how much time had passed after that. My inner chronical predisposition was telling me twenty-five hours had passed but there was no way of really knowing. Unwelcomed dreams invaded my consciousness each time I closed my eyes and each time my eyes opened I tried to throw it away.

I raised my hands only to realise they were already outstretched. I felt sand, earth between my fingers. I was moving between alternating warm and cold layers of pain, all the same I was alive. When my blurred vision finally focused itself, I found myself upside down next to an earthen wall with twisted straight square-like bars enveloping me. Now the ochre made sense. I was hanging by my feet swinging to and fro, between a rocky wall and a cage.

Each time I opened my eyes I felt that something grating roughly against my skin, burning it, as if something was rubbing me causing me great pain. My ears on the other hand could hear the clatter of an adolescent snickering from somewhere above me. On the fourth go I began to sense that there was a procedure being done to me. It was being done to me over and over by the crouched child above me. He or she was manhandling the rope and lugging it from side to side.

My head felt like it had gone through a blender and was now settling into crushed eggshells for a curry flavoured smoothie. What I had felt scratching at my skin during my unconscious purgatory was a huge pallet of straw propped against the cage before me, unlike the gravelly wall behind me. I leaned my head against the wall and listened to the most beautiful sound in the world.

My breathing.

I felt my chest rise up and down. I glanced down at the hand Naveen had slashed. Part of the wound was coated with a heavy film of dirt while part of my choli had been used as binding.

Why was I still alive? What were they waiting for? Why had they not just done away with me? Curious questions that were rattling in my brain and could be answered later. First, I had to get upright.

I need not have bother. A pair of manly feet in sandals came up to the cage and stopped. He exchanged words with the child, snapped at him before letting the child jump down and scurry away. A few seconds later I felt the owner of the feet manhandle the rope around my legs and slice through it. I crumbled down in a heap against the red sand below me as I heard him walk away chuckling.

I slowly untied the cord around my ankles and slumped down.

I pressed one hand down against the sandy ground and earthen wall for support. I slowly crawled with my knees around the cell like cage, trying unsuccessfully to avoid the straw pallet. I was more than a little dizzy. I was nauseated, which meant that at some point I had been drugged. What with, was something I dare not speculate on. The soreness of my neck from the tightening of the copper wire combined with the blade injury and blow to the head were all one big bruise on my person.

Though I felt drugged weak and ached all over I tended to try and get my bearings.

By the light above and the lowness of the moon I guessed the time to be about five a.m. Taking tentative steps until my shaking knees could support me, I found I was in a six feet high square enclosure with twisted square bound bamboo branches for barriers. On each square were barbed wires, meticulously coiled around the twisted branches forming a nice steel mesh on my cage and set between a wall of rock with a sort of crevasse opening. On one side between the enclosure and rock wall was a foot-high closed grate which I surmised was used for slipping in meals. The wires were great for conducting electricity. And since the three sides excluding the top were exposed to the elements with the wall attached to a four-foot exposed crevasse for backing, there was no great leap as to know why the wires were there or why they had built this gaol just here. I rested against the rock-strewn wall, keeping my distance from the blackened crevasse my prison was built in, knowing that when I had my strength, if I had my strength back and if there was a later, I could find some cracks in the three-sided cage or the wide-open rocky fissure.

Since the child had been crouched above me playfully conducting and enjoying my helplessness, I could assume that the wires where not charged with electricity at the moment. Though I could be wrong.

I was almost naked. The sari and choli I exchanged were gone, so was my Makarov and ankle boots. All I had on was my see-through nylon thighs, and my *Fleur Turner French* designed white luxury panties and bra. I bet they didn't take it off because of its sensual peek-a-boo cut-outs that make men go all progressive and conventional. Though a significant portion of my gadgets were missing, a couple were still on me. Thankfully, they had not relieved me of all my gadgets. Of the various gadgets there was "Cancer".

Cancer was the name of one of only four sophisticated organic powered subdermal-implanted transmitters, that was constantly linked to Galahad and planted under my left armpit. A personal guarantee against my being lost or kidnapped. The implants were partly made up of a rare isotope that continually sends a low frequency encoded signal to certain relay receivers via the internet. A signal that Galahad constantly monitors and while it worked it was a direct link to Seymour, the only man on this earth who knows me and everything about me. The man who had tried to foresee all possible catastrophes to befall me.

I was hoping if I was gone too long that this would lead him to me but if not then I would have to improvise with the other gadgets. Chief among them was in my tampon. I tapped my crotch and felt it. Inside the lining of my tampon were one transparent adhesive plaster wrapped in a wafer-thin silicone veneer and an upgraded concentrated *Belladonna* gas-form enclosed chemical in an eggshell-type rhizome. The plaster, like the bulb that I nicknamed *Hazel*, had in the soft padding, a strong combination of *Parasolutrine* and *Paracin Trichloride* mixed into it. The purpose of Hazel was to produce a quick paralysing effect on a single person or a room full of people. All I had to do was attach the sticky part to any two of my fingers, leaving the soft padding of the plaster exposed and press it onto my adversary's skin. I had used this method once before and hoped I didn't have to use it now, but glad it was there in the event it was needed. The Belladonna chemical that is primarily used for cattle anaesthesia in the rhizome was much simpler, its influence is like a knock-out gas. It just needs to be cracked open for it to do its job and was designed with three times the cumulative effect of the Parasolutrine and Paracin Trichloride chemicals. The belladonna could be used on a multitude of people, the effect would incapacitate those within any enclosed room within seconds only to wake up eight to ten hours later with a pounding headache and a vague or fleeting memories of what had happened.

I could hear indistinct chuckling and the sweet smell of *Chicken biryani and Assamese thali* cooking close by. I slipped off my bra and held on to it before tossing it against one of square barriers. Nothing sputtered, no sparks flew. That was a relief, it hadn't been electrified. At least not yet. I slipped my bra back onto my chest.

I leaned back further against the edge of the gravelly wall with the crevasse on my left, closed my eyes and started to concentrate. I needed to garnish my strength and get out of here somehow.

My mental power was bare and as motionless as my body. With my eyes shut, I forced my breathing to slow. Blocking all necessary senses of my surroundings, I engaged my mind and body to the art of restorative breathing as done the *jiujutsu* way, the adept Japanese art. With my mind's eye I summoned the essence of my chi. It is an intuitive mind trick to starve the imagination of unnecessary thoughts while at the same time restore your sense of self. It is something I had picked up in one of my imposed sometimes-worthwhile travels. When Seymour found me, he immediately sent me to every karate or ancient art survival sensei he could find to train me. Every three to six months during school holidays, I was under the tutelage of a master in survival or the finer arts of self- defence. He genuinely wanted me to be prepared for anything and everything. Given my virulent childhood, my wealth and cavalier nature, he sure knew as a target, I had to be tough and imaginative enough to combat any crisis imaginable. Be it business or combat wise.

I was two thirds within the inhalation of a breath, about seven minutes in my meditation when a voice sounded from above me.

'Good morning, Miss Dax. You slept the whole day; I trust you had pleasant dreams'

The voice emerged from the darkness above me, startling me with alarm. It seemed to be coming out of a voice distorter of some sort because most troubling fact was that the voice was definite frighteningly familiar without being familiar. I spotted a grated contraption just above my cell.

'Yes, well there you have it, Susan. Our man maybe on the verge of smuggling tens of millions of pounds of heroin, diamonds or whatever into the UK'

The voice, which was Sir C's, recited my conversation with him over the phone some forty-eight hours ago almost verbatim.

In my head I went "W-what the h-hell?"

'But that's the least of our problems' Continued Sir C's voice 'If it were just a matter of smuggling, I wouldn't need you to poke about.

'That's s-some trick' I managed to reply

'Isn't it though' replied a more normal voice without any acoustics. A voice I recognised as the Sin Eater. 'Hey! I know you're scared right now. You don't need to pretend. I'd be trembling in your position. You don't know why we brought you here, but I guess you know the answer can't be good. You're right it's not. We had every combination to your deck figured out, even when your hand came down on a familiar pattern we were there. Hey, check this out' there was a short pause then a different voice started speaking from the grate 'I'll be seeing that Shaggy blonde ballcock Boris tomorrow, where I'll tell him that we cannot interfere with his fucking little island problems, unless he gets down on his knees and kisses my shoes. He'll understand of course and thank me for the interest and my mercy'

There was a long silence while I contemplated what I had just heard. The voice was an exact copy of the United States President Mr. Trump speaking with distressing undertones about the British Prime Minister. This conversation might have happened or to what I assume, was an entire fabrication. It was disheartening and made me sick to my stomach. This Daayan was real all right, and they seem too cold blooded, ruthless, egomanias and above all clever. A destabilisation of harmony between friendly political leaders would certainly put the world on the brink.

I moved upright against the wall with my shoulder to the exposed crevasse.

'Have nothing to say?' Sigrid's voice asked me.

I really did not have anything to say, then again, I didn't want him to have the upper hand 'That was very childish of you Sigrid' I said with a sigh.

I heard chuckling 'It was, wasn't it? There was a slight pause before he continued 'So, you know who I am?'

'A Swedish accountant trained mercenary nicknamed by your guerrilla pals as the Sin Eater. Is it true you are the greatest combat fighter in the world?'

'Yes' he replied unabashedly.

'No ego there I see'

'Unnecessary, in my case'

'What a load of bull' I dared

Though I could not picture him, I imagined him sneering.

After a slight pause he replied very boastful-like 'You're trying to goad me'

'Is it working?'

'No, Pressure wasn't quite right'

'Pressure huh?'

'Yeah, see how I use it on you. *Få en belastning på detta*' He finished in Swede. I was quite sure, but he was more or less telling me to hold onto my nickers. There was a lingering silence, then I heard dialling, then a voice came on.

A tough Indian/Eton emphasised voice came on-line 'Anard'

'Hi, this is Susan Dax' said a very recognisable voice. My own voice.
'Ah Miss Dax nice to be hearing from you. Director … Mr Steele did mention you might get in contact'
'Yes. I guess he told you all about me'
'No. He was … how you say … cagey yes … he said just to keep you informed and provide you with assistant if and when you ask …oh and that you will reciprocate your services if you so desire'
'How coy of him'
'If you say so memsahib. I did go to your hotel but …'
'Yes well, I'm sorry about that … kindda busy but it concerns this organisation he asked me to look in'
'The Daayan … yes'
'Well, I've made very discreet enquiries and I'm sad to admit this, but it doesn't seem to exist, I did find out that Bada Nair and D Company were making some big strides in smuggling. Competing heavily. I think some bad blood may spill into the streets. But I think you can handle their little dust up'
'It's no surprise. The Punjab and Goa gangs are always up to something'
'Well they are, Imah is definitely thinking way above his station'
'A flaw of his'
'What is?'
'His ambitions' Anard's diacritic voice replied.
'I bet it is' my voice answered back.
'Is that it?' asked the disappointing voice of the intelligence officer.
'Yeah. I'll be leaving for London sometime tomorrow'
'Couldn't you enquire further?'
'I'm afraid I have other business to attend to and its very unlikely that our government will interfere with matters of your Internal Security. You understand of course'
'Yes, I do. Thanks for all your efforts'
'You're welcome. I'll give Sir Steele your gratitude'
'You do that'
The phone hung up.
Another long silence followed. The imaginary phone conversation of that little speech was impeccable and had been performed in an all too

familiar voice. Mine. I had just listened to my own voice, together with all the right intonations, voice inflection and speech patterns.

The Sin Eater and his Daayan cohorts had me cold and they hadn't wasted no time using me to get the Indian Intelligence and by extension MI6 out of the hunt. Indeed, by their own estimate I was also out of the picture on my way home, which meant my hours of life were limited.

'I'm impressed'

'I thought you might be' The Sin Eater's voice said 'How's the pressure? Feel it yet?'

I ignored his taunt, Instead I asked 'How did you get my voice print so …?'

'How does she seem?' interrupted a conservative but emphasised Indian voice I did not recognise speaking away from the mic.

'Suffering'

'Not enough'

'Would you care to try boss?' asked the Sin Eater.

'Give me that' the unrecognised voice said forcefully and arrogantly.

'Who the hell is that, Sigrid' I asked

'I am Brahma'

'Ah, the man behind the scenes'

'That is correct'

'That truly isn't your name is it?'

'Certainly not'

'I figured. Then you can answer the question?'

'What question?'

'How did you get my voice print so accurate?' I solicited

'*Yah koee bade baat nahin hai*' he said in Hindi.

"*No big deal?*" What an understatement.

'Of course, it was a big deal' I replied grasping his use of Hindi. I dearly would have given good money to see the expression on his face when he got to hear my reply. 'Go on impress me on how clever you are' I dared

There was a pause, a click 'We had your hotel room wired for sound' My own familiar voice replied. I could not help shiver at listening to my own voice. Why did he switch back to that contraption, could it be he wanted to illicit this response from me?

Trying to sound calm, I said 'I'd like to extend my compliments to your electronic experts. Indeed, they are geniuses. My bug detector never picked up a surveillance device in that hotel room of mine'

'You can thank Kavin Chandra for such subterfuge' My own voice replied 'It's the latest in all of his inspiring inventions, courtesy of the labs at Connexion. He says it is equipped with a floating algorithm Nano wireless receptor with an audio translating replicator and identification software programmed into it'

I scoffed 'I bet it's not reliable and has one of those inconsequential names like Kavinator'

'No matter what it does, he calls it "*A-tome*".

'Doesn't sound original' I remarked

'Named, he says in respect for some French bikini inventor from the forties. He operates devices twice the size of a pinhead. They're extremely efficient and reliable' the duplicate of my voice explained.

'That explains it, it would be like finding a needle in a needle stack'

My own laughter reverberated in the air from the grate speaker.

'You have a good sense of humour Miss Dax but Chandra in case you are unfamiliar with him is an Indian import who works for me and my organisation' my voice gloated

'Doing what, playing hickey with world leaders?'

'Surely you know Miss Dax since MI6 sent you all the way here to have a look. It's Chandra's accomplishment, this "A-tome" gadget you have come to procure isn't it?'

'No idea what you're talking about'

'You have no ideas as to how many countries would want his marvellous voice imitator. I find that hard to believe Miss Dax'

I had to pause. Could it be Sir C sent me on this trail so that he could get hands on this "A-tome"?

'That may be so but it's the truth' I said truthfully training my eyes on the grated screen as if I was watching his every move.

'A device that can replicate any vocal pattern and you don't think it has value?'

'It has tremendous value. It just depends on how it's used or by whom' I stated, emphasising on the word "Whom?".

'You think me crazy' said my voice

'Crazy? No Brahma, you are much too smart to be crazy. Crazy men never know they are crazy until it's too late'

'You are sly. But I appreciate your left-handed comment on my behalf. No, I am not crazy, not by my standards anyhow. As for the "*A-tome*" most agencies now know how utterly effective it can be. The previous incidents were just trial runs, experiments as they were. Soon after Chandra has done with his little tinkering, the tests will stop and the real fun begins'

'Fun?'

'Do you know the disposition of India on the world stage Miss Dax'

'A little' I replied while my eyes were exploring my cage. In truth, all my knowledge about India and China's temperament stems from the title of an old magazine, *"The fateful Race between China and India"*.

All my words and actions up to that point were carefully suggestible to put them off their game, it wasn't working as effectively as I hoped. Without making a sound I stood up. I hesitated to explore the crevasse. I was guessing it was my temptation or my folly because it was still concealed from inquisitive stares. It was not going to be concealed much longer, not if I had anything to do with it.

'Well Mother India is a wedge between China and your indisputable west. But with the help of my Chinese associates that wedge will be no more. My ancestor's dreams of unity with China will last much more longer than any in the world's history'

'The world could do with more unity And a Sino-Indian union will be welcomed. Just how one goes along with it is the problem' I said storing everything my voice was saying, while stalling for time.

'Quite right Miss Dax. An alternative to the Soviets broken bloc and the free world market, in a short while I will have the market world prostrating at India's feet. I have wealth and enough power to influence any outcome. There will be a union between China and India and my people will no longer be the half clothe starving horde you westerners watch on your TV during commercial breaks. We will become a nation as powerful as Bharat of old'

It was kind of weird hearing my voice speak of conquering and TV commercials.

'That is when they stop breaking heads and splitting penises from all the rioting, I assume?'

'Oh that's a small issue since I am instigating them'

'Including the ones abroad too? The ones in Orlando, Greece and Frankfurt?'

'Yes' said my voice incredibly pleased with itself 'By the time I'm done, the western world would be too busy with their petty problems they wouldn't care about our plans'

'Perspicacity incarnate' I replied almost exasperatingly 'It's the twenty-first century Brahma, people are not easily converted these days. Most are concerned with their twitter page or what the Kardashians are up to. As for your people, they should be concerned with filling their stomachs, providing for their kids, improving their health care rather than killing each other over antiquated laws or beliefs or prostrating themselves to icons of snakes'

'You know little of our cultural mentality Miss Dax. I am of royal blood. Blood that trace its ancestry down the ages to Kali and Naga, a serpent ancestor. My turban is that of a coiled cobra with its proud fearless stance poised over my head' Braham said. The voice, my voice had turned cold and reptilian. I was doubly amazed he could speak and translate his emotions through my voice. Chandra's device was truly remarkable.

'I suppose getting rid of crime lords and causing riots is one way to go' I heard my voice sneer 'Rajan and his brethren are just minor sacrifices to produce my wonderful age as is the riots. Cutting off the dead contaminated flesh of India will be a steppingstone of my new Empire of the strong'

'She's not suffering Brahma' said a voice away from the mic. The Sin Eater's voice

'How about feeding your barely clothe people first, Brahma?' I asked edging a word of two in before the idea of what suffering they had in store for me came into play 'If you have unlimited wealth, influence enough to make a difference you could do that without instigating riots. Or does the Daayan not believe in free thought. Or could it be you don't think your people will appreciate your efforts' I threw my head back and let out a sardonic laughter, mocking his dreams and the mad yet worryingly plausible ambitions he had set for himself.

The man calling himself Brahma was barely amused.

'We've had our chat, Miss Dax' he announced 'I just wanted to let you know you've stepped into a nest of vipers and you're not coming out. Your government is no longer the policeman of the world and we are no longer subject to its reign. They will not be able to stop me from obtaining my dreams. As we speak, Chinese troops are poised to join our own little militia to liberate us from the yoke of poverty and install a *Mahajan,* a new Gandhi who will bring prosperity for the subcontinent'

I had no doubt he was thinking of himself when he mentioned Mahajan or Gandhi. It was not exactly as smooth as Casanova's pillow talk, but one could no doubt get the gist of his tirade. This man was just using the Daayan Cult as a means to an end. He never cared about their goals if they had one. Who was he?

'There is a saying "Never sleep with a Chinaman, you might wake up missing more than you expect"'

'What's that supposed to mean?

'S-snakes lie, so do Chinamen' I asserted, shivering in the cold air.

'You do not know what you're talking about'

'The big boys from China are using you and you're swallowing their lies hook, line and sinker. The west you so despise will not stand idly by to see who reaps the spoils, all they need to say is announce to the world that this is for the sake of freedom and you will start a war that will wipe two-thirds of the world's population. If we are lucky, because the only thing around will be your precious cobras roaming the radioactive world you would have created'

I leaned against the wall to catch my breath.

'Enough of this'

How does one really try to reason with a psychopath? And how was I supposed to be reasonable when all I can think of was escape? I have come in contact with very unreasonable people in my life including this manic who has branded himself as Brahma. He didn't want to rule the world, he just wanted to return to the past, and did not mind letting the world burn by causing World War III in the process. He was blinded by his desire and dare not see the hideous danger his wild fantasy would dredge up. It sent a chill dredging down the centre of my spine.

'Yes, I agree' said the voice. The voice of Brahma said coldly. 'In any event Miss Dax you will not be around to witness my victory despite your ignorant remarks. Tell me what do you know about snakes and the survival rate of their bite?'

Due to my earlier Herpetology research I knew that snakes have no eyelids, are carnivorous, they swallow their food whole, are not aggressive unless threatened, are found on every continent except Antarctica and hate ammonia. Not that I was going to share that knowledge.

I leaned against the rocky wall. Pausing my search for a hidden escape opening.

'That depends on the snake'

'Exactly' Brahma replied 'Nice to know that you still have your wits about you. Here are some facts you may need'

'Will they help me from this prison of yours, Brahma?'

'I doubt it'

'Well go ahead' I proclaimed dryly 'You have my complete and undivided attention'

Brahma laughed rather cockily 'You amuse me Dax but let me be brief. I have other matters to attend to. You might not be aware, but Herpetology is a hobby of mine and I am in favour of five types of poisons emitted by snakes. Depending on which one inflicts its bite on you, you will suffer excruciating abdominal pains for days or die within twenty minutes from cerebral or internal haemorrhage'

'Ohhh can't wait'

I told him, my eyes alert for any flurry of movement.

'My favourite as you can guess is the King Cobra. Its bite will make you die of anoxia, a slow agonizing wake of asphyxiation. If by some fluke its cousin, the Asian Cobra gets to you before he does then you will die of a poison more deadly than strychnine. The choice will be yours Miss Dax. Personally, I will opt for the Krait or the Vipers. Nevertheless, I expect you to suffer the most grotesque and tormented death you can possibly expect'

'You expect too much Mr Brahma' I declared, calling out.

'Yes, I do.

For you there is no viable alternative I can think of'

'I would expect the Sin Eater to have another, more preferred option. Am I wrong Sigrid?'

'Mr Sigrid has no desires, be it for or against'

'I doubt that'

'Oh, just die why don't you' I heard my voice finally say.

There followed a silence, punctuated by the sound of my own laboured breathing. I knew his threat was not idle. Brahma fully intended to kill me using the most grotesque method he could think of. His maniacal means was by using his cult snakes.

My eyes moved nervously around my cell. Even as I continued to look for a means of escape. A creaking whirring noise caused my eyes to jerk back to the side of my cell where the foot-high closed grating was situated.

"This was it" I thought to myself as I watched the grate slide slowly upward.

I thought about Bilquees and Nadia, my two wards and beneficiary of my wealth. I also thought of Seymour. As his ward and executor of my will, I knew he and they would be fine. I doubt he would find it tedious trying to control a billion-dollar empire on behalf of my two wards. Bilquees at this moment was in the first year of college while Nadia was an intern at some technical college. How would they react to my death? I had no idea. Yes, they would take it hard but how would they mourn? I put an end to that thought and focused on the here and now.

The grate was electronically controlled, I never foresaw that. The grate slid out of sight, exposing a wide foot sided opening. Common sense told me to remain were I was and as silently as I could possibly be. Unfortunately, it is pretty difficult to keep one's cool when you know what to expect. A minute later, nine writhing, hissing whirly snakes came slithering into the hole and onto the earthen floor of my cell.

## SIX

When Brahma said I had stepped into a nest of vipers and I wasn't coming out, he was being literal in every sense of the word. There were four different types of snakes slithering towards me. Four were Cobra's, two vipers, one Python and two Asian. They were about five feet in length each. The Python was the longest and robust than all the rest. The Asian Cobras and one viper I recognised from various Discovery Channel documentaries. The others from various other places. The viper I couldn't identify was yellowish and gold and was much smaller than its precocious species.

In my mind, it was the most dangerous of the rest.

I pulled my hair back and made a tight bow.

The Cobras wide flaring hood rose fast readying itself for a striking position. They spread their apparent rage on each other and then on their counterparts. There was also something in the air that my flared nostrils did not until that moment notice was present. A scent that sort of drifted into my nostrils with a powerful rancid discharge. It was a chemical rancid aroma that resembled musk. Even as I breathe it in the thick, cloying stench grew stronger, making me gag.

This must be a chemical inducing smell, designed to heighten the susceptibilities of the snakes. A chemical agent that was sure to whip their olfactory senses into a veritable enraged frenzy. Brahma was taking no chances with me.

I slid against the crevasse along the wall trying to distance myself from them. The combine amount of venom like strychnine in all the venomous slithering snakes was enough to render me dead many times over.

Combined with the hissing, buzzing, and sizzling sounds the reptiles were making, my morning was indeed becoming unpleasant not to mention the echoing from the grated speakers was my uproarious and demented laughter. It filled the cell with macabre and tormenting refrains. Brahma or the Sin Eater were doing the laughing, I could barely imagine I sounded that way.

'Goodbye, Memsahib Dax' My voice called out gaily 'Have an eventful day' my replicated voice chuckled, echoing away from the speakers.

As my simulated giggle died out, a forked tongue from behind jewellike eyes glittered in my direction, just as one slid against the edge of the wired grated bambooed cage. It was some sort of Krait or Asian cobra. It slid along the edge of the grated enclosure and onto the packed red earth.

For some reason I thought about my wealth again. I had enough wealth to build a fleet of space shuttles, enough to feed three third world countries for years and yet none of it could come between me, a snake bite, and my death. I would agree with Alanis Morrissette and call this Ironic.

What was this *Nodus Tollens* feeling I was undergoing? The realization that the plot of my life no longer made sense to me. I shook that thought away from my mind.

My nostrils flayed wide as the rancidly powerful aroma smelling musk got stronger. The gagging stench cloyed up the confines of the tight air within my cell.

Brahma wanted me dead period.

The olfactory senses of the snakes intensified with the cloying stench of whatever chemical was being pumped in here. The snakes went into a whipping hissing frenzy towards me. The King Cobra grew twice the size of its neighbour, slid slowly and gracefully from the ground into the air. I moved slowly across my cell afraid of making any swift darting motions to encourage the cobra to lash out in a deadly lethal strike.

Just as I felt one leg touch one side of the wired grated bambooed cage a fifth snake made its appearance known. Dwarfed by the size of the King Cobra, it was the smallest of them and seemed the meanest. I was just as wary that its size like the vipers and the cobras had nothing to do with its ability to kill.

Whether I liked it or not it was time to make my move. I put a finger to the edge of my panties and slipped a finger into a barely noticeable opening were the back yoke ought to be and fished out a 22 inch long wire and with the flick of my fingers the wire turned into a flaming laser. It was one of the "necessary shopping" items I had one of my companies FEDEX me.

Some forty-six hours earlier, I had called Daniel Anderton, my most senior of directors in Axis Systems and trusted friend. He headed a multi-million technological research and development corporation, one my many shell corporations in America. A corporation that dealt mainly with my other research companies and a man I trust. From the beginning when Sir Steele mentioned Daayan and snakes, I had known that sooner or later I might be facing the pesky reptiles and there was someone who could provide me something innocuous and daring to go against them. If someone could find that item in my many companies, it would be Daniel.

Daniel has an IQ of about one hundred and ninety and once upon a time, he was a proficient hacker of companies. Using blue crypted boxes to make long distance calls, internet connections in coffee shops or libraries to steal home shopping appliances or steal funds from the massively rich for the underprivileged and getting into all sorts of trouble.

One unfortunate mishap saw him before a Judge, who gave him an option, join the army or be sentence to a four-year jail term. He took the logical option. His wild streak was curbed to some extent but not enough for him to stop hacking into secured networks. Some years ago, he was forced to resigned from the army after he was caught hacking into some defence satellite to receive better reception for a children charity organisation holding a party in the Middle East. As with all geniuses, he was quickly bored with life and with no real challenges. In search of some amusement, he found another hobby, that of finding fat cat executives or millionaires and milking or swindling them out of millions for charity. His golden goose was to be an elusive executive called *One Nine Eight Four* and he diligently followed a strange string of links until he found Seymour but before he could find me, I went in search of him and with a little luck found him. Our first meeting ended with me, despite his training, working him over good in a bare fisted fight. I bloodied his face and made him walk lopsided for a week and a half. Our second meeting was one of propositions. He made one and I made a much-improved proposition. One he could barely refuse. Anyway, since then he was one of my closest friends and most trustworthy males in the United States.

'Daniel?' I whispered into the handset

On the other end of the line came a grumbled voice 'Anderton here'

'Danny, its Susan'

'Boss' his voice changed instantly and became all humble and flattering.

'Daniel' I had said into the receiver "You busy?'

'For you? Don't be silly'
'Good'
'Your ears must have been burning'
'You say that every time. Whatis it now?'
'How's your stamp collection?'
'I don't collect stamps'
'Not even the Treskilling?'
'The yellow Swedish stamp?' The blue Treskilling was a 3-skilling stamp made by the Swedes in 1858. Due to printing errors, some were printed in Yellow and were as valuable to stamp collectors to the tune of $2.2 million.
'Yes, not the blue one'
'Like I said I'm not a Philatelist'
'Ok what about your necklace collection. Interested in Improving it?'
'What are you talking about?'
'I'm talking about a pear -shaped diamond that weighs about 14 carats worth about $17 million ...'
He need not go on 'The Blue Empress is on the market?'
'Yes'
'Get it for me'
'Will do. So how are things with you?'
'Daniel this is not a social call'
His reply was unsurprisingly straightforward. He knew this was not the time for any funny business.
'You in trouble, boss? What is it?'
'I prefer not to speculate' I remarked into the mouthpiece with a very condescending voice 'But I think I'll be dealing with snakes'
I was impressed as his voice once again changed, slightly 'Are you sure?' There was shock and surprise, but it was muffled. I could tell it was there, in the nuance of his voice.
'No'
I gave him a brief description on what I think might happen.
'We'll have something in sixteen hours' His normal nonchalant speech was replaced by combat ready deportment 'Where are you? Never mind' After a short pause, Daniel said 'I see you're in Delhi, I'll find out what you may need with the added accoutrements, I'm assuming?'

'Yes'

'You'll have it by breakfast'

'It has to look innocuous'

'Of Course'

'Thank you, Danny'

'Boss?'

'Yes?'

'Sure, you're alright'

'If I'm not out of Delhi in 72 hours' I said to him with a smile on my face 'Call out the hounds' I remarked before hanging up.

That was a day before my meeting with Imah Rajan and hours before Naveen's robbery. A parcel arrived with a note "From Ketteract. Wear with care"

Michael Ketteract was the chief scientist of ZenoTech, a man who had a brilliant mind and through hard work had obtained a scholarship followed by numerous grant proposals to study comparative biology's of the Neanderthal and present day man from Princeton, the American department of fish and game, wildlife, and many others. A few years back, something happened because he could not quite finish one particular proposal after a colleague fallaciously or unsubstantiated accused him of fraternising with a student of his. An accusation, which literally destroyed Ketteract's reputation with his academia, his personal life washing up in the wake. In any case, the specifics are not important, only that Ketteract at one point in his life wanted so desperately to eat a bullet. According to Seymour, he was way passing the crossroads of his life but a chance meeting with him, a contest involving matchsticks and his life changed. An offer was made by Seymour and a reciprocated promise from Ketteract was all it took for Ketteract to pull himself out of his despair and work hard enough to become a leading researcher in the field of the human genome. He was Seymour's friend and to my knowledge the one and only time I met him, I noticed he had a soft touch for bones, spores, animals and was a gentleman. He opened doors for women and loved helping old ladies up the stairs and take out their trash. However, to me, that was all a façade to hide his real impulses. Not that I cared about them.

The items in the parcel was an Epi-pen, a pair of Ann Summers see-through thigh lingerie and a pair of Fleur Turner French designer panties 12.8 cm and bra 32DE, both crafted to my correct dimensions and which I was currently wearing, with friendly instructions on how to use.

The Epi-pen contained a powerful Antivenin toxic to a snake bite which should be taken 24 hours prior to any bite. The Ann Summers thigh lingerie had been laced with a special chemical, chiefly among them was a component made from Ammonia. According to Danny's instruction it will repel eighty-five percent of snakes.

The flaming laser or "*Melee Whip*" as Danny coined it, was a powerful and dangerous of conventional weapon in use, modified to work like a whip-sabre. The internal workings were too complicated for me to remember but basically the visible wire harnesses a pliable plasma channel that is contained. It was 22-inchs in length with a weighted button tip that was used secondarily for grip to whack your assaulter with precision, but which actually housed a small lithium battery as a power source.

The body of the whip was made from a 3 -inch flexible high-tensive cable and when charged with the battery it tends to become white hot as a laser and do some unscrupulous carnage to any attacker. Carnage which had a limited time of effect.

Twelve minutes to be exact.

Giving my knowledge of fighting and weapons, the ability to use such wires demands great skill and a proficiency in weapons. I knew that using this with nothing, but wrist action can generate a good amount of force, causing enough sting to cause maximum damage. Because of its length I could be a decent amount away from my hissing and slithering feral companions in the cell. Not much but enough.

A quick flick of my wrists, three lashes and half my problems were a thing of the past.

With three lashes, I had succeeded in making an opening, albeit a small one and I had eliminated two of my fangled hissing friends. Their necks twisting lifelessly before my feet. The lash had cut not only through flesh but steel and wood.

Part of my six feet high square enclosure with twisted square bound branches for barriers now had warped sheared metallic lines from the effect of my Melee Whip. Also, its meticulously coiled twisted branches were now a garrotted mesh opening of cracked wood. My life now depended on the speed which I could get through the small opening. Another lash of the wire and the opening was almost wide enough to get me through.

Behind me as I raced to the opening, three of the deadly snakes remaining were all hissing and buzzing as if in a fit. I knew they couldn't help their senses being dosed by the intense fetid miasma of an unknown biochemical, I just wished their attention was not so focused on me.

As the sinuous reptiles made a bead for me, I made small swift motions activating reflexes which could be either terminated by a strike or a kill. By the time I reached the opening they were no more than a few feet from me. The melee whip was of little use, I had been advised that its killing setting had limited power. Six lashes at most was I going to have. I was going to try to reserve the last two lashes on something imminent. Not that this wasn't exactly imminent.

The hissing of the Cobra was so close, so loud that I had to stop all protestations in getting to the opening. I wasn't at all concerned if I was being observed. I doubted it. Both Brahma and the Sin Eater had left me for dead. To their best belief I was in a matter of minutes or hours depending on the bite. They didn't expect much beyond my death.

I bent down slowly and scooped a handful of dirt and devoid of hesitation I flung it into the leading cobra's foreboding face. Then flinging myself forward, I hurtled into the improvised opening. The last thing I was thinking of as I clawed my way through the deformed wiring and cracked bamboo was where it led or that there may be other poisonous reptiles awaiting my exit. Something soft struck the callouses of my bare left foot. A billion dollars couldn't bring any doubts as to what it was. Danny's Ann Summers see-through thigh lingerie had no effect against what snake did the bite. Thankfully, it could not penetrate through the tough soles of my feet. A condition I have had from walking from Siberia through to the middle east when I was much younger. My soles had developed hard callouses that were tougher than raw hide. Or just maybe Danny's Epi-pen was doing its work. Nevertheless, I jerked my foot back and scrambled faster forward, scraping my head body and skin through the low, narrow crude opening. There was not exactly room for me to turn my head to see how many snakes were attempting to follow me through. I was betting, all of them. I could still hear them hissing and buzzing as I pulled myself forward but thankfully a faint current of fresh air caressed across my face with an unmistakable draft as their sound grew less fainter as I pulled myself finally through.

No alarm systems were going off, no urgent shouts were being made, apparently Brahma felt that I was being taken care of.

I burst out onto some crude playground. A child of maybe six in tattered clothes peeing watched me as I burst through. The surprise on her face was indicative of someone not expecting what she was seeing. She watched me, still crouched, not saying anything as I got to my feet and brushed myself off. Wrapping the Melee Whip around my right palm I walked up to her. I suspect the sight of a half-naked woman suddenly appearing before her was quite a sight. '*Chalana*' I said to her.

She had no idea what I was on about as she stared back at me with black beady eyes. "Run?" from what? She must have wondered.

I turned my head. The sight of the slithering, hissing and buzzing reptiles coming towards us was enough to make her understand. She ran off crying on her small oxbow legs towards the constructed red buildings with guard lights on. It seemed I was in an overshadowed villa of some sort, the building she was running to connected all of the other buildings to them. Not exactly the place I would have a choice to escape through. I took off in the opposite direction down a singular path with a resilient type of bamboo fence bordering its side, away from the dying smell of chicken biryani and assamese thali.

As I jogged off, I thought of what I could do to repay my very inviting hosts on their intentions. Brahma and Sigrid Eatherly where the only things on my mind. Their clever little device the "A-tome", their intentions where not conducive to my thoughts and for that I was going to make them regret their actions. With the "A-tome" at their disposal the world might be incapable of dealing with Brahma's group and their intentions but since they had just given me a model for their plans, I had a fair idea who was bankrolling Daayan and Anurag Surte.

One thing though, I did not know was how he was going to put the "A-tome" to use. How would he wreak havoc like its counterparts' name and succeed with their peculiar and yet horrifyingly preposterous goals?

I had been tasked by Sir C to see if this Daayan really existed. I wondered if such an aged cult could be around and now, I discovered it is real. Or being part and parcelled as real by a devious megalomaniac.

Pity I could not put a face to the voice or the name.

I was consumed with getting away I forgot one of the first tenements in the art of war. *"Never let up your guard"*. I was approximately two, three blocks down the bamboo path when my eyes hit something which caused me to stop short. A high rock barrier with soft artificial light streaming through a secondary wooden enclosure. It had cracks in its square shaped wooden panel catching my attention and shorting my escape.

Nearing the enclosure, I pitched my whole body up onto the barrier with silence being at the top of my list of priorities. No sound followed or preceded my entrance to the wooden barrier. It was constructed in four narrow parts of hardwood. I put my eye to one of the cracks in the structure, having no idea what I might find. I found boulders, different lengths of driftwood, all seemed very ordinary, but it was a small stagnant of a black green pool of water that I noticed things I had no desire to find. Not just the pool but the ground was moving and the all too familiar sounds reached my ears. The hissing, vibrating buzz of serpents. By the left of my right foot there was a flap which I knew must be jerry rigged to be opened at certain times.

Now I understood why my cell was constructed where it was. The only escape, if there was an escape was the path in this direction and were it led to. Brahma must have had this constructed to lure hungry snakes from here to the cell, no doubt goading them with that fetid chemical smell that I still now sniffed.

The snakes were stirring from under the rocks, lifting their long necks and small heads through the surface of the pool, wriggling through countless others and slithering between, on and around the pool, wood and the earth. I heard a whine and my eye drifted to a contraption just to the left of the enclosure. It was a basket of some kind filled with assorted types of wriggling rodents. At the bottom of the basket was a translucent tube and from it dropped a chunk of raw bloodied meat. Almost instantly two large ravenous snakes consumed it, with the larger winning the larger piece. A large lizard was dropped from the basket to the tube and into the enclosure. A King Cobra slithered its body with no longing desire to forgo its innate compulsion in chasing and symptomatically rising up towards the scurrying lizard and striking with deadly precision. The lizard saw the flaring hood of the cobra and tried to evade. It darted sideways but the cobra sang its fangs into the scaly neck of the lizard. The lizard hunched up for several seconds and the cobra slid back. The lizard moved ever so slowly to the reactive poison in its system, like a drunken sailor on liberty. It dropped to its side, its claw appendages kicking sporadically before the cobra swallowed it, feet first. Satisfied, the sluggish cobra wrapped it bulbous length around one of the driftwoods, looking as if it were basking in the noonday sun. Rats, more meat, lizards were periodically dropped into the enclosure and when I had enough of the sight to see I peered away to search for my escape. But it was not to be that easy.

To my left was the path back to my cell and to my right was the whole stretch of rock wall with the snake pit. Before me, just behind the feeding contraption was an empty space leading away and hopefully to safety. At least I hoped it led to freedom, but I did not get an adequate view of the contraption feeding the reptiles only that I surmised it was one third full. I knew enough of snake's habits that they are sluggish after a meal. Hopefully, they would not be as aggressive as they were with me in the cell. But I doubted it.

Every reptile was going to prevent me from escaping if I made a move towards them, or through them even sluggishly after a feed. But it was worth the risk because soon Brahma's posse will be after me and know exactly where I've gone despite the cries of the oxbow crying child. So, I waited until after their feed. It was a nauseating sight to behold, watching the cobra's, the vipers and kraits attacking again and again, wriggling here and there, swallowing their thrusting quivering victims, and then finally laying in an inappropriate angle, seeming satisfied.

It happened suddenly. I finally got a flash of the feeding contraption and viewed the protrusion of a long sinuous arm dangling over the feeding contraption.

'You all eat better than Granny Harinakshi' I heard a humourless and sarcastic voice in Hindi say.

Just as it was with Brahma, it was a voice without a face. However, memory served me well all the same. The voice was shatteringly familiar.

The last time I heard it I was standing half naked before a corpse and just about to chase down a thief. Suddenly my rage caught up within me as if it were only steaming until now. It bubbled up from inside me as recognition hit me.

It was my comforting lover, Sameer Kannauj.

# SEVEN

I should not have been all that surprised. Maybe this was karma or just a seasoned cynical convenient way of him having been brought before me. It was hard for me not to be emotionless and brutally hard at this moment. After all I have put my life, not to mention my chutzpah on the line again and again despite my wealth and I could not help becoming violent to those who would be cruel and savage to the world they inhabit. Sameer Kannauj, I had taken him into my arms with a measure of compassion. Even if he were a stranger, I could still feel the heat and tension he generated in my loins, no matter how brief.

Hearing him speak just now erased all consciousness of the raw and exquisite pleasure we had given each other. It was replaced by the realization that he played a classic decoy honey-trap to perfection. Distracting me while Naveen and his gun totting partner rob me or better still, keeping me distracted while Naveen and his buddies bug my hotel room, in either scenario it caused me to feel a blind seething hatred.

Sameer's long gaudy arm slid away, vanishing from my sight, just as a scrawny black rat was the last of the rodents to grace the displeasure of the feeding contraption.

The poor black rat was attacked, subdued, and swallowed whole by a Krait and then silence reigned in the snake pit. I reached down and tried to pry open the wooden flap by my right foot used to aid the snakes escape down the bamboo enclosed path. It didn't take more than four seconds for me to slide the flap upward, nevertheless I needed to be cautious and feel a little temperance. My eyes roamed the pit in case the snakes discovered what was occurring. Nothing stirred and nothing moved with slippery purpose.

After getting it up I put the most crucial aspect of my plan into use. I ripped off my thighs and tossed them at a specific spot in the pit. I then raised myself and propped myself against the sides of the wooden panel, pulling myself out of harm's way when the snakes come racing away from the pit in fear of the ammonia in the lingerie. During their rush I was going to scale the wooden enclosure leap into  the pit and

using my gymnastic skills I was going to vault my way up and over. If I
not only get the timing right but land at the precise spot I have to land,
I'll be free and clear.

But it was easier said than thought of. Danger isn't exactly my forte,
then again it seems I crave it. I always like to challenge the potatoes of
my existence but not the sauce. I wasn't Susan Dax adventurer, trouble
shooter because of my beauticious looks or figure but by way of common
sense, wealth of experience and luck.

I hung back, avoiding all necessary risks until I was satisfied my plan had
more than a fifty percent risk of working and did it work. With my eyes
fully adjusted to the light the only thing that remained was my speed.
Speed, I told myself, that's all that was needed.

Still propped against the sides, I stuck out my head and shoulders and
peered over the enclosure and began to see the effects of my lingerie.
Several of the snakes had left their comfort zone and were sliding against
the sides in an effort to get away from the scented ammonia they were
simply sensitive to. A couple had found the flap and were streaking down
the bamboo path. It wasn't long before half the snakes had emptied out
of the enclosure. Holding onto the wooden enclosure was a strain on
my arms.

Still I held on and made several calculations in my head. It would take ten
feet by four yards to get across, the distance between a long agonising
breath of death or life. Suddenly my cell was looking more appealing
than this.

A stubborn King Cobra with its head turned away, lay on a strategic
boulder and several vipers lay about it in similar relaxed and unaggressive
postures, seemingly immune to the effects of the ammonia in my lingerie.
Speed, I reminded myself.

Steeling myself, I let the melee whip loose in my hand and rose up until
it seemed I was standing over the enclosure, my back against the corner
niche between the end of the bamboo fence and wooden enclosure. I
could hear someone moving about away from the pit, no doubt Sameer.
I hoped he was alone, but there was one way to find out. Inhaling
sharply, I brought my gymnastic skills into play. I vaulted up and off the
wooden enclosure forward and springing deftly in a high tee position
onto the boulder where the satisfied King Cobra rested. It wasn't at all

planned, nonetheless the essence of speed led me to spring my body upward and forward, evading the innate springs of the hissing vipers around my feet as I landed on the boulder. I leaped in the instant my feet touched the rock, while my hand let loose the melee whip for a fourth time. They struck the rearing vipers at my feet. I didn't look back to see what I missed as I sprung onto the other end of the wooden enclosure. Tightening my hands around the wooden high wall, I pulled myself up and out of the enclosure. Though my incursion was brief, I had managed to awaken the lazing reptiles. There were now sizzling, hissing sounds of the awaken reptiles. They spat and struck into the air at where I had just been. There was no time for me to rest or catch my breath, I was already running in a split second. In that instant I heard a cry of astonishment. If I had anything to do with it, it would have been the last sound Sameer would have uttered. He was six seven paces away carrying a bucket from which he had been feeding the critters in the pit when I rushed him and struck him in the throat, stifling his need to call out for others. The bucket cluttered to the ground as I jumped, twisting myself up and around him. I kicked him in the gonads from behind, letting him fall to his knees, before wrapping an arm round his throat, curbing any cry or protest he might have wanted to make.

'You say a word' I whispered 'I snap your neck'

Even if he put up a challenge, he'd be no match for me. He had already seen me kill a man, so he knew I wasn't bluffing. With my bloodied fingers I wiped them across his face.

'Surprised?' I asked him 'Don't tell me you didn't know I was here, you sonofabitch'

He was trying to speak but my grip was too tight. He nearly ended up choking.

I let my arm loose, a smidgen.

'I … I didn't k … know … I swear to …'

'Oh, shut it … just like you didn't know about Naveen and his buddy huh?'

He shook his head violently from side to side in protest to my accusation 'N-no … not then …' he griped, gasping for breath 'No Miss Susan please … please on Vishnu's head … please I beg you to believe me'

'Believe you and get a snake bite for my troubles or better still a bullet through my head'

'He never said anything about you to me. Only later'

'Who?'

'My *cha-cha* Brahma'

Now I was surprised 'Your what?' I exclaimed

'Har … my … uncle … Brahma. He's my uncle Miss Susan. Please, he's been my everything since I was a *bachcha* …just listen please and …' he pleaded exceptionally low pitched 'Afterward … please … if … still want to kill me then …'

He left the sentence unfinished.

My rage was still bubbling inside me then again something in me had slackened. Rage that was partly directed at myself, for being so gullible. Was I about to succumb to his plea? Could it be he sensed my arousal for him the moments before I scaled the snake pit? How come he could sense that feeling and capitalise on his pure physical chemistry? I told myself that it wouldn't hurt to hear him out, knowing that someone pleading for their life is much more revealing. He as far as I knew was the closest thing to the real identity of Brahma.

I eased my grip further 'Start talking'

'Yes … I was to make myself known to you. Get … whatever information I could get'

'The excellent honey trap huh? What did they want you to get?'

'I don't know' he whispered, his voice barely audible 'Why you were here, how long you were here for. Not … nothing … about the men who hide bug … in your room or Amand and Naveen who come later'

He strained to turn his head up towards me. If he weren't so innocent, he would be straining to scream my presence all over the place trying to attract someone's attention.

'So, you were to find out information about me? Why, Sameer?' I asked coldly. How the hell did they get onto me in the first place? I pondered

'He made me do it'

'He made you do it?'

'Y… yes …but after what happened at the hotel, I couldn't do it anymore. Not with Amand dead. I had to leave and forget the whole thing'

'He made you spy on me?'

'Please' Sameer begged 'Just … please let me explain'
There was no evidence he was stalling in any case there was no proof otherwise, in either case and yet he spoke solemnly with intent and an uneasiness that made me at least listen to what he could tell me. If he was being straightforward, he could be my possible link to the Daayan Sect and Brahma, and if he were being untruthful, I had little to lose. I made up my mind to listen to him and try to read between the lines to his words and try to spot any contradictions.
I let go of him and stood over him. Prepared to strike the instant something upset me.
Sameer made no false moves. His tone of voice was strained after my choke hold. He explained to me that Brahma had raised him and forced him into his service despite his solemn objections. Though he was his uncle, he was more of a father and his older brother. It's not like he could refuse despite his objections, after all Brahma's reach not only in the government or police were substantial. 'He would kill me the moment he feels something not right. He has threatened as much to me'
'Uncle huh. And your parents? Where are they?'
'Imprisoned somewhere by him. I don't know where'
I have always considered myself a pleasant judge of character, but my latest track record would suggest I take a careful account of whom I judge. Maybe it was still my rage and anger that was preventing me from seeing his sincerity I really did not want to.
'And suppose I believe all this?'
'It matters not. Whatever him and the big white man are planning it be done soon'
'How soon?'
He was about to reply when I heard footsteps behind me. I jumped and whirled fast behind him and waited. I let loose the melee whip and poised myself for whatever action might be needed.
'Sameer' An inquisitive male voice called out.
'Who is it?' I whispered
'Reeven. One of my uncle's men' Sameer whispered back.
'How do I get out of here?'
He gestured due west, at the buildings eclipsed by the villa.
'Give me your phone'

He panickily reached into his pocket and produced a Motorola. I tapped the settings and went to the "about phone" menu, memorised the phone number before handing it back to him. 'I'll be in touch, you better answer when I call'

It was risky to trust him, then again, I was willing to make a leap of faith. If he betrayed me again, things would get very hairy. I melted into the dark as Reeven came into view.

## EIGHT

I didn't exactly leave, I wanted to observe the scene before me, unfold. In the darkness, close to the hub of the Daayan cult I had the perfect advantage.

'What in Vishnu you doing?' Reeven demanded forcefully as he walked up. He was a middle- aged man with greying temples and just a little too much spring in his step. I recognised him as one of the fake waiters from the Colonial Café. He was in-fact the artistic looking Indian man whom I presume was the proprietor of the café. The one I had no doubt knew his dead employee's side job, from the way they conversed.

In his left hand I could see a Sig Sauer P226 handgun. It was half trained at Sameer. On his arm just below the rolled-up sleeve of his white Pagri shirt was the undeniable tattoo of a snake coiled cobra.

Picking up the bucket 'What you think I was doing?' Sameer challenged. He moved forward a little tense. I was uncertain if he would suddenly call out to him and reveal my presence. I waited because this was a perfect position to see if he'd betray me and if he did not, it was also the perfect reason and position to gather as much information as I could.

Sameer didn't bother to glance in my direction as Reeven stepped up to him.

'You took too long' he sneered lowering the gun.

Sameer glanced at the lowered gun and asked 'You never were concerned before, *ab asap kaon pareshan hain, Riven?*'

'You not know?'

'Know what, Reeven?'

'That girlfriend of yours she *saanp pinjare sey bacha gaya*' he said displaying an arrogance I had seen before.

"Snake cage" is that what they called my prison?

'My girlfriend?'

'You know, your *angreji ladki* from the hotel' he said with disdain

I shuddered inwardly at the moniker *"English lady"* he had used for me.

'She was here?' Sameer asked, simulating surprise.

'Yes. Your uncle is *narak kay roop mein pagal.* You didn't see her by any chance?' he asked as he tucked the butt of the Sig Sauer into the back of his pants.

I grinned as I listened. I bet Brahma's mad as hell at my escape.

'Why would I see her?' Sameer replied 'I didn't know she was here'

'Well she was and now she's not'

'Good for her huh?' Sameer joked

'Do not take that attitude with your uncle, *bachcha*'

'I take whatever attitude I like ... especially with my uncle'

'Child you push your luck against your uncle's patience too much' the middle-aged Indian replied '*Tum sach mein Vishnu tum par dekh raha hai aur nahin apne Chacha Dayan chudalilon*'

'Vishnu is kind. He sees all' replied Sameer

I did not really get that part about his uncle's Daayan witches.

'He does indeed. By the way he needs to see you in his study, Surte just left. *Ab*' he finished curtly

Maybe it was the way he spoke or his condescending manner, but I hated the man. His association with Brahma and now Anurag Surte whose name I hadn't heard since Imah mentioned it earlier was enough for me to strike. When he turned away from Sameer, I launched myself at him. I propelled myself at him with an intended Taekwondo strike. I came out of the darkness like a flee on the back of a tiger and struck. I hammered Reeven with a *Son-kai.* A knife-hand sort of strike. My open hand hammered down from the darkness, through the air to administer a chop to his neck. The force of my attack should have instantly broken his neck.

Some instinct within him was aware of my attack. He twisted away from me as my hand came down onto the side of his head. I felt my knuckles fracture some of his facial bones. In any case, damn the man, he was not ready to capitulate to a white girl, especially an *angreji ladki* whom he deemed inferior. Reeven turned around from where he fell and came at me with an anger, I had not seen in quite some time. He reached into the back of his pants in an effort to pull out his Sig Sauer, I darted swiftly to his left twisting round and delivering a *yiop cha-ki kick.* Bringing my left knee high up to my waist I balanced myself on one foot and with my knee locked in one position I slammed it out in a savage and perfectly executed side kick. I caught his hand at the wrist sending the pistol clattering across the floor. He opened his mouth to scream but I was literally at his throat. My grip on his windpipe wasn't exactly secure because the both of us careened back and forth within the jungle. Reeven gagged and out of desperation struck me twice in the breasts. I let go out of agonizing pain and he staggered forward, out of pain but unable to call out. He started to rush away into the night towards the buildings glinting with lights. I jerked forward still dizzy from his blows and leaped for him in an unadorned rugby tackle pulling at his legs out from under him. He fell to the earthen floor with a loud thump.

I was on top of him immediately. My fingers digging into the pressure points on his arms. For the life in me I couldn't get a grip to my satisfaction.

'You are one tough bastard aren't you Reeven?' I declared to him Instead of answering he shoved his entire body forward in an effort to unhinge me then again by the strangest of luck I caught hold of his *Spienius Capitis* just behind his neck and squeezed. For the longest of seconds his reaction was at it should be, then all of a sudden, his body lost all tension and it relaxed. Blood vessels burst across one of his cheeks as I got to my feet and stood over him.

He struggled to move but couldn't. 'What you do to me, girl?'

'Nothing a little pressure won't undo'

He struggled to free himself from the paralytic hold that he was under but try as he could, he could not. A thick glob of bloody phlegm crossed his face as he continued to struggle. He cast an eye at Sameer's revulsion. Sameer was now a willing compliant in whatever endeavour I was behind.

'Brahma will see you both dead' he spat.

'Maybe so, but you won't be here to see it'

I had no mercy for this man. He was a mercenary in the service of a murderous madman, and I had no time further for him.

I raised a foot.

'No memsahib I only take …'

'Orders. Don't we all Reeven as they say duty has no lovers'

I was about to bring my foot down on his neck and feel it break under my stamp.

When I had an idea. I wished I could see him crumple to the floor. Watch as he rolled to the side, his neck lolling to one side, his face distorting into a grotesque grimace of pain. But my idea would be worse for him. I got behind him, tucked my arms under his shoulders, tugged him halfway to his feet and dragged him to the wooden enclosure of their snake pit. It took me several seconds to haul up his body weight to the enclosure, with him protesting and cursing. When I did get him there, I propped him at the end of the rocky wall.

I loosened the melee whip from my hand and wrapped round his neck over his pagri collar 'Here' I acknowledged turning it on 'This might help' I told him getting under his knees. 'No memsahib no …'

'Have a great trip' I remarked as I hauled his whole body up and over into the snake pit.

He landed in the artificial pond where I had witnessed the deadly snakes rear their grotesque elapidated heads and make a meal of their preys.

There was wild churning in the water, a flash of an annulated tail. The melee whip lit Reeven's neck up and the pool lit up in a nauseating neon light of creepy crawlies. He convulsed in a hideous spasm of agony. He managed to push himself forward, trying to make his way out of the pool of stagnant water but one of the remaining deadly snakes sunk its small fangs into his forehead. It moved awkwardly with the grip it had on Reeven's forehead. Another snake, a cobra got a tight grip of his forehand and hung onto it with a strange horrifying tenacity. Reeven could move all the same not by much. My paralytic pinch on his body was in full effect. The type of death he was to experience was the one he and his cohorts were to make me experience.

Oh, death was sighing a sweet smell to what he was about to undergo.

Oh, how I wish Brahma and the Sin Eater would only experience it as well.

I glanced at a shock faced Sameer as I went looking for Reeven's gun.

I found and picked up the Sig Sauer.

'That's what your uncle intended for me' I said to Sameer.

'That may be my faith' he whispered to himself. He seemed far less in control of himself than I gave him credit for, disregarding what he had just witnessed. 'The things he's had me do. All for him and his cause …

his belief in a one India. Worship him as he were Naga of old. Reeven and his men deserve worse … trust me'

'Who is Anurag Surte?' I asked briskly.

'I d-don't know, I'm not present or always sent away whenever they meet. I-I do know he is a disruptor or controller. My uncle provides him with whatever he needs to organise riots, supplying weapons and information and money. Protesters, student rebels and campaigners like everyone. Hindi, Jihadists, Nazis, Shiites and Sunni or Sikh dissenters anyone who want to do some serious damage'

No wonder the mysterious Anurag Surte had no persona, he was a person with unscrupulous morals backed by a man who wasn't batting on full wickets.

Sameer's face seemed to be straining under pressure. I could see he was about to feel the release of emotion. I did what I would do in any situation such as this, I changed the subject.

I flicked the magazine release of the Sig Sauer P226, inspected the 13-round cartridge clip, slammed it back into its chamber and cocked the gun. The Sig Sauer is a reliable gun, hence its popularity but sometimes it tends to not cooperate. The mere action of my inspection was enough to stifle any mood swing he might have been considering. I increased his heightened emotional stability by asking him where we were.

'I will tell you everything but first you must tie me up. If my uncle realises, I helped you … my faith is certain and so are my parents' As he went in search of a rope, he informed me we were several miles away from Jaipur.

Jaipur! Where the suicidal killer Nadir with the daughter Amira had wanted to tell me.

I've heard about Jaipur, the city had something to do with the colour pink.

'If you can make it through the villa, use the lab entrance that building there' Sameer said pointing to the building connecting to the centre villa on the west side with garnished portico and colonnade structures 'It shouldn't be crowded but with your escape … my uncle's force's *baval mein hoga* … oh er … they be in … in … er … frenzy. Try to head left as much as you can when you get outside the road west will lead you right into the city … is long walk'

I ignored his concern.

'How many men does he have?'

'Excluding Mr Easterly, eight but they are no more fanatical that his followers'

'His followers?'

'About fifty I think' he added

'Don't worry I'll make it out' I announced to him half holding up the Reeven's gun.

'My uncle has taught me not to trust no one, somehow he's gotten into my head so it's hard to think for myself. I think I trust you Miss Susan. I have no choice now if you can help with my parents' his tone detached. Though he seemed distant, I could see there was strength and determination behind his frightened eyes.

'I'll do my best, I promise' I assured him, though I still had no way of knowing how I would be able to get to his parents out in time from a place that was unknow to me or him.

'I believe you. Why is that?'

'I have one of those faces?' I teased. Sameer shook his head.

'No. No, that not it'

'Maybe because we've been intimate'

'Must be must be' he whispered. He reached out and took my hand, curling his fingers around mine.

'Tell me about your uncle's box?'

Three wrinkles appeared across his forehead 'Box? What box?'

'"The A-tome?"'

'I know nothing about any box'

I told him what it does, and he made a small grunt of comprehension.

'So that's why Kavin been here for last couple of days?'

'You know this Kavin?'

'He's been in conference with my uncle and Mr Sigrid all afternoon. It was strange because guards were guarding the lab too closely than normal'

He informed me of what his uncle used him for. Because of his looks, skill and popularity with the sitar, he was reluctantly used for the vilest of sports, seducing women for unspoken perversions perpetuated by his men and him, all designed to fulfil his uncle's and his men's sado-sexual pleasures and amusement. Some of his victims he was sorry to say ended up dead or on a sacrificial altar up in the mountains. He informed me he would help in any way to get away from that sort of work provided I could help with his parents. I informed him of my assignment, and we made plans to meet up the next day. He could be trusted now, by not interfering in my fight with Reeven or making my attention known, he was now a valuable ally whose life I did not want to jeopardise.

'You don't seem to be an agent Miss Susan' he wondered.

'I'm not'

I informed him I was doing a favour for a friend.

'Friend? He inquired. 'Must be good friend' He said still searching for some sort of rope.

'He deals with thieves and liars all day'

'Still he a friend' he said as he cast about his eyes looking for some damn rope 'We better get you going before someone comes looking for Reeven'

'Don't worry he won't suspect you' I asserted as he bent down to retrieve something.

'No, he won't … not unless we find …'

'We won't need a rope'

'What you mean …?' he started to ask, before he could finish, I cut short the rise to his feet with the butt of the gun. I clipped him hard across his temple and his body crumpled back to the ground. For added insurance, so that they did not suspect him, I brutally punched his face and body till it was a barely recognisable pile of flesh. It was the best way I knew I could ensure he would be alive for our meeting and days to come. His uncle would assume I was mad at his betrayal and dealt him a beating he would not forget. I felt his strong pulse before leaving him to the faith his uncle would design for him.

*     *     *     *

Platitudes, like clichés only become platitudes because they succinctly prompt things that border on being universal truth. They are stereotyped and simply so glibled to the fact that they fit a multitude of sins and circumstances.

One platitude that came to mind as I left Sameer Kannauj beaten up, alone with a collection of venomous snakes and the dead body of one grotesque café cum mercenary, was when it rains it pours.

Things did not happen in drips and drabs, no … oh no … they were coming at me fast and furious, ever since I arrived for the restructuring of INFLUX.

In a short space of time, I've speculated on the wild goose chase Sir C had sent me on had any credence, been robbed, become a witness to several brutal murders, literally been led into the lair of the Daayan cult and been fed to ravenous reptiles. It had not been a stress-free or convenient route. And though I had not seen the mysterious Brahma behind the Daayan cult, I had certainly been given more than I can chew on to prove it was no fiction and that he and them, was an absolute threat.

Though I had faith that, that too will be a thing of the past, now with Sameer's assistant. First though my escape to Jaipur before he and his heavy breathing grunts make a meal of me.

The building Sameer had indicated was to the west of the compound. Entering through the first door I understood why he referred to this building as the laboratory. There were specimen cages, small glass cages in rooms that looked like a combination zoo and herpetology laboratory behind white doors. With the gun poised, I crept down the constricted poorly lit hallways just as a voice echoed in the air. Reverberating from the opposite way of the hallway.

'Reeven? What took you so long? Sameer taking his time with those cretins?'

It was neither Naveen nor any voice I recognise but I read the impatience in the man's voice. I ducked around a left-angled bend in the hallway just as the sound of a quick footed person came round toward me.

I glanced back to see someone with a wide- open pagri displaying a glittering garrotting wire that hung from his neck. He was knocking on one of three doors behind me. Ducking back, I rushed down a hall which had an atrium and ducked round it. It seemed I was in a maddening house of maze with doors. I did not know which one was going to lead to my desired place. I turned into a north hall and into one corner and literally bumped into a man almost three feet taller than me, wider than me by two breaths, with a gnarly looking forehead and almost a hundred pounds on me. He too had an open pagri shirt but instead of a garrotte, he had a kukri knife tucked in a sheath on his hip. Why would they have a weapon that must draw blood before it is sheathed? A question for another time. Before he could mutter anything, I leaned into him, pressing the muzzle of the gun into the side of his stomach, and fired twice with the Sig Sauer. The Sig Sauer clicked roughly on the second click, but the damage had already been done. I let the big man crumple down the side of the wall with a big O on his mouth and a surprised expression on his face. The sound was somewhat muffled by the big man's muscles, then again, I doubt it was enough. Someone would have heard it; the Sig Sauer was a loud gun but somewhat disappointing. Instead of leaving the jammed gun with the dying man I tucked it into the small of my back, in-between my panties and proceeded onward.

Less than thirty seconds after I killed the big man, I pushed an ornately carved door open, squinted and blinked rapidly to adjust to the overhead front light of a courtyard.

The inner courtyard appeared to have been renovated from some lush Mediterranean region to a landscape of dense foliage. A colourful array of peacock colours in full bloom. Brahma had not spared any expense in recreating a bushy topiary that resembles a south French country villa. Closing the door behind me I half expected the sum of Brahma's security force to be waiting for me. Instead there were only two big kneeling goons, praying in the courtyard on a path that was covered on both sides with a dense wall of yews and wild junipers. They got to their feet when they heard the door close behind me. I could not help noticing that each worshipper had a pistol tucked into each of their pants. When they saw me from eight paces away, they unhooked their guns and aimed.

Dead eyes, as deep as the darkest depths of space stared out from behind low cheekbones. As the world crawled down to a slow motion before death, I walked down towards them. They raised their weapons. In that instant, I could see the spittle of phlegm on the first worshiper's face. It was dry and cold as the weather. His companion was almost the same except he had a scowl. I spotted a small silver and abalone pendant in the design of a King Cobra attached to one of the necks, a necklace dangling from a neck.

With a jammed gun, no melee whip, I was practically unarmed and helpless, or so they were made to believe.

Then, I moved.

I flung my jammed gun at them just before they squeezed their triggers, the distraction of something small black heading their way was enough to make their first shots go wide.

There is an art of expectancy that some of the great *ninja* and *shaolin* masters have taught their students. An adept knowledge of walking through a crowd without being seen. My body seemed to be stationary, my mind blank and yet I was pulsating forward ever so frightfully fast. Apart from the perpetual focus of my unblinking eyelids, I could not be seen.

Any killing object like a bullet, comes in fast. Most people think bullets are fast, and they may be right but, any object shot or flung at a student of *Su Chen*, the master of *Wing Chun* and *Wudang*, be it a bullet, a grenade, an arrow, a knife, a spit ball, as long as it was five six paces away, had the same chance of striking home. Namely none.

Twisting and turning, I their target was everywhere, their bullets were not. When I was within arms-length of kicking distance, I twisted on one ankle shooting up high into the air, I struck at the nearest worshiper. He flew away as if a bolt of lightning had smashed into him. The second worshiper was felled when his frustrating aims got the better of him. His gun clicked harmlessly just before I performed a perfectly executed a 90-degree *Yeop Chagi*, a sidekick. He too flew away just as a large commotion behind me could be heard from within the villa. Before anyone came to investigate, with no time to catch my breath and still on my bare feet I hunched my head and neck and took off into the wild juniper hedges. I knew it was only a matter of time before I would be humped if I stayed on the path.

Pushing forward, zig zagging my way through I ran, clearing the foliage barrier before me with my bare fingers. It took me a while to get clear.

Some yards in, I noticed a warm feeling dripping down my left side. I glanced at it and saw the culprit. I had been shot through the side. I guess dodging that many bullets was not exactly in the cards for me. However I was lucky, the bullet was a through and through and since I did not exactly feel it, it meant I could not do much about it but stem the bleeding. I did know it was going to hurt as hell later, even if I had treatment. I paused, picked up a handful of dirt and made a makeshift dry poultice using my bra and the leaves about the place then slapped it over the wound. It stung like a sonovabitch when I applied the dry pack. I held on to it for a couple of seconds before inspecting my work. The dry poultice had stemmed the bleeding and should hold for a time but not for a protracted period of time.

First, I had to get away. With the poultice secured I continued my trek. As I moved within the forest of banyan trees, yew plants and juniper bushes, sharp nettle branches and leaves tore at my naked skin, whipping across my face and eyes. From behind me I could hear the faint audible commotion grow a bit louder. I paused, making the unwanted rustling sound of leaves and branches stop. I hardly thought it would mattered. The commotion seemed to be one of criticism and culpability.

## NINE

It was just as the sun started peeking out from under the horizon that I think I finally got clear of Brahma's villa. On the other hand, I wasn't sure, until at last I barrelled my way through stinging hedges and burst free out onto a dusty track which must skirt the villa. With sun giving me bearing, I headed west.

It was not long before my pulsing heart, the bracing sunrise morning and joy withing me to be alive gave me cause to run. Small acrid dust clouds rising in the wake of my steps showed how joyous I must have felt. Soon the morning noises caught up with me. The low-pitched melodic droning of some strange insect or bee followed me for a while only for it to be replaced by another.

I did not know which part of the country I was in. I certainly didn't know where Jaipur was, but I was going to follow Sameer's instructions. I think I had until now.

The narrow sandy path was replaced by a wider even dustier road. Eventually I made it to the main road, though it was still narrow considering my British standards. A partially carved -out single lane thoroughfare which served as a road for traffic going both directions extended before me. I bet that during monsoon season this road and the rickety constructions in the remote distance would not be anywhere to be found, including the flat sparsely parched countryside. My black hair had come loose and partly covered my face, I brushed part of it away with a jerk of my hand as I looked down the road in both directions. Nothing was detectible to assure me which direction I should head. In the distance, there were several faint curls of smoke rising into the hazy dawn from some cracked structures in both directions. Sameer did not exactly give me explicit directions, he just said "head west", so west I headed.

Bedraggled trees dotted the sides of the road, dogs baying in the distance and quite crazy enough perched on stunted branches were hushed, gaunt, featherless, evil-looking Vultures. The carrion eaters of the east.

They eyed my wounded side with great interest as I walked past. My pale naked skin was just as appeasing to them as were the snakes in my prison. In the distance, before the rising sun, I could make out cuddled together a couple of adults with three smaller beings, children I was guessing. Taking my chances of probably annoying the vultures I ran full steam towards them. Squinting through the glare of the sun, I noticed the family unit squatting around a meagre flameless fire having a meal. Like the Vultures they eyed me with interest and unrestrained curiosity.

It was a full-on emancipated Jainism family, Father, Mother, two girls and a younger boy with loin cloth and all the little sundries included. A family unit devoted to the Jainism tenet that suggest enlightenment can be achieved by practising a rigorous austerity. According to Jainism writings, "*Infinite knowledge of self and the universe can be attained after the annihilation of all through ascetic practices*". I have heard of them and for all intent and purpose I thought that kind of lifestyle was over since the 18th century. So, it was quite a surprise to see one here and now. They watched me arrive and walk up to them. The emancipated family unit just looked up me with their weathered face, stained fingers and cracked yellow teeth.

'Jaipur?' I asked addressing them all and one of them, the Father figure stretched to his full height and pointed. Despite myself, I was heading in the right direction. I bowed, thanking them for their help, but before I could continue on the mother figure grabbed my hand and gestured to my side. Not one of them spoke but from their gestures, it seemed they wanted to tend to my wound. I didn't know if them helping me would be dangerous for them. I was assuming it was. So as politely as I could, I tried to refuse their care, but they had already gone ahead and removed my poultice, exposing my chest and breasts and applied some leafy concoction that stung and made me cry out. The children chuckled at my painful moan. Two minutes later they had wrapped a string of bamboo rope round my torso securing the new poultice they had used. Thanking them for their help I was off towards the rickety structures in the distance.

I was jogging again but within a couple of minutes I felt a sharp stitch in my left side were my knotted injury had opened up. I tended to it as best as I could but try as I might I could only manage to stem the bleeding.

All I could do is hope and pray that assistant from an approaching vehicle from either direction would grant my wish. I would appreciate a lift about now.

They say a man's inspiration is visual, for us women it is in the sequence of events. However, as clichés go, I would settle for a visual inspiration about now but instead of the sound of a vehicle or the bray of an Ox or Cattle towing a cart the sound that reached my ears was the sound of a sputtering motorcycle. Its grating roar came up from behind me. I was hoping it was one of the millions of *"Bikecab"* or *"Becak"* or *"Tuk-tuk"* in India that act as transport, A rickshaw would be a godsend, but I was not betting my luck on it. I kept running heading towards the ramshackled erections a couple of hundred yards away. I looked back every couple of yards judging the distance before it came into view. I turned off the narrow thorough road and hit the dirt just in time for the bike to come into view. I don't know what type of bike it was, but it was equipped with an apparatus that could hit anything within a hundred yards, chiefly I think were the vultures, because they jumped away from the bike as it sputtered past them. This has to be something from Brahma's villa.

Feeling the sharp stitch in my side, I rose and started running again heading for the first building. Wishing for some change of fortune, where a car or a truck would come by and I would finally get a hitch into Jaipur, was going to be wishful thinking.

Turning into a dusty avenue of shrubs from the track bordering the ramshackled structures, I heard a sharp explosive crack and the whizz of a slug past my knee and realised someone had a bead on me. I dove into the ground again.

Whoever had done that piece of shooting had an adept and proficient eye. Was it the biker? I doubt it. Shooting with such proficiency and riding a bike in this terrain was next to impossible. I crawled a few feet forward before getting to my feet and running towards the plume of smoke rising from one of the fractured formations ahead of me. I ran in a zig zag fashion, always forward. Another crack of explosion of a gun being fired, this one narrowly missing my left shoulder. I ran faster than I ever did. With the bike closing in on me, I made a dash for the seemingly make-shift building. As luck would have it, the dust the biker kicked up in his path was blurring his vision.

I took advantage of his limited view and raced into a junk strewn yard just as I heard one voice over a walkie instruct someone called Gornak to stop and follow me by foot. I wasn't sure but the instructor's voice sounded much like Naveen.

Of course, Naveen would be in the vicinity at the helm of recapturing me. I dashed past a splintered wooden door that was hanging on the last of one of its eroded hinges into a room whose pernicious and revolting smell instantaneously assaulted my nostrils. The vile stink of animal excrement and blood was enough to knock an elephant over. Even so I doubt it would pause the determination of Brahma's men.

I was in what was once an abattoir. A slaughterhouse for the Muslim's since the conventional Hindi's don't eat beef. The slaughterhouse dated back at least fifty and some years. It was an oasis of death. I had to pause and for a fleeting moment imagine at the amount of death that had taken place here. It was enough to make me consider being a vegetarian if I ever got out of here. With the air close and tight, I imagined all those braying, snorting cattle and bulls, impatiently stamping their bovine hoofs and the slaughterers with their astonishing precise gear preparing to stumble into a not so easy or convenient sanctuary to do their due.

Behind me I heard an exchange in a language I did not understand. Then the rush of footsteps racing in my direction.

'Memsahib Dax' called out the heavily accented Hindi voice I presumed was Gornak 'Please stop we wan' offer you 'ompromise. Brahma 'ant offer you arrangemen' when you keep life'

How nice of him. Offering me something that is not his.

I didn't pause, I kept running through the dilapidated structure that barely had a complete wall standing. Another shot went off and whined close past my shoulder, bouncing off the broad side of a drooping door frame.

As I ran, I wondered if I was heading towards a dead end since there seemed no visible way to avoid my pursuers. The bike's machine had stopped reverberating behind me because I assume its rider was now on foot, a sniper was taking pot shots at me from somewhere and someone was closing in on me. My cliché of a thought came true as I dashed into a room with no exit except the way I came. The room had no roof and the walls were all splintered, it was a miracle they hadn't fallen apart long ago. I was about to turn when I spied something half propped down one cracked wall that might give me an advantage.

The business end of a three-prong digging fork. Its handle had broken off long ago and the prongs were all rusty.

'Memsahib' the voice called out again 'It all over, I 'eg you please come out'

'Not on your life' I yelled back as I scrambled to grab the rusty digging fork and propped myself behind the door.

Another shot went off just as a figure presented itself before me. I flung the digging fork as hard as I could, like you would a javelin. The digging fork caught whoever's figure it was full in the chest. I stood there as a youthful looking Indian with the digging fork in his open chested pagri staggered into view. His mouth open, surprise on his face, a hand clutching the broken wooden shaft end of the improvised deterrent.

'W-why?' he questioned with his voice and his look. I was not sure he was asking me why I had killed him or why I had turned down the offer he mentioned or why I had the were-to to kill him. What I did recognise though was that his voice was the one belonging to the one called Gornak. Another figure from behind him also stepped into view. The copper-toned face ignored the thick gushes of blood emanating from the young man's chest or the genuine fear on Gornak's face.

He glanced at me and cursed '*Sala kuttaa*'. Calling his fallen companion a "stupid bastard" without concern or explanation he put his hands on the end of the broken shaft and tried pulling the digging fork out of his companion's chest.

I was away again out of the room and heading out of the run-down putrefying structure, but I heard Gornak's gurgling tormenting cry turn into a murderous howling pain as the digging fork was wrenched out of his chest.

I stopped and turned. It was time to increase my odds. That decision almost cost me my life. If I had continued on and not stopped and turned, I would have missed the flying digging fork heading at my back. As it was, I saw it in time to leap out of its way but not before one its prong seared part of my skin on my shoulder. The force off its throw made me fall into a crevasse with a sharp burning pain. I lay there trying to keep my eyes open, fighting the darkness that seemed to want to grab me. I rose up on one elbow just as my assailant presented himself over the rise.

'You not some tough shit, are you woman?' jeered the man before me. I stared at the man standing over me. He was an Indian in his thirties, maybe 150kg in weight, with a half-nelson beard, a measured scowl on his face, an open pagri shirt and a garrotting wire hanging from his neck. I was beginning to think that the open pagri thing was a motif for Daayan members. His tattooed arm of a Cobra head was clearly visible to all in the morning sun who could see.

'So how many of you are out there for a feeble girl like me?'

'Just Naveen and Ranjit' He said staring down at my naked body.

'Ranjit?' I asked as he slipped the garrotting wire from round his neck. He licked his lips before answering

'They say he be sniper in army, big shot think he can shoot. I get your ass, not him'

Could it be that this Indian wanted a booty taste of my arse?

'Yeah you did' I answered alluringly, hoping to determine his motives.

'And Brahma's offer?'

The scowl on his forehead deepened 'Offer?'

The disbelief on his face was genuine as he took the second step down towards me and I knew the offer wasn't genuine. At least for him. It was then I moved like a cannonball. With such speed I careened into him just below his chest plate and he flew through the air falling backward, a spittle of blood spewing from his lips as he landed. He still had grip of his garrotting wire as I started for him again. Just as I rushed, he flicked his wrist sending the garrotte at my neck. Remembering my hockey days, I twisted and leaped sideways just out of its reach.

The Indian cursed.

Snorting frustratingly, my assassin got to his feet. I started for him again, this time he came to meet me. He slammed a shoe into my naked breasts making me reel backwards, slam my head onto the floor and for an instant I felt my breath catch on fire from the pain, just as I saw stars. I rolled away from the other slamming foot and kicked aimlessly as hard as I could. Part of my foot caught him in the groin, it was on target and strong enough for him to grunt in pain. I got to my feet just as he sprinted at me. I let him come and when he was in the right position I swung, hitting him on the point of the jaw that meets the ear. It was a perfect blow. His eyes crossed and he fell backwards but only for a moment. My blow would have killed some men or taken out most others. This guy was getting to his feet once again.

He was tough but some of the starch within him had come loose. I swung again, this time with my fist, a sharp carving blow that opened a three -inch gash under his right eye. I followed with a left, but he turned his head in time to avoid taking it on the jaw. It caught his lean, jagged cheekbone and I felt it crack. He put his head down and leaped forward like a bull, I tried to dodge him, but his long arms encircled me, and I felt the grizzly-bear strength of the man at once. With his head down, he pressed himself against my naked chest, pulling me forwards at the waist. One of my arms was pinned to my sides, unable to break his hold and I felt my ribs about to crack.

I brought one of my knees up hard and fast and kicked him in the groin. I felt him gasp in pain and I was flung into the ground. I bounced once as I hit the floor, my hand brushing past something metal. The pain to his groin had taken its toll but it also sent him into a murderous rage. He dived forward, coming down on me. My breath left me in one huge huff as pain shot into every part of my body. A building falling on me couldn't have felt worse.

If not for the wild fury expression on his face I would have thought this Indian wanted to get fresh with me. Shaking my head, I let all my automatic reflexes come into play. I drew in a breath as he got up, grab me by the neck and lift me to my feet. He started to squeeze but I was ready for that act. The metallic item my hand brushed past was a garrotte. His garrotte. The one he tried to strangle me with and ended up flinging at me. It didn't take much for me to reach up and wrap it round his neck. We both stared into each other's eyes as he squeezed at my neck and I pulled at both ends of the wire. His face contorted in pain just as I think mine was all the same more than that, I could feel the greying darkness about to cover my eyes and in those few moments it took more than seconds for me to get the upper hand. I pulled enough to make his skin rip apart and his eyes bulge out of his head. His grip round my neck loosened as he dropped to his knees, but I held on.

Another couple of seconds passed and he began to choke as I exposed his oesophagus.

He got one hand to his throat, stared at me, reach for me before succumbing to the tearing of his flesh. He started to get up, but fell sideways, and I stumbled forward looking down at his dead eyes.

My whole body was quivering, and throbbing and I was gobbling deep drafts of air.

In all my years of combat I had never come close to death until now. The young Gornak was dead and so was his companion that being what it was didn't let me assume the other two, Naveen and Ranjit would stand by and let me mete out my own brand of justice. No, since I've had no other shots coming my way, they must have made themselves scarce or were searching the abattoir. I did not care. I stripped him of his white stained pagri and slipped into it. It covered my torso down to my upper thigh.

Making my way back to the narrow thorough road I glanced at my body. I was no pretty sight. I was filthy and stinking, my whole body torn and scratched covered in sweat and blood. If Seymour or Sir C saw me now, I thought, what would they think?

I was practically destitute, armed with naught but my wits and a brown belt in almost all five of the eastern disciplines, but that wasn't my concern now.

When I first sighted a vehicle, I thought it was Manna from heaven but the battered Suzuki heading towards Jaipur passed me without stopping. I caught a glimpse of a craggily face and silver hair before it disappeared. I kept walking, not about to stop and smell the roses, or in this case smell the dust and the rot. I think I was suffering from *Kuebiko* at that point. A state of exhaustion inspired by sudden acts of senseless violence.

I needed a bath, a change of clothes, a weapon, and some sleep. Most especially a bath, that would resolve my kuebiko. First off though, I needed to find somewhere to lay my head, a hotel room somewhere far away. In any event I still had to take things one step at a time. Going by the sun the hour was past ten and there was still a lot to be accomplished so I gave myself a good pace and began jogging. Naveen and Ranjit were still behind me but I think I had a good couple of hundred yards on them.

A few miles down was still a strenuous run. The noon day sun ascended high over me making the sky a vast sunshiny bowl of striking shadows and insincere mirages. I must have gone like that fifteen minutes after the midday sun climbed high when a team of half- starved oxen were pulling a rickety cart, came my way. On the back in the cart it was burdened high with bales of straw.

I waved the driver down, a bearded brown-whiskery peasant who seemed more like a *Sadhu*, a holy man that littered the countryside throughout India and Pakistan, than a Ferrier of hay. He pulled in the reins and guided the oxen to the side of the road.

'Speak English' I asked

He shook his head. 'No English' he said

I switched to Hindi 'Can you help me get to Jaipur?'

He examined my half naked body draped in a dirt bloodstained pagri shirt before answering 'Jaipur?' he asked beckoning his liver-dotted hand from side to side gesturing the word 'Almost', In the universal sign language.

'You can get me close huh?'

'Yes'

'May I?' I asked, seeking permission before I climbed on board his livelihood.

He flashed me an interesting grin granting his approval. I climbed onto the rickety cart next to him. He flicked the reins and the oxen continued their bumpy, spasmodic ride. It was slow going but still it was a hundred times better than making it on foot.

With the rhythmic swaying and creaking it wasn't that hard for me to doze off to sleep. I did so several times. My body needed to rest, and it was necessary for me to sleep. It was the third or fourth nod of my head when I heard a persistent buzzing sound. It was a steady drone followed by a chugging sound that grew louder and louder. I recognised it as the bike Brahma's man had following me, but it had been joined at least two others.

Instantly alert I looked over my shoulder, dust was billowing in the distance which temporary obscured their view of them except for the noise they made. Not about to take any unnecessary risks with the life of brown-bearded driver or mine, I hurriedly climbed into the straw and burrowed myself into it. The driver did not complain or ask for an explanation, he just continued urging his oxen on.

The purr of the two unrecognisable engines and the sound of a sputtering motorbike was getting closer. The combined gruffy roar came up from behind us. As they roared passed heading towards Jaipur, I happen to notice that Naveen was one of the bikers continuing the search for me. His bandaged head was unmistakeably recognisable. I sank further into the bay of straw, but they did not give the oxen cart a first or even a second look.

The other bikers had new faces I would hardly recognise before. I was betting Ranjit was one of them. Four men excluding Naveen, all Hindi's sent by Brahma to find me and hunt me down or find me and drag me back to the villa so that I could be taught to die like any other human being.

This has been one hell of morning, what would the rest of the day bring forth? Brahma didn't seem the type to give up and neither was the Sin Eater.

No. Oh something told me that this day is about to get hectic.

## TEN

Two hours later, the grisly old bearded man dropped me one exit away from the town of Jaipur. I made it into the municipal city just before three p.m. and I could see why pink was predominately linked to the city. The colour scheme was preponderately pinkish. It was a town of dusty paved streets and winding alleyways that would confuse the casual tourist or visitor.

My situation bordered on the comical side. I mean here I was far and away from any tourist, British or otherwise, half naked, draped in a bloody pagri and devoid of passport or rupees. I had that subtle Monachopsis persistent feeling of being truly out of place.

I thought of hiring a car to take me back to New Delhi, but I estimated that the journey would take a good four to five hours. I had to contact Sir C now so he could scramble SAS unit 3, big guys with big guns and itchy fingers and also prepare myself for the scheduled meeting I had with Sameer later this day. Jaipur was a large enough town to search, a feat that couldn't be easily accomplished by more than four men on bikes. I immediately spotted one of the town's police station and had a mind to go in and call Sir C, but I figured that this close to his home base Brahma might just have it under his control. Plus, since I was fourteen years old, I haven't had faith in any police station. My last experience involving a police station was not exactly a good one. No, I figured somewhere else other than a police station to make contact and it could not be by phone. Maybe an SMS text would be simpler or a message through the MI6 website. It wasn't exactly secure, but it would have to do.

Spotting a group of kids tossing a cricket ball about I made my way towards them. They eyed me suspiciously as I approached them. Two of them pulled out a phone and started filming me. The 12 to 14-year olds seemed more interested in filming my pale grimy-coloured, partly exposed breasts and legs as I made my way towards them than anything else.

'What the hell you kids doing?' I asked all three kids

They gaped at me with surprise on their faces. Finally, the bigger of all three kids asked, 'You not American?'

He had a Sikh accent which meant that this town might be predominately Sikh or Muslim.

'Nope'

'You English?' asked the smaller of the kids in a similar Sikh accent

'So?'

'Never know the English to show skin, you all proud of cover skin' said the big kid

'Yeah well we are very prudish, now one of you let me borrow your phone'

The smaller of all the kids tapped a button on his phone and was about to hand it over to me.

'Why?' asked the big kid.

'Nonaya' I replied

'Nonaya?' he asked

I snatched the kid's phone away from him and quite simply said 'None of your business'

The kids' phone was a TechNo X2 smartphone, one of those fancy Chinese phones the manufacturers IDC succeeded in getting rid of because of malicious malware. It had a sophisticated android text program which I hoped was enough to counter any encrypted monitoring device. I hurriedly tapped out

"79262416 1119121322 +/- S1614. 8221323 2112924228, 21181323 518151526 222687 1221 1726181169, 25926191426 +42226111213, Dax"

A simple ambiguous substitution cryptic message which simply said;

"Track phone +/- 8km. Send Forces, find villa east of Jaipur, Brahma + weapon, Dax"

I was about to punch in the numbers of Sir C's phone number when I realised, I did not know it. I did remember Mr Ambrose, his second-in-command's mobile number though, so I inputted his and sent off the text, then deleted the message entirely.

I tossed the phone back to the kid.

'What you being into lady?' asked the big kid who together with his playmates had been examining my body

'Nothing really' I said in Hindi running a hand through my hair. Another surprise for the kids 'You go out for the night and before you know it bad men want to get into your panties'

They each took a step back. Eyeing me ever so cautiously 'Your pants huh?'

'Yes. Now will any of you kind boys direct me to the nearest hotel'

'There be three in town, nearest one be …' said the boy who had not spoken until now. He must be the smart one.

'The Punjab' The big kid finished for him.

'The Punjab, huh?'

They pointed. They each gave me their version of how to get there except the smart kid.

'Is that how I get there?' I asked him

'Mehdi is right, lady. Left down there then right. You not miss'

'Thank you er … what's your name?'

'Hameed'

'Hameed' I acknowledged stretching out a hand. He took it 'I will not forget'

'Forget what?' asked the big kid

'Never you worry' I said turning away from them and walking in the direction they signified.

I spotted the white brown brick seven-story building that had dying flowers surrounding its lobby entrance. I had been in tight spots before, with all my stuff locked away in a hotel room a couple of hours away and without money or a passport or even a weapon to deal with Brahma's men if and when they appear it was going to be a hard sell to anyone who wanted to accommodate me.

No sooner had I stepped into the lobby when the uniformed guard accosted me at the door. I could not blame him, especially when anyone seeing me as I saw myself reflected from a mirrored wall, half naked, filthy, blood stained and reeking from God knows, I would do the same come to think of it.

'Ma'am can I help you?'

'No' I declared walking past him. He hung back some several feet behind me in case I made up a fuss. As I approached the lobby desk, the face of a girl with deep red talons for nails behind the desk, tightened.

'I'd like a room please, there's been an incident' I said to her as she blew out a breath of smoke from the cigarette partially hidden from view.

She paused regarding my shabby filthy appearance and dismissed me as female homeless but despite herself because of the colour of my skin she had to give the impression to be interested in my plight, though she was less than attentive. Her eyes flicked up momentarily at me 'Um … er … you don't have any luggage pukka hippie' she said inferring – if not stating straight up – that I was a homeless hippie, undeserving of a room.

Granted I smelled like something a rat peed on and far from the elegance and splendour that graced this establishment I still didn't deserve to be addressed like this, but I let it go. I was in no mood to argue with this girl. 'Do I need to have luggage to check in?' I asserted between clenched teeth. The guard behind me placed a hand on his service revolver. There was no need for that.

'May be not but I doubt you have a credit card, do you pukka?'

A small fire started deep in the pit of my stomach. I half twisted my neck to address the guard 'Relax, I've had a hell of a night' I turned back to the girl 'What does …?' I began to ask.

'Miss Dax?'

I turned my head towards the enquiring voice. I half expected one of Brahma's men, instead it was an immaculate trimmed Indian, someone dressed in a tailored pinstriped suit that he did not seem all that comfortable in. A person whom I had never seen or met before. His expression told me he did not know me but half expected to meet me.

'Yes' I answered

'Hello Memsahib' he said welcoming me with a handshake and a kiss on both cheeks 'I never imagined you would grace our hotel' his eyes gave me the once-over from head to toe 'You've been busy, haven't you?' he said grinning. He snapped at the girl behind the desk and barked some orders at her in Sikh. She in turn hurried to hand him a key card 'Please follow me to your room, I assume you would want some rest. Mr Krakauer said you might and that I must accommodate you with anything you will need'

'Mr Krakauer?'

'Yes'

'How perceptive of him'

Oh Seymour, it was just like him. Anticipating my needs before I had them, though this one was a bit hard to acknowledge. How the hell did he know where I would pop up. Then I thought of Cancer, he must be tracking me.

'I wouldn't know Memsahib never met the man' replied the suited man 'Spoke to him though, he's rather aggressive, isn't he?' he asked as we approached one of the two elevators.

I ignored his question and asked him one of my own 'And sir you are?'

'Me? Oh, I do apologise memsahib, I am Vijay Shah, the manager of The Punjab. Of course, with you as the new owner you could change the name to whatever you want, even replace me … if you want' he said with a stifled laugh.

New owner? I was the owner of The Punjab? How in the blue blistering barnacles of hell did that happen? Seymour.

I stopped 'If that's the case' I turned, re -entered the lobby and walked up to the girl behind the lobby counter who was now puffing away to her hearts content 'What's your name miss?'

She glanced at Vijay behind me before answering 'Mishka'

'Mishka, I don't like your insolence'

'My insolence?'

'Yes, and since you like smoking you are relegated to the kitchen because smokers don't belong in hotel lobbies, they tend to reek the place up. You'll only get back behind this desk if and when your attitude improves'

'What? Who in hell are you?'

'You heard me' I announced, ignoring her query 'It's the kitchen or you're fired' I said then turning to face the guard 'I like your attitude but you need to relax and be less of a bully'

'You can't do that' yelled Mishka as I walked away running a hand through my hair, leaving a dumbfounded expression on her's and the guard's face.

'Mr Shah please educate them. Not now but afterwards'
Mr Shah pulled his eyes away from me and glanced at Mishka and the guard.
'Yes mem-sahib' he said as he made me follow him into the elevators. I had two reasons for doing that. One, I really did not like her attitude and two, Brahma's men were due to find me, what better way to make it sooner rather than later or easier than harder for them. Optimistically, after and not before my appointed meeting with Sameer in a couple of hours.
The good-sized Deluxe room Vijay Shah had reserved for me was a contemporary, clean, and comfortable. It provided a concentrated view of the Aravalli Mountain Range and the Hawa Mahal, 18th century sandstone palace that Jaipur is also famous for. There was also a reliable atmosphere, light and tastefully style touches of India. It was nicknamed the Hawa Mahal room because of the view and was tiled with multicoloured mosaics. It had two couches, drapes that caught the soft breezes, a flat screen TV, a sound system and a fully stocked mini fridge. The rooftop floor I was on had a large communal area with internet access, a small library and a restaurant called the Lantern.
My main concern however was for the bathroom. In it was not what I hoped. It had a black and white tiled floor, a shower, a toilet bowl, and wash basin but no bath. Disappointing as it was, I headed into it, nevertheless.
I stripped off my pants, the borrowed bloodied pagri shirt and set aside my tampon with Hazel inside before I stepped into the shower and let the warm water flow over me.
It took me more than twenty minutes to get myself clean, at least on the surface. When I was done, with a towel wrapped round my chest I headed to one of the couches, cuddled into it and waited until Vijay arrived with staff member who had a first aid kit. She tended to the wound on my side and the other cuts and bruises as best as she could. While she was seeing to my cuts, I demanded that Vijay hand me a third of on-hand- cash he had in the till before leaving me to dial the phone through to Seymour's special number.
The staff member left just as the handset on the other side was answered.

'So, you're alive huh Susannah?' was his first words when he heard my voice over the phone line. It was filled with anger but separate from that, a much more anticipated feeling called relief. From his voice I could tell he had had a couple of frustrating nights. Nights no doubt worried for me. He was angry at me hence the choice of name he called me. He never calls me "Susannah", unless he's somewhere between angry and joyous.

'Yes I am. It wasn't easy though'

'I can bet it wasn't. Where the hell is Jaipur and what was Sir Conrad thinking?' he asked. Him knowing where I was, was the benefit of the tracking app on his phone that was quite similar to Daniel's or Cancer's tracking efficiency. 'Sending you on some bullshit assignment. You are not his lapdog you know mistress'

'I know, but his bullshit assignment wasn't just that'

'Really? Last we heard you were somewhere in Mundak with the now late Imah Rajan'

'Ah, so they found him then?' I asked

'Yes. His boys are somewhat miffed, mistress and want a word or two with you'

'So do I. Let them know I know who brought the hammer down onto their boss and I want something out of it if I let them have it'

'What makes you think they'll not just take it out on you?'

'Well that will be petty of them'

'Petty. Petty? These are gangsters we're talking about'

'Don't fuss Seymour you'll get wrinkles'

'I've been on pins and needles for two days and she tells me not to fuss she tells me ...'

Something occurred to me. If he thought I was in Mundak then how did he know I was here? 'Didn't Cancer help out?' I asked

'Its signal was intermittent and nowhere near Jaipur'

I rubbed the area under my left armpit where my implant was.

'We have to see about that'

'Yes, we do'

'Well, do you want to hear what happened to me or not?'

'Oh, please ma'am do not grace me with your misguided exploits'

Despite his protest I briefed him on what happened because I knew he couldn't wait to hear what had happened to me.

In-between "What's" and "You didn't" I could hear beams of pride, in-between his amazement at the skills I implored 'Great mistress, I trained you as well I can, but two days you were gone, two da …' The phone crackled 'Hey guess who is on the other line. Our own two-faced aristocrat Sir Conrad' grumbled an irritated Seymour.

'Ah please put him through' I pleaded with Seymour

'Hi Sir C, how's your day going?' I brazenly asked when he came on the line.

'My day' he snapped 'I spoked to Anard already. He told me about your call, so do not start with me. Yes, I was wrong, now I have to generate a new pool of suspects before my meeting with the PM in an hour's time'

'I take it Ambrose hasn't decoded my message yet'

'What the hell you talking about …Ambrose? What about Ambrose?' he grunted, then it seemed that he addressed someone away from the phone 'Ambrose what is Dax talking about?'

'Ask him to check his text messages'

'She says check your messages' he said

I heard Ambrose's voice ever so faintly 'My messages?'

'No, no your text messages. You did say text message right Susan?' Sir C asked

'That's right'

There was a brief pause.

'A substitution cypher?'

'Yes'

'What does it say … save us the trouble?' said Sir C

'I go through all the trouble of sending you a well encrypted message and you want me to just decrypt it for you'

'If you please' Sir C insisted

'All right it goes something like this. Uh… track phone 8km plus or minus from it. Send your boys, find villa east of Jaipur and Brahma with weapon"'

'The Daayan exists?'

'More or less. Daayan is very much alive and so is Brahma but hopefully not for too much longer'

'What are you talking about?' Sir C asked 'I thought you were on your way back home and what is this about a weapon? What weapon?'
'Maybe next week if I finish our business here. Seymour brief him please'
Seymour informed him of the details I just recently briefed him about. I filled in the specifics from my initial experience with Brahma and Sigrid. My capture at the Shreyansh Fort and everything else that had taken place afterward. When he heard about "A-tome" he was literally quiet. His voice became tiny and small, I didn't need to see his face to know that he was very disturbed about the weapon.
'You know what I want from you, Susan?' Seymour asked me.
'I've got a pretty good idea'
'No, she's not doing it. Get your guys up there fast and deal with it yourself or have those ruthless boys from the Maratha Infantry to handle it' Seymour insisted.
'I can't Seymour. It'll take several hours for me to organise help in that area, besides, it seems the Central Bureau might be compromised. Susan is already there'
'And let me guess, you want her to get this "A-tome" witho …' Seymour was saying
'I want more than that from her'
'You want more! Oh, do not tell me, you want her to clip Brahma and Sigrid's wings. You do know about Sigrid, don't you?'
'Yes. I do not want her to just clip their wings but pluck their feathers by destroying the Daayan if possible so that they are in no shape to resume their activities' Sir C said
'Oh, is that all. She isn't Wonder Woman y'know' Seymour protested
'Look Moscow and Washington are already in an uproar Seymour over this phone hacks business and now this. The US will never allow China's involvement in devouring a sub-continent come to fruition and neither will we. A stand will mean war and we will make a stand'
'So, you want her to prevent a war?' said Seymour rather insolently
'In other words, yes. It's not her first time, if you recall. You more than anyone should know that' Sir C defiantly replied
'Oh don't remind me. What a sartorial tragedy that was' Seymour said
'That's the worse of the problems we seem to be having. My friend Mahatma Bhave seems to have gone missing'

'And that is her problem too, is it?'
'She's provided more info than two international spy agencies combined and gotten close too'
I could see where this was going. Seymour trying to protect me would go to any lengths to prevent my involvement. Sir C knowing my skills, desperate for my involvement will do anything to persuade me to continue on. I had already made my choice.
'Hey gentlemen don't argue over a decision that's already been made' I proclaimed over the line to both men. My reply informed both men that I would be doing what Sir C had proposed.
'Damn it, ma'am you've done enough'
'I know, but there's this niggling desire of mine to pounce back into Daniel's den'
'Jeeze, I thought I taught you about controlling desire's'
'You did, but see revenge is a very palatable desire'
'So is love. Why don't you find a nice young man and get married? You know with you married my blood pressure will definitely come down to a reasonable level'
'Hey old man are you suggesting what I think you're suggesting?'
'Yes'
'This is definitely not the time'
'If not now when?' He had a point. 'Marriage is not that bad a word is it? Hey, how about that photographer friend of yours … er … Steve Duggan? He's a nice young man who definitely has the hots for you and you for him'
'Marriage is a sentence, a life sentence' I replied
'You two finished?' Sir C interrupted 'Hear the news out of the Philippines?'
'Sorry been a tad busy lately' I replied
'Not you Susan, Seymour. 34 dead by Jihadists' he stated '18 dead in Germany and god knows how many with the anti-Trump riots in Orlando'
'And that's her problem too huh Conrad?' Seymour complained
'No but …social upheaval seems to be popping up all at once, all over and if this Brahma is claiming to be partially respo …'

'You do know, gentlemen' I interrupted both men 'I'm seriously out of supplies out here'
'Don't worry I'll handle that' Seymour said acquiescing to my wishes.
'The priority is "A-tome" and this inventor … what was his name again?' Sir C asked.
'Kavin Chandra'
'Right. I could have Anard meet you if you need help or would you prefer an old friend'
'Briggs?'
'Yes'
'I knew it. You sent him as a minder for me?'
'Relatively speaking. Could you use their company?'
'Certainly, and we need to set up a suitable contact code just in case. How about the second stanza of my favourite poem'
Only Seymour knew that my favourite poem was "The Rime of The Ancient Marina"
'"The Rime …" you mean?' Seymour asked
'Huh huh'
'I let you know Conrad' he said to Sir C
'Good, we will co -ordinate later' Sir C responded, 'How about your contact, this er … Sameer, when do you meet him?'
'In about three hours'
'Can you trust him?' Sir C asked
'Trust is a big word. But I have little choice if I want to take on India's answer to Poi Pot'
'Or Hitler' Seymour added
'Adolf was never this clever or tenacious Seymour' Sir C observed
'Good luck to you both and let's hope I hear from you soon Susan'
His end of the line disconnected.
'How you doing, Seymour?'
'I'm not pleased mistress. Does that answer your question?'
'No' I declared, wanting to have an answer to the one question that was bugging me ever since I entered the Punjab 'But I have been wondering about something'
'And that would be how I knew you would be there at the Punjab?'
'Yes. Pray tell, how did you know?'

'I didn't'
I was taken aback.
'Then how come …'
'Your implant proceeded east from Shreyansh Fort. When my search team couldn't pin you down, I went with Plan B. I didn't know where exactly you'd pop up, but I knew if something was wrong and you somehow escaped your abductors, you'll rather head to the nearest hotel or church or in this case a mosque instead of a police station. So, I just bought every hotel within a four hundred-mile radius area in your name and had a word with each of the managers in case you showed up'
I was flummoxed.
'Smart. Every hotel in four hundred miles?' I marvelled 'It's not as many as you think. 127 I think'
'How many five-stars rated?'
'Thirty-one'
'Good on you. Now as for supplies'
'You'll get them before sundown. I'm sorry to say I won't be able to make it'
'Why not?'
'I'm in Quebec at the moment'
I was not only astonished but enthralled. I thought he was much closer, like New Delhi 'Ah'
'I'm on my way though'
'You coordinated a search and a trade sale from Quebec?' I asked with wonder in my voice.
'Yeah'
'Seymour I'm impressed'
'I bet you are milady'
'Try not to be in too much of a rush to get here huh?'
'Yes, milady and ma'am please be careful'
'You know me I always try'
'We both know that's an understatement'
'It may very well be. Good afternoon Seymour'
'It's just after 8 here ma'am'
'Well then good morning'

He hung up his phone, but before I could hang up mine, I heard a very unnatural click, as if someone had cut off another line. I placed the handset onto the phone. Could it be someone had listened to our conversation? I thought about the intelligence leaks and dis- information. I never did work out how they got onto Imah's and my meeting at the Colonial Café.

Fuck.

Sundown was going to be a lifetime if I could not figure out what was going to happen next. With my meeting with Sameer close at hand I had to find out if he and me were compromised.

An hour or so later I emerged from my hotel room looking very much the opposite of what I had been when I walked into the Punjab hotel. I had darkened my exposed skin and ditched the pagri. In their place Vijay had purchased a pink coloured Shalwar and matching Kameez. I still had my panties and bra and complimenting them were leather strapped sandals and a hijab completing my native look. Brahma's men were looking for a female westerner, my disguise could buy me some cover, not much, but some. Vijay Shah had handed me a hand-fisted roll of cash before I left after of course I paid a visit to the kitchen for one or two items. The rupees he handed to me was more than enough to hire a pedicab or rickshaw.

'Where can I send off a fax?' I asked him

'A fax, miss?' he inquired, a tad confused

'Yes'

His confusion took on a bewildering expression 'Don't they still do that here?' I asked him. He rolled his eyes, his thoughts racing in a daze of confusion.

'C'mon Shah think, where can I send one off?'

'Try the business centres down Pratham Street. One of them might have the facilities'

'How do I get there?'

He went behind his desk and pulled open a drawer. He fished out a glossy map of Jaipur and marked a place on it. He handed it to me. 'It's not far, two rights and a left down Harappa road, you cannot miss it'

I folded the map before thanking him.

I hailed a three-wheeled "tut tut" vehicle two blocks from the hotel 'Pratham Street' I told the driver in Hindi. The driver glanced at me and eyed me with the same curiosity a dozen others had since I left the hotel. I may speak the language, then again, my accent and manner of speech did not match my skin colour or attire.

I said nothing to alleviate his concerns. I was anxious to get off a fax and that was it. My conversation with Sir C and Seymour may have been compromised and I had to do something fast to correct it. The driver didn't try to put one over me, he took a direct route to the market street called Pratham. I was alert to everything around me, particularly those on motorbikes as we journeyed.

As much as I knew, Brahma's men were still on a one-woman hunt after me and I had to make myself as inconspicuous as possible. The outfit and grease paint aided the ruse, but I wasn't about to take superfluous risks. Thoughtfulness is a key principle in a world governed by ruthlessness and craftiness. I was going to be as cautious as conceivable.

'Memsahib is *Kuchipudi* dancer, yes?' the driver asked when he pulled up three blocks into Pratham Street.

'Dancer? Me? Why you think so?'

'You have high arches, just like dancers'

I looked down at my feet. He was not wrong, I did have high arches just like a dancer 'You have good eye' I said to him, relatively agreeing with his assessment.

'Perhaps mem-sahib would honour me with autograph?' he asked fishing out a pen and paper. I smiled and scribbled the name of the first dancer I knew that came to mind. Vaidehi Parashuram. He grinned 'Plenty of thanks mem-sahib'

I did not wait to see his reaction when he deciphered the scrawled signature of a *Kathak* dancer who retired from dancing and was now an actress. It was as light-hearted as I could be given the circumstances. The first three business centre didn't have what I needed but the fourth one hidden in a hole had a phone cum fax machine that hadn't been used since the late 05's but it still worked.

I handed over the hourly fee and was directed to an adjourning room where there was a fax machine, several phones for long distant communications and several computers all separated in box glass terminals. I sat down on a wooden stool in a workstation designed for the fax machine and scribbled a note, marked it, and punched in the website fax number of the MI6. The word "PRIORITY" printed in marked ink on top of the page was I hope a signal that the note was to be taken seriously.

My business concluded I tore up the fax and got up to leave, just then the phone on the fax machine began to ring.

I picked up the receiver 'Hello?' said a British female accentuated voice.

'Yes'

'Who is this?' The voice asked. I flinched inwardly. I've always hated such questions. I have no idea why, I just despise that type of query. Also, I hate the question "Who or what are you?" and statements like "Who do you think you are?". At the present time it was not a time for me to be overly cynical.

'Who is this?' she asks again.

'I'm nobody'

'Did you just send a fax ma'am?'

'Yes' I replied

'Could I have your code?' she asked curtly

'Code? I have no code but if you want to get technical, I suppose triple S would be a good start'

There was a short pause before she came back on 'Thank you ma'am, where are you now?'

'I'd rather not say'

'If you are in a foreign country be aware that your activities are being permitted under that countries courtesy. We will disavow any illicit person or activity as not approved by the host nation'

'In other words, MI6 are not accountable' I stated

'Yes. Thank you for listening, your message shall be sent onward' She hung up.

I rose, one hand reaching for the handle of the sliding glass door.

Someone was standing right outside, blocking my way. I looked up into his face and could not believe who was standing there. I felt a chill tickle down my spine because he was no stranger.

# ELEVEN

I did not know whether to say Hello or Good Afternoon to my very unwelcomed guest.

The latter was infinitely more preferably considering the man was one of the three Hindi faces facing me from the other side of the sliding glass door. Faces I glimpsed as ones on bikes riding into Jaipur, all with curved kukri knives tucked into their hips. In one of the Hindu's hands was a snob nosed automatic whose exact make I couldn't exactly make out. However, his intentions were perfectly clear.

'You look very distracting Dax memsahib' he said through his bandaged face as he slid his knee across the glass door, sliding it back several inches.

'We have got to stop meeting like this mate' I said to him forcing out a hollow laugh.

'Indeed, we do'

'So how do we do this, anyway, ask me to walk ahead while you and your fellow heavy breathing arseholes follow me?'

'Oh, you are smart memsahib, I hoping you end our conversation violently. Not so smart you insult us' he said levelling the snob nosed automatic at my chest

'I've never been a bad sport no matter what Tracy Tuttlebaen said'

'Who this Tracy Tuttebe …?'

'Tuttlebaen, she was a classmate in boarding school who accused me of being …'

He moved the gun nearer to my chest 'We not want to hear?' The Hindu was not as thick-headed as I thought.

I was playing the fool to buy time, but he wasn't having none of it. He slid open the door further to let me out of workstation cubicle. He gestured that I walk in front of all of them.

'Make my day and tell me how you found me?'

'You always being this sarcastic mem-sahib Dax?'

'Only when I know I'll have the upper hand soon, memsahib' I announced, no longer being subtle with my intentions. I was addressing his masculinity and mocking it.

The Hindu responded by shoving the gun further up the small of my back as he carried on a relatively false conversation as we walked through the business centre offices.

'By the way what you do to Mishka?' he asked me

I was almost disappointed to hear that it was an employee of mine that gave me up, even if I did hope she would. Now I felt fear. Not for myself but Sameer. If it was Mishka at the other end of the line, then she heard what was said about Sameer. This close to the hour of our appointed meeting I had to get to him before anything befell him.

'How much?' I ask

'How much?'

'What was her price?'

'She not want anything, that's why I ask'

'Just her, that's too simple'

'Not just her. We also think Miss Vaidehi is actor not dancer anymore' There was almost an endorsed ring of triumph and vanity in his voice, however, I was less concerned about his ego than my present predicament and those that may get caught in the crossfire if he and his companions grew a bit too eager. The tendrils of my instincts had been reaching out, measuring, and appraising. Through the door I could see the market was building up into a little frenzy and in the foreground were their two other companions with motor bikes sitting high on their machines. One of them was no doubt Ranjit or could it be one of the ones with me.

Just beyond the door, ahead of me was a plump man carrying a wicker basketful of Khameeri Roti coming up to the door with agonizing slowness.

'The cab driver. That almost makes it worthwhile' I said about to push open the front door. 'Though I don't think killing a bunch of women and children are on your agenda. Imagine all that needless blood'

'It is your blood I wish to see memsahib, not others'

'In that case do not take this the wrong way'

'Take what …'

I was two paces out the door when showing none of the outward appearance of the fierce concentration within me, I smoothly dived forward, forearms angled flat in front of me to cushion the impact with the ground. As my arms touched the ground, my legs were half drawn up my head to sight the Hindu over my shoulder. Naveen thought I tripped at any rate he was wrong when he saw my feet rising. He tried to swerve away but he was too late. My feet shot out like a mule kick catching him square in the chest just as he squeezed off a shot from his gun which went wide. The impact of my kick lifted him a clear foot off the ground and flew into his two companions who were following closely behind.

The plump man ahead of us hadn't been looking up. When he saw me, I was dashing towards him and relieving him of his parcel. He opened his mouth in astonishment as I tossed the dough bread one after another at the two bikers. The bikers scrambled off their bikes and hid behind them, ducking from the flying bread.

Naveen behind me was not done. I did not know if Brahma's order to his men where to bring me in alive or dead. From Naveen's actions I would say it was still uncertain.

I straightened myself as I heard him, and the others scramble to their feet. I could have crippled him or lain him out senseless with a different placed kick, but I wanted to see what his orders were. If he knew I could easily kill him, like our first confrontation, he didn't show it.

Naveen exited the door slowly, breathing fast, the gun nowhere to be seen, his bandaged face mottled with anger and shock. His two companions with kukri knives in their hands followed him and moved quickly to one side. Though I was not out of their reach they made no attempt to come at me. This more than anything informed me that they needed me alive. Death was a possibility, but their orders were to bring me in alive.

My mind moved ahead. This fight was going to have to end swiftly, I remarked to myself given that a small group or shoppers were gathering around us. Hardly the attention we both needed. Naveen was the head of this little group and beating him conclusively "might" just take the fight out of the others and disperse this crowd.

Might.

He moved in with one foot slightly forward, crouched a little, hands held low and half clenched ready to strike with fist or edge. With my arms folded loosely across my breasts I walked straight at him. My unorthodox move confused him, worried him. I had taken that pose deliberately. I had wanted to see if he had his gun and fire at me, gun me down, fight or insist to continue with his escort of me. He hesitated looking for the trick as I went at him. He swerved to dodge the kick that did not come. A pace from him and he struck, his right hand slashed edgewise at the side of my head.

I blocked it with the point of my suddenly raised elbow. The impact was audible to all with ears. Naveen bared his yellowish teeth through the white bandages in a grimace of pain as my other hand smacked him viciously across his face. A quick shuffle and I was out of reach again of his long arms. Even as I was shuffling out of reach his right leg shot out in a quick counter, heading for my groin. It was a move I anticipated and hoped he would execute.

I made a two-footed jump, six inches back and an inch clear of his foot, bending slightly to catch hold of his rising ankle against the niche of my crossed forearms. My arms bore the brunt of the impact from his kick as I gripped his heel and toe of his boot and wrenched it round in a swift, explosive twist.

Naveen cried out wordlessly as his arms flailed and his standing foot jerked clear of the ground. He spun in the air on the axis of his standing leg and landed with a *"huff"* on the ground face down, arms spread.

In readiness for my escape, I snatched up another roti and tossed them at Naveen's knife-ready compatriots beside him. Had I known they were armed with more than a knife I would have thought twice. A hot slug of lead whistled through the air.

The gun blast brought everyone to a stop. The old heavy-set trader of roti let out an intense shout. The gun man shoved him down to the ground in a panic. The people in the business centre and on the street were yelling and running in every direction as the Daayan gunman tried to make a quick getaway. But I wasn't about to let him get away that easily. My foot shot out in a snap kick to the back of his knee, he faltered and staggered forward. He stumbled into the putrid gutter than ran alongside the street.

Another shot rang out. This one creased my forehead and I felt a sharp pain as it seared my skin. I ducked, leaped forward as another shot whizzed over me.

Bloody hell! I was wrong, they did not care if I came in dead or alive. I rolled over to avoid the next shot I was sure would follow. It did and so did Naveen. I saw him painfully hobble towards me and tower over me, the sonovabitch had a positive talent for getting to me when I was at my least.

I rolled away from him, but he brought both his hands down on me like a sledgehammer, the blow caught me between my shoulder blades with tremendous force that I lay spread-eagled on the ground. His foot followed, catching me alongside my temple. I felt myself slither almost two feet. What followed was a beating I half expected. The amount of hands smashing into me was untenable until at last the edge of a gun barrel slammed into the top of my head and I dove into a pit of darkness.

# TWELVE

It could have been an eternity but in truth it was only a hundred and seventy minutes, when I slowly began to surface from the blackness. As I started to regain my equilibrium. I heard humming of a sweet tune and felt something wet and soft patting my brow and eyes, cleaning what I assumed was the blood from my face. This was damn nice of them, I thought fondlingly.

I was not stripped naked this time. Maybe they will when I recover myself. When I finally got my eyes open, I saw that they were not being nice at all, they were being thorough. An old scraggly Indian woman dressed in a blue and green Sari was wiping off the dark colouring on my skin. She had started with my arms and now it was just my face that needed cleaning.

I felt my arms tied behind my back at the wrists. My ankles were also tied together, and I was propped against a rocky stone. Behind the old woman were silhouettes of faces and shapes as I began to focus. The eye picks out the biggest things first, in this case it was the form of some huge presence. A bald-headed presence that I could not identify. Beside him was the mountain figure of a grey-haired man who I had no trouble identifying as Sigrid and next to him was Sameer Kannauj's average-built body now in a white Pagri and yellow slacks and several other men.

One of the men standing behind Sameer was holding my Chinese Makarov by the barrel, a gun he could not use because of the digital fingerprint sensor. Speaking of weapons, I could feel the small utility knife I retrieved from the Punjab's kitchen safely strapped to the inside of my leg. They had not bothered to search me or if they did it wasn't a thorough search.

It seemed that I was in some sort of mountain temple. The humming I heard were from the people gathered in a semi-circle of sorts. They were all Indians with chalk painted faces in the shape of a cobra's head and staring forebodingly at the centre of the temple as they hummed a trancelike tune. If this was the Daayan cult I was in so much trouble because in the flickering light they all looked strange with haunted expressions on their faces. The group was made up of mostly women with a good sampling of men. Most had craggy, old faces with a sprinkling of fresher and muscular faces. A number of them were crippled and suffering from what appeared to be polio and leprosy. The old woman beside me finished with her work, got to her feet and limped away.

Beyond the onlookers, I could just make out darkened and lighted corridors and an archway leading away from the main part of the temple. Against the far wall were rows of candles of all types burning around and behind a kind of altar. A long, flat slab of rock with a peculiar sculpture of a cobra's head hanging above it.

One of the silhouettes voices brought me to my attention 'I was impressed by your escape Dax' The voice unmistakably owned by the Sin Eater said, 'How the hell did you manage it?'

'F-fortitude' I grunted

'It was unfortunate, of course. I had underestimated your reputation. That will not happen again'

'I know I can't take you, but I'll be willing to give it a go' I ventured. My dare annoyed one of the men who reached one hand down to me. Sigrid stopped him. 'No let her alone' he said with merriment in his pale blue eyes 'She can do us no harm' The man stopped, reluctantly straightened up, licking his lips with his small beady eyes glittering at me. He said nothing and I wondered if he was as subservient as Sigrid seemed to think.

'Where have your boys brought me?' I asked glancing at Sameer who had his back to me.

'You are at our home Miss Dax' replied a voice I never heard before. 'Your escape of us was an inconvenient set of circumstance'

The voice belonged to the huge balding man. He stepped partially into the light and though I couldn't see parts of him, from the bottom part of his chest, I saw a very impressive man wearing a coarsely woven tunic of expensive white linen buttoned probably up to the neck from which hung a gold Khul's amulet the shape of a Cobra's head which was reflected back to me. His whole persona evoked a strange nightmarish prodigiousness that attacks the human spirit. I still could not see his face much less identify him and it seemed he was keeping his right profile out of sight nevertheless, I felt like a child again in his presence because strangely, it was when I was a child that I fought my most frightening battles alone.

He planted his plimsole covered feet firmly within sight of me and remained still.

I looked up, still not able to make out his face 'You must be Brahma, sir'

'Yes' his voice said brusquely 'I take it the mystique is lost now that you see me'

'You could say that'

'You've been terribly busy during your escape. Killing four of my people'

'You lured me to your villa and fed me to snakes, so let's call it, even shall we?'

'Touché. However, my people don't see it that way' he said directing his words at the staring men and women. As he spoke, he was careful to stay in the shadows, hiding his face.

I glanced at his people staring at me, every eye had a moist tinge to them. Helpless, restless and troubled were the haunting looks that stared back at me and I had a bout of Occhiolism. Realising for the first time the smallness of my perspective and I realized that this Brahma, Sameer's uncle had set up a kind of elite of the damned with what seemed to be political and moral overtones.

'I bet they don't, seeing as they couldn't afford the simple vaccination that could have cured their ails' I replied.

'How impudent of you. Everyone here is a victim of the immorality of present-day science and geo-politics. A victim of political agendas that do more harm than good' He seemed to be singing a different tune than the previous tirade. 'With sixteen families here all sterile, crippled physically and emotionally by constant government mismanagement and corruption it is only a matter of time the people will retaliate'

'Your riots are seeing to that. I must say your Anurag Surte is most efficient'

'You know about him then'

'I do. You know if you want to overthrow the government you vote to get them out like everyone else'

'Funny, and the venality that exists within the ranks?'

'That's a bit beyond my prevue'

'It's beyond everyone's prevue'

'Oh yeah? And where do the Chinese or your "A-tome" device come into this?'

His voice was hesitant for an instant. I could see he didn't want to discuss this in front of his people. 'They're a means to an end. Anyway, I digress' he gestured to one of the men behind him 'We're here for a sacrifice, bring out our guest'

We all heard the shuffling of feet behind us, an English assented Indian voice cursing in what sounded like Bengali *"Kuttaar Baaccha"* which my poor interpretation deciphered as "Son of a Dog" or "Son of a Whore" I did not know which. Before long, a silver haired Indian in his sixties, wearing a bloodied Bengali *Kurta* with *Chikan* embroidery was flung onto the rocky earth next to me. He had been beaten badly and was looking seriously dehydrated.

He cursed his chaperons *'Betichod'* I understood his curse because it was in Hindi. He had told his escorts that they were "Daughter fuckers"

"Who the hell was this?" I thought to myself

'Ah another culprit who dared to upset your plans?' I asked leaning up

'Very good Dax. This is Mahatma Bhave, Administrator of these parts who only last year complained that there is a selective silence from AAP and congress regarding the riots and that it would behoved of congress to deploy an adequate number of armed security forces personnel to combat the rising cases of riots and like you a capitalist'

This was Sir Steele's friend, the Governor of a district state, the one that went missing.

'I guess, you didn't like that?'

'The problem was "Armed", I didn't want armed cops on the streets, we want dead cops and protesters on the streets'

'A curse on all your mothers' The Governor of Maharashtra yelled at them in Hindi 'You will all pay for this you daughter fuckers, especially you Harsha'

'I doubt that Bhave'

'You wait and see dog fucker'

'I must agree with my friend here' I interjected

'I thought you might. They tell me you own all the hotels in Jaipur, Muslim and Hindi alike, is this so? How did you manage that?' Brahma asked stepping backwards

'Are we going to compare wealth's now?' I asked

'That's a good question, what do you think, Ranjit?' he asked turning to the man left of him.

'I think we should kill them at once my Lord Brahma' replied the man who had hold of my Makarov which was conspicuously absent. He gestured a hand at us while his little eyes that were hard as stone stared angrily at me. I must have offended him some way.

'I agree' Brahma said curtly with a voice of granite. His belly did not lull where he stood. His heaviness I guessed was of muscle rather than fat. 'One less headache to concern ourselves with. See to it will you?'

'Will do, *Mere Prabhu*'

My attention was on the man next to Brahma who called him his Lord. Ranjit.

No wonder he had bad intentions for me. I had made his sniper skills seem like he was a novice. Or was it something else?

Sameer was still there but his eyes were on the floor, his face was swollen and garnished with black and blue bruises. I knew that if I were to get out of here, it might depend on my former lover, Hazel and a utility knife.

A middle-aged woman touched Brahma on the shoulder '*Mere Prabhu*' she said getting his attention.

He glanced at her as she whispered something in his ear. He nodded, turned to his nephew and put a hand on his shoulder. All the while he stayed in the shadows. The huge man's figure hid everything as he walked past me towards the doorway with Sameer following. A muted stone dropped from Sameer's hand and rolled towards me. The stone did not bounce of make a sound like a rock would. I looked at it and noticed it had a soft wadding around it like paper wrapped round it. I surreptitiously picked it up and held onto it.

'Where the hell are you going, the world knows about you now, if they don't get you I will'

He stopped in the archway of the doorway and turned towards me his face and right area still seditiously hidden in the shadows. 'Miss Dax in a few minutes you are going to be feeling everything imaginable lest make good on your boast. As for the world, let me worry about that'

'You won't succeed' I yelled at him

'My dear lady I already have' he said, 'That reminds me, Mr Eatherly would you hand my nephew the drive' he turned to Sameer 'Sameer would you mind?'

'No, uncle' replied Sameer.

As Sameer went over to Sigrid, he cast a look in my direction, never seeing the slight nod from his uncle at Sigrid. As Sameer neared Sigrid he delved into one of his pockets and brought it out again. He held out his hand as Sameer reached for it. He could not see Sigrid's hand was empty. His face showed his confusion when he noticed it. As he looked up at Sigrid, Sigrid reached forward with one hand in lighting speed and caught him by the neck and lifted him off the ground as if he were a truss of hay.

'Noooo' I yelled but it was no use.

Both Mahatma Bhave and I stared as Sigrid slowly squeezed the life out of Sameer. Sigrid had a bright satisfying smile on his face as he squeezed. When he was done, he let go of Sameer's lifeless body, it crumbled like a bunch of old newspapers onto the rocky earth.

'*Chutiya*' cursed Bhave in Hindi, literal meaning "Bastard" or "Fucker". The revulsion on his face I bet was similar to mine.

'Betrayal is not something we tolerate around here' Brahma's voice said with a sinister invisible grim resonance.

'He was your blood, a noble one if what you claim about Naga is true'

'That doesn't exclude his actions' he said before turning away and disappearing through the archway.

I cursed inwardly knowing the truth of what he said. Whatever his plan was, it seems he would definitely make his point clear.

The other men began to drift off, disappearing one by one into the various corridors that led from the central point of the crumbled old temple.

I untangled the crumpled paper round the note Sameer passed to me. All it read was

"*Parents at Vadh dvaar. West ridge, boat. Dass and Anurag Surte same person — DO NOT TRUST. Box still at villa. Drugs leaving for Kerala port*"

Dass and Anurag Surte were the same? How convenient and sensible did that make, it would explain a lot. As for the drugs, I assumed that it was the heroin Sir C was first concerned about. With the "A-tome" still in Jaipuri, his parents at a slaughterhouse and there being a boat in the west ridge, well how useful was this information now or what could I do about it, I questioned as I chewed on the note.

As for everything else it seemed to be falling into place and making sense. If Safi Dass, the deputy director of India's Central Bureau of Security was not to be trusted, it sort of made sense that he was the one who grassed on me. He is almost the top man in the organisation, all orders go through him before filtering down. How else would the Daayan cult know I was meeting Imah? Why they killed him and why I was lured into a trap. Dass is obviously under the influence of Brahma and his unholy cult.

'Who are you?' whispered the old man lying next to me.

I winced inwardly at the question.

'A friend' I answered back 'Sir Steele sends his regards'

'You know Conrad? You one of his agents?'

'No'

There was a short pause and then silence as the temple stood almost empty.

'You are Susan, yes?'

'He mentioned me then?'

'He has high regard for you'

Just then before I could reply we heard the sound of an engine. A large engine tuned by a heavy-duty truck of some sort. We listened as it trudged away and finally faded away from our hearing. Suddenly Ranjit appeared with two men and two women with him. One of the men was Naveen.

'Take them' Ranjit said quietly.

I groaned at the fresh hell I was about to experience.

Bhave looked up as the men moved quickly to him, seizing him by the arms and lifting him up to his feet. The women did the same with me. Bhave comprehended what was about to happen but he looked composed as to others who would be pleading or screaming their heads off. I kind of admired him for that. We walked some distance towards the main hall of the temple and altar.

'What are you dog fuckers going to do to us?' he asked in Hindi

'They aren't dog fuckers they are snake lickers' I corrected

Ranjit's response was to stop and slap me across the face. It made my head swivel. 'S … see … they have … no sense of humour' I chuckled. To Ranjit, I was an *Angreji Kutiya*. An "English bitch" who did not deserve to breathe the same air he was.

He grinned a deadly evil smirk at me as he ran his hand down over my breast. I tried to twist away but the women holding me had a good immobile grip of me. 'We see who have humour' Ranjit said

He turned to the women holding me 'Prepare the altar, then her' They flung me down and walked away. The men flung Bhave down too, beside me and did the same as the women did.

I heard him grunt painfully as he hit a rocky stone. When he finally looked in my direction his already bloody pale blue lip was bleeding. The blood was flowing freely. It was a bit unusual, so I asked with my voice low 'You diabetic?'

He nodded.

Damn it.

'Hold on' I whispered

I saw Sigrid walk up to us. He didn't say anything, he just grinned that damned bright disarming smile of his at us as he walked past.

'So, they're going to …' Bhave was saying with a touch of fear in his voice.

'Kill us' I said flatly. They was no need sugar coating it for him, he was going to find out soon enough.

The women returned with buckets. One went to the altar and began washing it. The other came over and started cutting away my clothes with a small pen knife. She was bound to find the knife, so when her eyes met mine, I head butted her. She turned away crying out with pain and a bloody nose. It made the other woman come over from rearranging the candles.

It was all I needed to tear off the Sellotape strapping the utility knife to my inner thigh, using a cheap laugh and her groan to conceal the sound of my flicking it within reach of Bhave's hand.

He at first was confused at what I did, then saw the knife and did his best to conceal the small knife.

Ranjit appeared with one of the men to see what the commotion was. There was no need to tell him, he could see what I had done.

'I thought you smart woman' he turned to the bloodless woman as he took out the kukri knife on his hip and handing it to her 'Deal with her' The woman grinned and slashed me down the left side of my torso, slicing off the bandage already holding the wound there. The nose bleeding one kicked me in the chest. I saw her foot coming and though she wore sandals it still hurt like hell.

Her companion began ripping the remaining articles of clothing from my body in a frenzy when she joined her. In their rage they did not notice a loose strap of Sellotape on my thigh. There was no pained embarrassment or fear when they finally got me naked. The men just admired my white coloured flesh, especially my perked breast stained with blood that ran down my left side.

The women went over to the altar.

The men stood watching us closely as the women returned. pulled me to my feet and hauled me to the altar. I already surmised what they were about to do but horror caught up with me as I saw the arrangement of candles over the altar. They had rigged the candles over small bamboo shaped beakers held by strips and suspended by leafy balanced ropes. The hollow bamboo beakers were empty. The intention was to let the hot wax drip slowly into them and when they were filled it tilted sixty to forty-five degrees and drip onto my body from the bamboo beakers.

I struggled against their hold as they laid my nude body onto the slab. One of the men assisted them in spreading and tying my legs with ankle straps while Ranjit stood watching with my Makarov in his hand. One of the women started cleaning my body with water from a cut gourd and a white napkin.

'Yes, this is right' Ranjit said walking up to me as I lay on the slab studying the candle setup while his cohort and woman cleaned and tied my hands to my side. 'These special made wax candles boil for a long time, they will pour down on you little by little by morning you will be covered by wax' 'You will die … little by little' said the lady with the bloody nose 'You will be our sacrifice to Daayan the guiding spirit of pain. Pain of the body, the spirit, passion which has guided our lives'

The other woman was lighting the carefully prepared candles that were part of the choleric contraption. Turning my head, I saw Naveen enter at the head of a procession of men and women with painted faces, walking slowly crooning a mantra.

Death was coming, I knew it however I did not believe this was how I end. Rubatosis hit me as I suddenly became unsettlingly aware of my heartbeat.

The two women, Ranjit and his cohort joined the assemblage as they kowtowed around the stone slab. As Ranjit and his mate joined the group chanting, Naveen and the men with him stood up and began rubbing their hands over my naked body, smearing it with honey. I had no idea what that would accomplish. They stopped suddenly and joined the others in their chant just as a group of old wrinkled women with long hair, weird headdresses and long dirty fingernails approached me and started waving their hands over me. Their hands were not empty. They held amulets with mirrors and adorned gold-plated jewels on them. Where these the witches the late Reeven had mentioned to Sameer? I wondered.

They didn't once touch me, they just fluttered the amulets and their hands over me. Two of them suddenly screamed and took a step back. 'This one is not right' one of them cried out in Hindi.

'This is our doom' The other old woman sobbingly concurred.

I was barely listening. I was waiting for the pain that I knew would come. I had long tested the bindings tied to my wrists and found them too tough to loosen without help.

The old women stopped and withdrew. The two old women who for some reason panicked joined the others and began to chant.

The candles were burning steadily, and I could see the bamboo beakers starting to fill up with the hot liquid wax.

Laminachi, my first teacher was a Siberian hermit hunter. He taught me plenty about hunting, striking within one's ability and knowing where to place a shot on any animal. He taught me little about how to focus my mind. That was left to my other teachers which I put into practice.

I let my emotional energy become bare and as motionless as my nude body. I engaged my mind and body to the art of meditation and breathing as done the jiujutsu way. Closing my eyes, I let my breathing deliberately slow. For a moment, my mind went blank, everything went black. A numbing, perplexing feeling came over me, then my head refocused with total concentration like a bee being balanced on top of a needle. As I gradually immersed myself into a meditative state, I could feel the fear of death and the pain to come slowly abate that when it finally came, I barely flinched.

All of a sudden, the chanting stopped and the whole ensemble rose and soundlessly funnelled out of the main temple.

It took a while, before I knew we were alone to come out of my contemplative state, and for me to again test the bindings on my wrists.

My eyes swept across the empty hall just as something tugged at my wrist. Bhave had propelled himself across the hall inch by inch and had now manoeuvred himself along the edge of the slab using the utility knife to cut through the bindings on my right wrist.

He was not in the right position to cut through my bindings, so he manoeuvred himself where his battered head rested on one of my nipples. He glanced up over the rise of my breast and the dark mound just in front of my eyes. I could see a touch of embarrassment in his eyes as he moved the knife up and down against the strap securing my right hand. He had just cut through it when fresh pain hit me again.

Three drops of wax hit me all at once. My involuntarily flinch made him unintentionally drop the knife. I heard it clatter onto the floor as Bhave lost his balance and fell forward twisting his body to avoid my breasts.

A funnel of molten hot wax lay cupped over my stomach emitting little wisps of steam. Another bamboo beaker was nearing its limit and about to tilt and send another stream of liquid wax down on me. It almost didn't matter. With one hand free, I hurriedly loosen my other hand. Pulling myself up on my buttocks I leaned forward in an attempt to loosen the ankle straps around my legs. Just then the old woman who attended to me earlier limped into the hall. I caught sight of her just as Bhave rose to his knees with the utility knife in-between his teeth. She was about to cry out at what I was attempting when I snatched the knife from Bhave's teeth and threw it at her with pinpoint accuracy. The knife buried itself in her throat. I finished loosening the straps and leapt off the slab altar.

I went over to her. She was bleeding from her neck profusely and her attempt to stop the bleeding with her hands was hopeless 'Sorry mother and thank you for your care' I said to her hazing eye as I took her face in my hand and twisted her neck. It snapped with decisive precision. I was sorry to do it, but it needed doing. I yanked out the bloodied knife from her throat.

I went over to Bhave and cut his bindings off.

We both heard the sound of voices approaching.

Two voices, Indian voices.

Male voices.

'You stay here' I whispered to Bhave

I hurriedly tiptoed to the corridor were their voices were coming from. As they appeared, I grabbed the first one by the chin and wrenched it hard across to the side, breaking his neck in that one move. The other, startled by my sudden attack reached for the blade by his hip and was about to pull it free when I thrust the utility knife up and under his chin burying the whole five-inch blade into his bearded submental space, the submandibular tissue space under the midline of his chin. He jerked upwards before quivering on his feet as I wrenched the knife out. He was on his feet for ten whole seconds with shock on his face before collapsing in a heap.

I didn't notice who the men were until after I had killed them, I noticed the face of the first man whose neck I had broken. It was Ranjit. How surprising this twist of change of fortune this would be for him.

Me alive and he dead, oh what a reversal of fortune. I bent down to search him, but my Makarov was no where on his person. Not even his blade. How unfortunate for me. His companion however did have his kukri knife and I gently relieved it from him.

Bhave was up on his feet when I got back to him with a weird expression on his face. He was shivering with a chill-like -sweat on his brow. He was going in some type of shock. I hoped it was not a diabetic kind of shock because I would not know what to do. I escorted him to a dark spot in the hall.

'Sit down' I said to him then bent over him. 'Let's have a look at you' There were contusions all over his body here and there.

'This will have to be quick'

I placed my hands over his diaphragm

'What are you doing' he asked

'Making you strong enough to walk' I announced as I began to massage his chest, trying to avoid the gashes on his skin. He flinched several times but gradually the pain and sweat on his face began to ebb. Next, I started on his arms, legs and calves. I whispered to him softly compelling him to go into a quiet dark void. Gradually the numb nerve centres of his body began to re- establish their places with the area of the body they controlled. Slowly his deltoid muscles began to react to the soothing massage of his nerve centres.

'Now we have to get out of here' I told him when I had finished

'Not like that' he said looking at my nude body. I had almost forgotten. As I went over to the old woman I spotted where they had piled my clothing. It was all in shreds except for my panties, sandals and Kameez. Retrieving them and hurriedly stripped the old dead woman of her outer covering. It wasn't much but it would do. I dressed myself and approached the corridor where Sigrid, the men and women disappeared down to.

'Hey' I said to Bhave handing him the kukri knife I took off the man I had just killed 'I just have to take care of something'

'N-no no, let's go now'

I glanced at the exit Brahma had used, undecided of which tunnel to go through. It was then that Sameer's note made sense to me. "West ridge, boat". We escape through the west ridge where a boat will be waiting. Where was that I wondered? I glanced west at the less used darken corridor and pointed 'Head down there. If I am not back in five minutes find your own way home and alert the authorities'

I slowly went down the corridor listening and smelling the air. I heard the group chattering at the end of the corridor. I could smell a poorly cooked *Vindaloo* and a faintly steamed *Thali*, it seemed they were having dinner.

I ripped open the tampon from my pants and retrieved the eggshell rhizome and squeezed. Holding my breath and without looking I tossed it low into the room. Ten seconds passes until the padding broke from its shell and spilled its odourless gaseous compound of *belladonna* throughout the room. I turned away and made my way back to Bhave. I knew the occupants in the room will all be paralysing for ten to twelve hours, time enough for us to get the authorities here. I thought to myself. We had to escape first.

More than keeping them secure until the law arrived, I wanted to give us plenty of time for our escape. I did not want what happened last time, happen again.

I found Bhave huddled close to the entrance of the corridor I had told him to wait. He smiled at me when he saw me approach. In his hand was a head torch and a box of matches. Where he found them was not as important as it was. It was just possible we were going to need both items.

'Enjoying the scenery?' I asked him taking the head torch from him. 'It's not exactly the Taj Mahal'

'Oh, I have no idea … but if you can imagine it, you can see it'

'You're a peculiar woman Susan'

'Don't be so fascinated with me yet, we still have to get out of here'

'I'm not worried, I know you'll get us out somehow'

His confidence in me was very infectious. It made me want to walk as if I were ten feet tall but all I could manage was my normal 5ft 10in.

The corridor led to a cellar on the far side of the temple. The closed cellar window opened up to the rocky face of what I supposed were the Aravalli Mountains. We had just reached the entrance when a low droning alarm went off behind us. I could see the sick fear and shock on Bhave's face as the distance clamour continued to sound.

'Don't worry, they'll think we left the back way' I said to Bhave hoping to restore his composure. The last thing I needed was him being agitated.

'Isn't this the back way?'

'Yes, but ssshhh … don't tell them that'

'Tell me … you called Brahma … Harsha back there …' I was beginning to say

'You don't know who he is?' he asked staring back at me as if I were of the informationally challenged of the species.

'No'

'Harsha … is Harsha Kannauj, one of the richest men in India. The sixth actually. He is worth about 6.7 billion dollars and owns the Mundra port and other ports across India. He also owns Avis Cements and was once my supporter'

So that's why he is so influential.

With a name like Harsha Kannauj no wonder he animatedly, articulated the brooding intense character of a cult leader and the name Brahma.

6 billion dollars huh, that is a quarter of what I was worth.

'Why would he make a display of killing his nephew?'

'Nephew?'

'Yes, Sameer the man we just watched Sigrid kill?'

'I know him well and I didn't understand what you meant back there' he said 'He doesn't have a nephew. He doesn't have any family. A wife but I think they're separated'

Huh, Sameer was not his nephew, but he regarded him as family just the same, why was that? I wondered. Maybe Sameer lied to me.

I tried to get my bearings when I considered Sameer's note and we headed west. We had not gone more than twenty yards when the mountain kind of just ended, blocking our way. It would seem that I had chosen the wrong way when I spotted it. A narrow cave that had been blocked off was open before us.

I turned to Bhave. His movements were laboured but controlled and he seemed very calm.

'You're not claustrophobic by any chance?' he shook his head

'That's good because it seems we're going spelunking' I told him 'Caves can be dangerous places if you're doing it for the first time. Do not waste energy on what you can see next or time, cold or anything else except what you doing at the moment'

'I've gone mountain climbing before, I think I can manage this'

I gave him a small smile 'Sorry for being such a bitch, I can't help it' (Paragraph)

'Oh *Bheti*, I wouldn't describe you as a bitch, that be stupid of me. So, can we go?'

'Yes, we should. I'll help you through the rough patches. Ready?'

'Yes'

'Ok'

The excursion through the cave was abominable. Combined with the penetrating cold, the slides down and up proved to be challenging. I had shut my mind to hope and fear, from anxiety and speculation, hoarding the steel fitness of my mental and physical energy. If I were able to do this, I feared for Bhave and did my best to accommodate him.

Three quarters in I glanced back at the gritty but cultured Indian who was gawking almost drunkenly about him. I stopped and turned to aid him to his feet, but his legs did not seem to want to respond.

'You quitting on me?'

He shook his head, breathlessly and shivering as he clutched at me 'My dear … that will be … the day. My wretched … body … won't co-operate. Give … me a moment'

I squatted beside him, kneading his chest and said 'Take it easy. Let's have a rest for a couple of minutes yeah. Breathe deeply … slowly and exhale …' I stopped. I had heard something. I slanted my head, staring at the narrow rift which we had just emerged from.

Yes, there was it again. A scrape of metal on stone moving swiftly. Someone was coming and from the swiftness I could only guess who it was.

# THIRTEEN

He was coming. Sigrid was coming. The greatest combat fighter in the world was coming to put my lights out.

I had no illusions about that. He emerged from the hidden dark of the cave entrance into the morning light with a machine pistol in one hand. I knew there was one type of business he had on his mind. Kill me and the aged man in my possession.

A head torch like the one we used was on his head. He stood up straight, sniffing in the fresh air and looked about him. He immediately caught sight of me and the boat behind me ferrying Governor Mahatma of Maharashtra away.

The grin his mouth made was all so familiar, filled with confidence and amusement.

I moved across the ground a little in profile to him. Standing with feet apart and head slightly back. A pose of challenge.

Sigrid understood it, tossed away the machine pistol and relieved himself of the head torch

'I was hoping for this' he said

When I remembered how he killed Sameer I could only have one reply for him

'So, have I'

Sigrid moved.

It is only prudent that Bhave say a few words here because I was really out of it at this time.

*　　*　　*　　*

*The Governor of Maharashtra, Mahatma Bhave's Tale.*

I am not one for storytelling but from what I see that morning was something to treasure.

This big white man whom I just witness killing another man with so much ease and no remorse was coming to kill us. This girl who I just met was about to sacrifice her life so that I could get away was standing naked, her hair drawn tightly back, gleaming like a gilded titan waiting for that killer.

Oh Shiva, if only I could have taken a picture. Susan had insisted I leave but something about her stance compelled me to let the boat float in the middle of the river and watch the spectacle in front of me. Standing there still. Only the soft rise and fall of her beautiful bouncy breasts showed how womanly rampart she was, like a crowned golden goddess she was.

Conrad had told me about her, but I barely listened at the time. What stuck with me at the time was he used one word to constantly describe her. "Indescribable"

Yes, she is that, Indescribable.

Lord Shiva once set a task for Vishnu and Brahma but cursed Brahma for lying. Consequently, Shiva insisted that Brahma can only be worshiped once a day. If he was worshiped more than a day, then Vishnu had the authority to beat the daylight out of him. This was a story I have told my kids among many others, but it seemed this was the very same bedtime story unfolding before my eyes. Now standing before me, I did not know who in that myth was Brahma or who was Vishnu. I was hoping that Susan was emulating the role of Vishnu.

My blood was pounding in my brain and I felt the sense of my own reality slipping. I think because of the cold and the climb I just took. In my tired mind, despite the pounding in my head, I could hear the brash lyrical music of the *Bharatanatyam* based on the mythology interpreting the fight before me. With the weight of all my gods bearing down on me, I gazed from the middle of the slow-moving green river as myth was quickly becoming flesh.

I saw the man Mr Sigrid appear from the mouth of the cave, stop to survey the situation and smirk a very ugly grin. He was wearing a warm yellow striped cardigan and blue jeans. He said something before throwing away the pistol and head torch. He walked some paces towards Susan then stopped.

'Isn't there a chill in the air to be in your birthday suit?' he asked Susan who stood like a statue, neither responding to him nor acknowledging his presence. Mr Sigrid took a step forward, testing his footing. Then suddenly he moved very lightly and with deceptive eloquence which obscured his speed as he went after the girl in front of him.

For my life I cannot exactly remember the first sequence of the deadly confrontation. I just knew that the goddess Vishnu was matching the lying god Brahma blow for blow, kick for kick, block for block and speed for speed that my old analytical brain reserved for fencing could articulate. I remember the impression of the two figures closing, intertwining and splitting as if they were in some strange eerie *Jhumair* dance. There was the flashing of fists colliding with elbows, forearms, hands and the impacting of feet. Once Mr Sigrid tried a leaping karate kick but slipped almost losing his balance, he dived. Hitting the ground, rolling in a perfect break-fall as he lightly rose to his feet.

Susan muttered something like 'Show-off'

His recovery was so beautiful that I had to internally applaud.

One thing that fastened my attention was Susan's body, her pink mocha skin glowing in the morning sun from the honey and oil on her skin. Her firm breasts, long limbs always orbiting back, always back, gliding with her bare feet, turning in whizzing pattens and counterpointing advances from Mr Sigrid that seemed to fuse with his prearranged synchronisation. The boat engine oil on her skin was serving her well in deflecting some of his brutish moves. Once Mr Sigrid caught her briefly by the hand and once by her foot, each time I squealed silently with panic, knowing that if she fell I would too, but she just twisted her greasy limb and wrenched it out of his grip before his fingers could close.

It was about two minutes into the fight when I noticed she was bleeding down her left side. A bruise seemed to be swelling up on her face and left torso. There was blood but she seemed unaware of it. There was no hint of desperation on her face. Instead there was a cold impassivity, a burning, animal glare in her eyes. She seemed to be possessed by a ferocious and unyielding will to survive. Everything else had been stripped away from her. The cockiness and kindness I first noticed about her was nowhere to be found.

Why Mr Sigrid didn't see it was remarkable. If he did, he should have given up and walked away or shoot us both and be done with it.

They were getting closer to the edge of the river, his back was to me, crouched a little, arms slightly spread, edging towards her. It was then she took him by surprise. She moved forward for the first time. Suddenly flowing at him with bewildering speed into his steel-plated arms, a move so wildly insane that it took Mr Sigrid unawares. If it took him by surprise, he did not seem fazed by it. They clashed again but this time they didn't come apart. Her face was against his chest, her arms round his waist and she was encircled by his grasp, too close that she could not drive a knee into his groin.

Instead she did a strangest thing with her palm. She seemed to palm him three or four times but like before it didn't seem to faze him.

He laughed knowing from where he stood, he had the upper hand. I had to agree because there was no way she could throw him and no way she could escape. Hooking his hand behind her back he prepared to crush her. However, it seemed Susan had other ideas. She was still moving, carrying him back and back. In the instant of shock, I think he realised her purpose only it was too late, he seemed immobilised. I noticed Mr Sigrid bleeding from the nose and his ears an act he did not seem aware off. Locked together, they fell. He snatched a frantic breath as his back hit the water.

Mr Sigrid it appeared was unprepared for the seconds of almost total paralysis. His grip seemed to slide off her body and her slippery body eased off from his fixed grasp. Fighting sudden panic he tried to kick his way to the surface but for some reason he couldn't, It was at that point I saw Susan slip behind him wrapping her forearm under his chin, clamping tightly against his throat as her other arm was tucked through one of his arm against the back of his neck in a lock that should have broken his neck if not for his abnormal strength. Her legs coiled about his legs propped to hold his thick thighs in place as they both sank and disappeared from my view.

Agonising seconds of fear wandered into seconds of waiting.

The ripples of the water were dying while I knelt in the boat by the river's edge waiting, staring hard-and -fast at the water, hoping and praying for her to appear. My nerves flayed with tension when one of her legs broke the surface briefly, but that was a full minute ago. It was over, Vishnu had taken Brahma to Shiva via Nirvana. They were both dead. Susan had gone taking Mr Sigrid with her.

Tears welled up in my eyes, a profound feeling of despair overcame me and I really did not know what to do. Just then water splashed several feet away from me, my head whipped round and I saw the most delightful sight I could ever have seen, that is apart from my children's birth of course.

Susan's body gleaming on the surface of the water against the greenness of the water. I heard her take in great sobbing inhalations as she sucked great mouthfuls of air into her lungs. Her hair had come loose and covered her face. She threw it back off her face with a jerk of her head and took four slow strokes to reach the edge of the river. By the time I paddled the boat over to where she was, she was lying on her back breathing hard.

'Aaaaahhh …. Aaaahhhh …… aaaaahhhhh ….' came the sounds of her racked breathing echoing in the morning air. I climbed out of the boat with the bundle of the clothing she tore off her body and crouched beside her, patting and rubbing her shoulders futility, croaking 'Well done well done, bheti …. You did well … we must get you warm … the cold …. well done' I blabbed

# FOURTEEN

For the longest minute I lay on the ground by the river unaware of where I was. Someone came up beside me congratulating me. I did not recognise him even when he mentioned the word "Cold". It did however spark a realisation that I was naked and cold. Barer than a new-born and colder than a well digger's arse.

Struggling to my knees, I whispered the words 'Clothes' and the man beside me covered my front with a thin cloth before aiding me to my feet and then proceeded to dab my back. I was not aware I was bleeding because the man seemed to be tending to it. I couldn't care less. I snatched a clothing item and proceeded to dry and warm my legs.

I realised that I was afraid of something and at the same time, angry. Scared, not for myself but for something else, maybe it was retrospective fear, I had no idea. Angry at someone and not something. I got dressed slowly, it was then the situation began to dawn on me as I snapped out of my fudge state.

I could not believe I had bested the greatest combat fighter in the world. The Sin Eater. I should feel pride but all I felt was anger.

Now I realised why I was afraid and angry. The man beside me, Bhave Mahatma, Sir C's friend. I was scared for him because he was still here. What if I had lost the battle?

I turned towards him 'W … what the hell? Why are you … still here? I did say go; I think I said it … Go … I was there and I remember me saying go … why are you here?'

'My dear … I couldn't …' he simply said

'Couldn't?' I proclaimed angrily 'Of course you could … you men … Bollocks … you … never doing what you're told … I did say go … what if I had lost? … men … Seymour knows better and if he were here, he'd go'

Bhave started laughing feebly 'Who the Vishnu is Seymour? If he were here, my dear I doubt he wouldn't do the same and if he didn't, his arse should be severely kicked'

Suddenly all the anger in me melted away and I forced a smile.

I was glad I was alive. Colours were now suddenly brighter, sounds were pronominal and smells, scintillating.

'We should get going' I said to him as I wrung my hair dry.

'Yes ma'am'

As I climbed in beside him into the canoe the surface of the river rippled abruptly, perturbed from below. Something rose, slowly from the dark green water, a yellow cardiganed arm, then a mop of soaking silver hair, then Sigrid's sightless white face appeared. His body lulled for a few seconds then rolled over before slowly sinking. Before it disappeared, I saw the effect of the *"Tie Sha Zhang"* or The Iron Palm blow I had applied and the effect of my strangle hold on him. His bloody eyes, ears and nose were still seeping blood, his head was slumped at an awkward angle to his broad shoulders and his stomach had an unusual a redness to it.

'You wanted to make sure, didn't you?' said the man next to me a little shaky.

I did not answer.

'I'm glad you did' he said

'Glad? Huh!' I straightened up 'He was good, his reputation of being the best fighter in the world was well deserved. I never could have taken him on his own ground. Be thankful he had an aversion to the cold, and I am well versed in a blow that could kill any man'

'He wasn't the best. He clearly underestimated you'

'That may be, I'm glad I don't have to do that again'

'So am I'

'Good, how are you feeling?' I asked Bhave

'Just a little skittish' he said smiling at me 'But immensely happy to be alive'

'As am I. Soon you will be home, dry and safe'

It was twenty minutes later before we were safe from the machinations of the Daayan cult, arriving in the town of Agra and four hours later when we walked through the doors of the local Western Union office in Jaipur.

No sooner had we stepped into the highly polished marble floors of the office than a uniformed guard accosted us at the door. Just like the hotel guard I did not blame this guy, especially when I caught sight of us in a glazed window. Torn, battered with bruises was no way to make a way into official offices.

'We'd like to see the manager' I told him

'He's in a meeting and can't be disturbed' the guard replied, implying that we were the wrong type to call on his manager.

'This is an emergency'

'Sorry but I can't disturb him' the guard replied.

'Go get him now' Bhave said angrily beside me.

'And why would I do that?'

'If you want to keep your job you better do as she says'

He glanced at me and scoffed

'And who in Kali is she?'

'I'm nobody' I unceremoniously stated.

'Well if you're not going do as she says, then tell him his governor wants to have a word' he insisted

'Governor?' the guard enquired

'You don't recognise me?' He asked then turning to me he said 'That's the problem with the grassroots, they don't take the time to study their candidates'

'How would I know' I replied just as the guard clamped a hand hard down on my shoulder, while his other hand rested on his holstered service weapon.

'That's no way to treat a lady' I said between clenched teeth.

'You no la …' he began to say when I issued a quick effortless chop to his kidneys which sent him sprawling across the air-conditioned office. The other guests and customers gawked with surprise.

'No need to get excited' Bhave said aloud to the gaping customers and guests just as one of the tellers stood up from behind her window enclosed cubicle and walked round the enclosed workstation towards us.

'Mr Governor is that you?'

'At last someone with a good education' Bhave said quietly to me. When the young woman came up to us, she regarded us curiously before smiling at Bhave 'I thought that was you' she said in Hindi glancing at me.

'A supporter, how fortunate' Bhave said in English grinning at her

'Actually, I voted for your opponent sir' she replied taking his example to speak in English.

'Ah … and still you recognised me?'

'Yes sir. Ever since you paved the roads in my neighbourhood' she glanced at the guard who was rising ashamedly to his feet and casting me with angry eyes 'So why did Amir deserve to be punched sir?' she asked

'He was being rude'

'Ah I see'

'We need to see your manager. We have business to attend to' Bhave said. Either it was the tone of his voice or the speed which I used to dispose of Amir the guard but whatever it was she nodded and asked us to wait there as she hurried round a row of desks.

It wasn't a minute before someone exited the room where the woman disappeared through.

He was not an Indian but a tall lanky Asian several years my senior wearing a proper bespoke black business suit. His outfit was as immaculate as ours was filthy.

'Can I help you?' he asked, his eyes appraising us as he outstretched his hand to take Bhave's hand.

'You are expecting me' I said to him

A curious expression went over his face as he looked at me 'Miss Dax?' he inquired

'One and only'

'Of course, my apologises. I'm Richard Leong' he said with an accent I readily recognised.

'You're Canadian?'

'Yes, I'm the regional manager here' he said as he glanced over at the guard who was glaring at me. 'Did you upset Amir?' he asked me.

I shrugged my shoulders

He chuckled 'Amir why don't you go for a break?' he said to the guard

'Governor, Miss Dax please come with me'

We followed him down a row of desks, through a short passageway and into a wood panelled office. It was a Wall Street-type refuge smack down in the middle of India.

As we entered the office a familiar figure standing at an attention greeted me.

'Inspector'

'Briggs?'

'Commander, sir'

'It's Susan, Sergeant remember'

'Sir, yes …Susan sir'

'At ease Briggs'

He slumped his shoulder, easing his intent body. He gave me a big grin. Standing before me now, I could be happier that he was here.

'Sir C got my fax?'

'Yeah'

The fax I sent at the business office was to change the venue of all communications and contact through any Western Union office in the Jaipur region via code using the second part of my favourite poem.

'Briggs this is the Governor of …'

'Governor of Maharashtra Mahatma Bhave, Sir Steele's old classmate' he finished for me extending his hand to the Governor 'Pleased to meet you sir'

They shook hands.

He gave me an evaluating look 'You don't look worse for wear' he told me. He had a right to say that because in truth he had seen me appear worse.

I explained to him that the Governor had got caught up in the Daayan's revenge schemes. He sympathised. I turned to Mr Leong, 'Do you have some chocolate, something sweet …'

'I think …' he went round his desk as I examined Bhave's eyes. They looked just a bit jaundices and pale. Leong produced a half-opened bar of a milk chocolate. I gave it to Bhave 'Chew, slowly, it should help' I turned to Briggs 'How's Margaret?' I asked

'The missus had a touch of the Indian flu, so I sent her home' he explained in his soft liquid Manchester accent.

'Good for … I mean … how sad'

'Indeed, it is' he said going behind the desk in the room. He produced a cream coloured 8-wheel luggage expander and a medical travel kit. 'Here is a care-package from Seymour, Mr Leong, you have a place where she can change?'

'Yes, please follow me'

'Governor please excuse us' Briggs said to Bhave

We followed the regional manager down a passageway to an office furnished with just a desk and chair.

The manager left Briggs and I in the room. The was an inquisitive air on his face when he did so. I suspect he didn't see the reason why Briggs would stay behind.

'First let's have a look at you' Briggs said opening the medical kit.

I stripped and he turned his head 'Commander please some decorum on your part should be necessary. You are after all a lady'

I ignored him as he tended to the exasperated wound on my left side and face, he followed by seeing to the various bruises and cuts on me. The medical case had some wonderful antiseptics and antibiotics. One set was a bunch of pills and plaster, the other was an antibiotic infused flexi-pen.

Opening the case, I began to brief him about my escapades since I left The Punjab hotel assuming he had already been briefed by Seymour and Steele about my activities up until then. I instructed him with some special directives concerning Imah Rajan's guys before informing him on what I had learned about Anurag Surte and Safi Dass. He wasn't surprised.

I inspected the contents packed in the wheeler case. Inside were a container of wet wipes, a towel, a pair of native Indian attires and a pair of my own western clothes, including a tanned coloured Tripmaster jacket with a special distinctive surprise in the cuffs and collar. A pair of ankle boots with "*Dons*" implanted in the heels, a polymer-knitted black silicon carbide Kevlar bodysuit with ceramic matrices and laminates, a pair of Celine black pants and bra courtesy of Daniel Anderson's connections. In the make-up kit-bag was one of my personal brand of make -up Guerlain Ombre Couleurs, my Yves Saint Laurent perfume that cost £800 an ounce, an Olay regenerist skin cream, a bristle and nylon hair brush, a stylish hair comb, a nail kit and Veenor tampons.

Also within the case was a new blue OnePlus8 Pro Phone complete with all the necessary upgrades, a brand-new Beretta Nano BU9 with three cartridges, its holster and an adaptor to program the digital trigger code, Peko my stiletto knife, its sheath, a Bronze Damata hand wallet and a Dior digital watch that acts as a transmitter for the detonation charges in the ankle boots. Interesting though, the watch also had a GPS, I think it was Seymour's way of boosting my subdermal implant.

As for each of the heels in the ankle boots, they had a bap of densely packed plastic explosive demolition charge. A B111 Taggant composite next-generation explosive gel with an adhesive tab on each of their bases. The British army calls it *Hodex*, I nicknamed them my *"Dons"*. They give off no energy signature and were completely inert until activated. Under the base of each don there was a small plug-in screw hole made exclusively for the flex cord wire at the base of the heel or the plug-in dial from the Dior watch. They were companion pieces for the Dons, neither one works without the other.

I quickly cleaned myself with the wet-wipes and towel and dressed.

I left out some interesting bits in my brief but when I was finished, he was silent then added in a hesitant acquiescent 'Ok how you wanna deal with this Harsha Kannauj?'

I shot him a glance. How the hell did he know Brahma's real name?

'You looked surprised, Lieutenant Commander? I did tell you … I always keep my ear close to the ground even out here in slum-dog millionaire country' he saw the inquiring look on my face.

'The movie?' he added

'Never saw it'

Briggs chuckled 'Mishka might have mentioned him after some applied pressure'

'I hope it was messy' I said wincing from pain.

'Getting Brahma's men to take you out or whatever … stank of desperation and now getting your friend killed makes me wish I had applied more' he said as he handed me a vial full of Ibuprofen.

'You figured she did that all by yourself?' I asked him.

'In-between tea and aidin' that agent from the Security Bureau to track you … yeah'

I picked up the Beretta and Briggs used the adaptor to program my fingerprint into the digital trigger.

Someone rapped on the door of the office.

'Come' Briggs answered

Leong came in and glanced at me before addressing Briggs.

'Sir!'

'Mr Leong'

'I think we have a problem. Somebody is asking for the Governor'

'Are they now?' I asked as I tucked the gun into its holster in the case. I thought for a moment. Someone apart from the young teller must have recognised Mahatma Bhave. Whoever they were, they might regard me and the Governor as a threat and knew we were here. Why or how they could be here I hadn't an inkling, but them being here perched on an official building suggested we were in danger in some way or perhaps there was the rudimentary off chance that they were here to on the governor's behalf. If they were Brahma's men how they knew we were not cooking under hot wax or pushing up daises, isn't what mattered now, it was what to do with them now, that was significant. Me, in danger will certainly put those I associate with in danger.

Considering all situations, I finally came to a conclusion. Identification first. Both men were waiting on me 'Do they say why they're here or who they are?' I asked without emphasis to Leong

'They say they are his security detail. They've been searching for him for the last 18 hours'

'Make Bhave identify them, if they are what they say they are, then join them, keep him safe' I said to Briggs

'Uh no. No. I'm under special mandate not to let you out of my sight'

'Briggs!' I exclaimed, suddenly getting an Mauerbauertraurigkeit urge.

'It's no use beseechin' me, I'm joinin' you to handle your end of this caper'

'Vincent, despite Seymour's intentions, I need you to keep Sir C's friend out of harm's way' I pleadingly said. That made him stop his protest. For as much as he respected me, in his mind Sir Conrad Steele was his and my superior. 'I have no doubt that if they are who they say they are that someone in his detail is not what they seem and they intend on betraying him. Besides, I need you to watch your back concerning a certain Anurag Surte'

He knew what I meant.

Safi Dass and Anard.

'Ah!'

'Besides, you have to get the authorities to the mountain temple in a hurry. I doubt my potion will hold out that long' I insisted.

He nodded. 'And see to Imah's guys and the drugs' he protested.

'Yeah sorry about that. I have nothing to impart D Company apart from where it might be now'
'Kerala port, yes I got that' he said, 'Why them and not the authorities?'
'They'll find it faster. Make sure you emphasise to the new head honcho that half of it is ours, no dead bodies during their raid and if they cheat me, it would be at their own peril'
'I will. You think they'll go for it?'
'Half a truck full of £10 million pounds worth of free heroin? Yeah, I think they'll go for it. If they don't, I'll burn it all up. Make sure they understand that'
'May I ask what you intend to do with your half?' he asked me
'I don't know' I mused 'Dump it in the ocean or flush it down a toilet' He didn't show any surprise or challenge my decision. He knew very well I hated any narcotic drug.
'So, what now?'
'I have to get my hands on that box and pay Brahma a special kind of visit, so I think I'll head back to the Punjab and get some sleep'
'Good. You look like you need it'
Picking up the 8-wheeler case, I asked Briggs 'Is Mishka still there by any chance?'
'She was when I left'
'Good. Mr Leong would you please show me a backway out of here?'
'Of course'
I turned to Briggs 'Well then Briggs go make yourself busy' I said dismissing him.
On the way, I asked Richard Leong why we were being afforded this much cooperation from him. He answered 'When your CEO calls you personally to accommodate a certain request, you have no choice in the matter'
I wondered if it was Sir C or Seymour who was behind that particular favour.
I bade him a fond farewell and hailed a rickshaw to take me to the Punjab Hotel.
When I arrived, Mr Vijay was nowhere to be found neither was Mishka. The guard lowered his eyes as I approached and he greeted me with the kindest words, he thought he could muster. The man behind the desk

found it odd until he mentioned some words to him. 'Madam Dax will have her key, Sharma'
I went up to my room with a staff member and my luggage in tow.
I hit the bed as soon as it was in sight and dozed off.

# FIFTEEN

My sleep lasted for six hours, by the time I woke the sun was setting. I felt the first pang of pain when my eyes fully opened. I took the pills for pain relief Briggs had handed me before entering the bathroom. I did my business before I jumped into the shower. When I was done showering, I stood in front of the bathroom mirror stand and examined myself.

I wasn't the typical large or slender person. I was curvy in all the right places but there were days when I really did not think I'd fit in my garments. Days when that yucky feeling makes girls like me feel all bloated. There are a few new things a young woman looks out for when examining herself.

The world or more precise, my style of living had definitely changed me. I had not moisturised my light golden-almond skin for some time and yet it was smooth, tough and taut from reeling in muscles and running hard. My hands were coarse and scratched with small cuts, tainted by my recent rigorous activities, my arms were smooth and clear except for the odd blemish of old wounds and my breasts were taut and erect. I had a muscle tone that was not perfect, but my abdomen was hard and supple, just what a fighting woman needs. These days, every woman instinctively knows that she cannot naturally change the length of her calves or width of her hips without serious and dangerous cosmetic surgery, but she can with limited effort definitely change the length of her hair, the perkiness of her breasts and shape of her nose. My areolas were firm like muscles and my neck was tough but relaxed. Of course, there are certain areas of my body I'm not keen on but for the most part, I believed that though it was not perfect, I did not despise it.

If you believe professional aerobics instructors, there are perhaps only two routes you can take to ensure a firmer shapely body tone, like mine. Diet and regular exercise, not counting plastic surgery. I believe I have been in shape since I was old enough to stand, though eating right has not been high on my list of priorities. The odd pull-in plies, sweeping squats and leg lifts are an uncharacteristic routine that I adopt when I have the time to exercise. Nevertheless, to test my body all I need do is do a handspring.

My speckled eyes held a lustre of wet patina, but I suspected it was due to the shower I just had. Probing my body further, I could see that apart from the recent wounds on my left side and the other cuts and bruises, there was the faint scar from old injuries. On my shoulder, my upper arm and torso and an even older wound on the inside of my thigh, low and indistinct enough to make me a bit sceptical about wearing bikini, though it hardly ever stopped me. Apart from some slight callouses, my feet were perfectly formed and I was a bit proud of them. I went red when I saw that my toenails and fingernails were heavily chapped. My nail kit wouldn't be able to repair all the damage. Nothing I could do about it now but a visit to a nailing and hair salon wouldn't go amiss when all this was over. Testing my muscles, I lay flat on the floor and did a handspring before getting dressed. Apart from the pain, my muscles felt taut but all in all still capable.

I called downstairs for some light sandwiches and a soda then using my phone I goggled Harsha Kannauj.

From what I could surmise he was a recluse worth 6.3 billion dollars according to Forbes. He's rarely seen socialising and there was seldom a picture of him, his last picture was five years ago and the photo before that was his engagement photo even then the photo didn't show his full profile. Both had a trademark of his which was a black turban. He seemed to invest in stock market capitalisation, stock market investments and domestic consumer markets that serve innumerable mom and pop shops. He has a place on the most popular street for the rich in India known as D-Street but rarely spends time there. He's restrained when it comes to funding charities and social causes. His marriage to a certain Saanvi Stasey, a British born C.P.A. Accountant it seemed was short-lived because he was divorced from her shortly after. It wasn't clear how he made his billion's but for a billionaire he was living time below normal.

From the lead captions on the breaking news app, I noticed that the anti-Trump pickets in Orlando had now become violent with several men dead and eleven others injured. The Jihadists in the Philippines were getting bolder, adding another twenty-one deaths to their repertoire. Then there was the race riot occurring in the Mississippi, where the cops had shot two black men and almost lynched another one. As for England there was a brewing group in Trafalgar square challenging the conscious Orwellian bias on issues like race, gender and surveillance by MPs in the commons. Things seem to be getting worse the world over. Brahma and his plans were sort of making their point.

I turned the phone off.

Feeling the polymer-knitted Kevlar bodysuit that could withstand a shotgun blast from two feet away against my skin, the Beretta BU9 Nano automatic that Seymour had gotten me snug in its holster tucked against my side and "Saint Peko" the thin stiletto lying snugly in its customised echelon against my forearm I felt powerful. And why not, the stiletto nicknamed after the Finnish *Karelian* saint or warrior who provides rain to the fields only provides death and destruction whenever I chose to. While the Beretta, though a muted pistol, it was a powerful handgun because it possessed a custom-made compensator with bored chambers and combined with its customised digital trigger scanner it makes it a most reliable automatic.

I decided against taking the OnePlus8 Pro phone even if it was an all-purpose multi-android phone that did everything from surfing the net to scanning and locating or disabling other electronic devices. From the apps I could see it also had imbedded in its matrix a 3-D block array with non- patterned rotation. A self-destruct worm embedded in its base code in case any other person apart from me attempted to use it. It didn't have the latest contact details of any of my friends, but it had particulars of associates who could help me out of a jam if and when the occasion did arise.

A waiter appeared with my sandwiches which I wolfed down with such speed I almost choked.

After satisfying my hunger pangs I felt it was time to get down to business. I was about to disregard one of Sun Tzu advice from the art of war and embrace another. *"If your enemy is secure at all points be prepared for him and if he has superior strength evade him "*. No, I was going for the frontal approach. Hold out myself as bait to entice Brahma, feign disorder and eventually crush him.

With the dimming light I decided to take an evening stroll, grabbing my Damata hand wallet and Tripmaster jacket, I exited the hotel. As bad as I wanted to get to Brahma's villa, I did not think riding up there and knocking on the door was a good idea. I needed to be in the company of his men, I needed an escort and that was what I was waiting for.

Leaving the frescoed hotel with painted murals and gilded inlaid tiles I walked under the now purple sky. The sun was just a faint orange smudge at the further edge of the far horizon. I listened for the sounds of footsteps that echoed mine. Listening for footfalls that clicked in par with my ankle boot heels.

It was thirty minutes into my walk as I turned into the near deserted alley of Fatehbur when I heard it, it roared into my ears. A sound that would have made most people's blood run cold. Years of training and experience had toughened me, steeled my nerves, that made my reaction not like most women or even men. However, I would be lying if I weren't a tad worried.

The humming roar reverberated through the alley and I was temporarily blinded by the glare of a motorcycle's headlight that caught me full in the face.

There were three Hindi's each one mounted on their respective motorbikes like some modern version of a cavalry detachment. They began to circle me, jeering me with laughter. Onlookers at the end of the alley were very conscious about not interfering.

Brahma was once again calling the shots and I was the one willing to play into his hands according to his rules. I was going to be one dead female this time, if I didn't appear to be at least playing by his rules but I think Susan Dax was certainly not going to let that happen.

*      *      *      *

I recognised one of the riders immediately from my previous encounters. He was one of the goons that waylaid me at the Business Centre. He wasn't turbaned like the others, but I knew what he was thinking even if we'd met just that once.

'You hard woman to put down, memsahib Dax' one of the men called out 'That is why we here'

I remained still and unmoving.

'So, you're here to shoot me dead?' I yelled over the roar of their bikes, knowing that Brahma had too much of an ego to not want to witness my death himself. I shielded my eyes from the winding glaring headlights. I noticed each Daayan member was armed with a revolver, three .45s which were levelled at me. One at my chest, one at my head, the other at my back.

'Shoot you, Dax memsahib?' one of the men snickered. He was one of the two I hadn't seen before. Like his unknown compatriot, he was a tall powerfully built young man who was obviously relishing my discomfort. 'That be too easy. No, our master has ordered us no such luck. We are to bring you to the villa. Our lord will deal with you personally'

That was a mistake telling me that.

'Just the way you deal with Reeven' the one I recognised added.

The image of Reeven flashed through my head. Me tossing him over the enclosure and him falling into the snake pit. Reeven paralysed trying to evade the writhing of ravenous snakes that attacked him again and again. The screams he tried to make but couldn't because of the paralytic touch I had inflicted on him and I knew the rare delight that would afford Brahma if he could see me undergo that same hideous and agonizing faith over and over.

These men had been ordered to bring me back alive, but not necessarily in one piece. It was an advantage of mine and yet a disadvantage because they would protect themselves against any harm if need be.

'Will he? Apparently, there's no way I can fight back, is there?' I called back, flexing my right forearm muscle to release Peko, who fell into my palm 'Three against one isn't exactly cricket guys. I'll come quietly' I said raising my hands in a submissive gesture.

Dropping the Bronze Damata hand wallet, I waited for them to make the next move. The biker pointing his gun at my head dismounted his bike and began to approach me, his gun shakingly levelled at me. I walked slowly towards him slowly letting my hands fall to my sides. He was two paces away from me when I buried the stiletto's blade in his right eye socket. He gave a piercing scream as I pulled out the stiletto slicing his eyeball in half with one fluid movement. Thick curds bloodied jelly burst out from his face and the silver helm of the blade.

I wasn't around to watch him scream his head off as he grabbed at his face and dropped to his knees.

I had broken into a run flinging the stiletto at one of them as they squeezed their triggers. Their aim was way off and they knew it, because unthinkingly they had made an attempt to avoid the stiletto flying at them. One slug chipped the earth at my feet while the other whizzed by my arm. They jumped off their bikes another mistake of theirs. Pulling out my Beretta oblivious to anything but my targets I pulled the trigger twice. My aim was precise, I shot the revolver out of one of their hands while I shot out the kneecap of the other.

One of the bikers, the one I recognised wasn't out of commission, but he wasn't in good shape either. He was bent over moaning the loss of feeling in his left hand, the revolver I had shot out of his hand had only slowed his movements.

I could hear the screams of genuine terror from the eye missing biker as yet another bullet whined through the air from the revolver of the biker down on the ground with one missing knee. It was an incidental shooting because he was firing blindly at me as he yelled from the pain of his bloody knee. Another bullet he fired whizzed through the air grazing through my Tripmaster jacket and my right arm. The searing pain gave me a red-hot brand as it went through my flesh. It was enough to make me wince but not agonizing enough for me not to squeeze the trigger at the knee missing biker, shooting him through his nose before the Beretta dropped from my fingers.

The recognised biker had picked up his gun and aimed it right at my chest 'Stop Dax or I shoot you now' he cried out.

'And disappoint your Lord Brahma?' I sneered at him.

'I not care' he squeezed the trigger and I steeled myself against the explosive pain that would follow. For all intent and purpose, I should have been hit, he had me dead to rights and I was supposed to be moaning from the pain of getting shot. However, his gun failed to fire, instead it exploded in his hand with a bang. Shooting the revolver from his hand had somehow upset the machinery in the revolver making it defective and unable to fire true.

I lunged at him, my fingers curled roughly around his wrist to grip his now smouldering hand with all the constricting tightness and blood-stopping pressure of a tourniquet. The gunman yelled in pain and tried to jerk away from my hold, my other hand, held in a *sohn-nal* configuration, stiff and rigid became a scythe of bone and muscle.

My fingers shot out and hit him in the kidneys, I followed my strike with a snapped right foot across his ankle, breaking it. Using his body weight, I twisted him away from me as did the blown-up revolver. I could have killed him, but I needed him.

I knelt beside him and pinched his *sternocleidomatoideus* muscle in the lateral posterior border aspect of his neck, causing his heart to pound out of control. As he moaned from my touch, the pain in his side and ankle I said 'Kill me now and Brahma will feed you to the snakes. Help me. I have important information for your lord and if he doesn't hear it from my own lips you might as well forget you or the Daayan ever existed'

His eyes flicked to the body of his fallen unrecognisable comrade I had shot through the nose, his face contorted and livid with rage. He turned back to me and bit hard on something in his mouth before I knew it, he was choking spit and mucus from his closed mouth, quivering against my hold. I released my grip on him as he then threw himself backward. Disparagingly he had bitten down hard on a capsule, probably filled with cyanide. 'Blimey!' I cursed

Just like Nadir, this gunman had chosen to take his life rather than consider my offer.

I reached for his oral cavity and tried to pry his lips open with my fingers, but he crunched down harder, keeping his mouth firmly close. His eyes told me he rather die, than oblige me. I stepped away.

His features softened into pride, gladness and a little bit of pain. He had beaten me and that was gratification in its own right as he saw it. Ending his life against my wish for his beloved Brahma was the best thing that could have happened to him. With such logic I knew Brahma was more dangerous than ever.

The moon was beginning to rise over the alleyway of Fatehbur making the shadows long and dark, obscuring the murky face approaching.

Behind me I caught a sudden flurry of motion. The eye missing gunman had dived. Karate or no karate he had caught me quiet unawares. Before I could stop him, he hit me like a wrecking ball. I could not help my breath fly out of me as I fell back, my head hitting the ground of the alley. Something warm and gummy dripped onto my face smarting my eyes, briefly blinding me.

When my vision cleared, I looked up and saw my eye missing killer standing over me. His wounded eye, the little that remained from it was dripping a blood-tinged jelly like substance like a leaking bath faucet. In his hand was Peko.

'Our lord will just have to live without killing you now memsahib' he spat at me as his foot shot out as I tried to get to my feet. Why he didn't use the stiletto, I wouldn't know. I gritted my teeth as I felt the steel shod toe of his steel laced boot smash down my shoulder. He was the only one of the three who was not wearing sandals but biker boots. He followed his stomp with a kick to my breasts.

That he made himself understood despite the oozing of his eye was quite impressive. 'I kill you now and that be end of you' From his tone I knew he meant every word. His other chums were dead, so he saw no other preference but deal with me with extreme prejudice.

He came at me with a furious anger, kicking me with random abandonment. It was during his fourth strike when he was poised to stab at me with the stiletto that I jerked up like a bucking bronco trying to unseat its rider. Reaching out with both hands I caught his ankle and twisted his foot violently to one side. It was futile to maintain his balance but try he did. He wasn't successful, he went down in a crash, Peko flying from his hand. I followed my initiative with a kick to the small of his back. The impact of my foot against his back sent him skidding along the alley earth. I glanced over my shoulder, a considerable crowd had gathered at the end of the alley and the two downed gunmen together with their bikes were still.

I turned my attention back to the Indian before me who was struggling to his feet. Just then something whizzed through the air and pain exploded down in my leg. I grunted with pain as I looked down to find that a razor -sharp kukri blade had dug its way into the thick fleshy muscle along the side of my thigh.

A knee buckled and I dropped to one knee.

I wanted to scream but I kept the cry of pain from escaping my lips. The pain burned its way inside of me tunnelling upwards to my guts and my nerves. The blade dug in deeper and deeper not content until it claimed my body, exposing the very core of my physical endurance.

There was no way I was not going to let that happen.

I heard someone say in Hindi 'Veer, make yourself scarce'

My knee buckled again as the missing eyed Indian dashed to one of the bikes and mounted it. He wasn't responsible for the knife in my leg. He gunned the bike and went full throttle roaring into the early evening. Clenching my hands into fists, gritting my teeth, I tried to conquer the savage pain. I reached down, closing my eyes for a second and grabbed the hilt of the blade, wrenching the quivering knife out of my thigh. There was no way I could staunch the flow of blood but luckily the kukri knife had gone in cleanly, hopefully missing major arteries and blood vessels which supplied the muscles of my whole leg. I pulled myself to my feet, my gimpy leg stretched out alongside me, but lost my grip as something disturbed my equilibrium. I felt dizzy and my eyes though open began to cloud over. Could it be that I have been poisoned? I smelt the knife in my hand, an acidic smell brushed my nose. Yes, I had been contaminated but it seemed to be with something mild.

I turned towards the crowd of onlookers, the only place where the knife could have come from. I could just make out an Indian in a white cotton gown walking out towards me. I tensed and held my breath at this nameless Indian advancing towards me, I had no doubt he was part of Brahma's private cult.

I squinted, trying to pierce the gloom. My opponent wasn't taking any chances, he was moving slowly in the shadows towards me. I realised that apart from the wrenched kukri knife in my hand I was unarmed. 'You must be afraid of me' I said softly steeling my tone against the uncertainty I was feeling. 'Only a woman would use poison, so come on mate and finish me off, I haven't got all day' I called out, daring the psyche of his male pride, trying to locate his form in the darkness. A rush of air signalled movement, something hard and unyielding lashed out at me catching me right above the smarting of my thigh flesh wound. I grunted with fresh pain.

The darkness over my eyes was preventing me from getting a view of my assailant. However, if you've spent three months with your eyes bandaged tightly so that you could train under that condition you get slowly adept in listening for attacks and / or defending yourself.

Using the knife as guidance I remained still, listening and reaching out with my skin and mind at where the next attack would originate from. A crashing weight slammed into me throwing me back, my injured leg pinned beneath me. For a moment, I felt the weight of a human boulder and I could have sworn it wasn't a man. The roundness of the chest was a good indicator that it was a woman attacking me.

I pushed myself upwards, steadying myself, listening, waiting for the next attack. When it came, I was ready. As air rushed to my face, I deflected the oncoming blow with a *Chookya Makgi*, a rising block that absorbs the impact of a blow with a bent hand raised a little over the shoulder. As the other blow came, I slashed at the arm. I heard a cry of pain, a woman's cry of pain.

'Ah bitch you've bitten off more than you can chew, haven't you?' She didn't like my choice of nickname and as her next attack proved, it was quite effective. She came in close, too close that I could smell her hot sticking breath across my face. She wasn't a beast, but she was a lioness in her own right. She had responded to me without words just her fists and her knee. After a flurry of blows, she got my hands pinned down, she then exerted a force along the inside of my arms, kneeing repeatedly at my flaccid leg at the same time.

I think she was surprised at the effectiveness I used to defend myself despite my obfuscation and her venom inside me, because she screamed at me as she had me cornered, restrained against the wall.

The flesh wound was bleeding worse than ever that I feared I would pass out due to loss of blood on a plus side my vision was clearing. During her attack it occurred to me that she didn't realise that I was still armed or maybe she believed the poison within me should have had a more powerful effect on me. I had plenty of opportunities to cut up on her but hacking up on the female of the species seemed very indelicate and anomalous to me. In any event I thanked the stars that the effect of her toxin was fleetingly temporary.

Then staring into my eyes, she spoke for the first time 'I will bring you to our lord Dax' she hissed as she held me down against the wall by my wrists 'But not in one piece'

Her dark penetrating eyes and lilt Indian accent reminded me of an enraged Ellen.

'I'm impressed' I said wincing as she dug her knee again into my bleeding thigh. My hands and fingers were feeling numb. It could have been from her grip on me cutting off the blood flow in my hands or the residual effects of her acidic poison. I was hoping the former.

Despite her hold on me, her strength which was equal to mine and the position she was in, I felt noticeably confident that I could turn the tables on her. She wasn't as experienced a fighter like me, she was fighting on instinct and I was armed.

'What's your name?' I gasped

'My name?' Her expressive delight in pinning me down was overtaken with surprise.

'Woman to woman we should know each other if I am going to kill you'

'You dream woman' she said with a scornful chuckle 'And it is me Jia who is going to do the killing'

I jerked my knife hand to the side and began to bend my hand down and forward, inching the sharp bloodstained kukri knife up into Jia's side. The bent peak of the blade cut through her cotton white blouse like butter. I didn't stop there. I stared into her eyes as I shoved it deeper and deeper. An Opia feeling came over me as her lips were twisted back in a spittle-flecked grin, exposing her smooth even spaced white teeth and *paan* stained red gums.

She changed her game plan, but it was too late. Jia had tried to raise a knee to my side, but it slid off from the slippery blood. Shock overcame her, she couldn't stop me, her death was eminent, and she knew it.

'Sorry Jia' I said to her as I rammed the kukri knife into her, between two of her ribs, cutting through flesh and muscle like a butcher quartering a slaughtered pig.

I rolled her against the wall as I let go of the kukri knife.

'Bitch' she gasped 'S-see y-you in … h-hell … you will d-die … die … Da …'

For mercy's sake I pulled out the knife and plunged the entirety of the blade into the middle of her chest hoping that her last words weren't prophetic.

A faint gurgling sound welled up out of her throat, she was no longer able to speak. She made a spastic jerk and an involuntary shiver went through her body before she became still.

Blood poured out of her as I withdrew the knife out of her chest. My hands were sticky, slimy and slippery with Jai's blood.

I took a step back, my wounded leg stretched out in front of me. Quickly I ripped off pieces of her the blouse I had mistaken for a white cotton gown and wrapped it around my thigh wound, stanching the flow of blood. Tying it off as tourniquet with the Kukri knife, leaving just a lazy trickle of blood dripping out of the deep puncture wound.

I wasn't sorry that her body lay stiff against the wall, not when it clearly had been a matter of survival.

Afterward, getting my bearings I found my bronze Damata hand wallet, Beretta and stiletto. I heard the parp of the sirens before the flashing lights of the police squad vehicles arrived. It was time to bring in the authorities, knowing what little it might do.

Before they could surmise the situation, I used a payphone to put a call through to Briggs and asked him to put Anard on.

When the Indian Security agent got on the line, I expressed to him my circumstances and he said he'd take care of it. I knew he wouldn't be able to do it without the authority of his superiors, one in particular. Safi Dass.

If what Sameer and I suspected was true, it won't be long before I'd be out of police custody and back on the streets to be scooped up by Brahma's men.

It was ten minutes after the commotion that I looked about me, surveying the scene. The squad car cops were there taking statements from the handful who saw the altercation and were trying to make sense of the scene. A sergeant was there scanning the block taking in some of the stone faces of the tenements, a downtown inspector who was frowning as he took in the scene and a lab coat specialist who was examining the scene.

While I was being handcuffed, a photog was snapping away with a police mobile photographic camera and scrounging for IDs on the two dead men and woman. He found none. One of the cops who led me away into a police squad car had searched me and found the beretta, he didn't find

Peko. They confiscated my bronze wallet bag and the Beretta. Several cops admired the Beretta as they took more than another look at me, not believing I had caused this much chaos. The drive to the nearest police station was not long, the place was a near modern-day hub of police authority, and it was ready for me. They seem to be into everything behind their lined wooden desks searching for anything and everything from birth certificates, to ballistic reports to crime data.

From the curiosity of their faces I could see that someone had already given them an heads up on me. A male sergeant took me by the arm and led me into a one desk room with a couple of chairs, a standing fan, a disc camcorder standing on a tripod and a one-way mirrored window. He closed the door behind him after taking off the handcuff around my wrists.

A medic came into the room and saw to the treatment of my thigh wound and the scorched wound across the top of my right arm. He was careful to treat my Tripmaster jacket with care. He cleaned and bandaged both wounds very competently. The lateral wound on my left side was sealed tightly enough that he saw no need to tend to it but he did his best to re-seal the other visible cuts and bruises on me then left with a smile after leaving a pint of water in a bottle on the desk for me.

Two detectives came in closely on his heels with notepads and started questioning me, like a pair of Miami cops, first in English, then hesitant French and then Hindi. Try as they might they couldn't pull off being east coast cops from America but like a pair of characters from a muppet show they questioned me on and on. My silence was like a tic to them which grew and gnawed at them with every passing minute.

First, they sympathised with me for being brave enough to withstand a three- pong attack and as far as they saw it, I was acting in self-defence. Next, they tried to blame me for the excessive force used and that I may be charged for using an unregistered weapon and negligent homicide. Next, they tried to implicate me in killing the woman intentionally, which would incur jail time. Just as they were deciding to get rough with me one of their cell phones rang.

'Hassan' answered the taller of the two.

The voice on the other end was deep, yet soft. I watched his reaction to the instructions being filtered down to the Indian detective who glanced at his comrade, hardly believing his ears.

'Good, sir. We see to it' he said in his broken English Indian accent trying to sound too damn courteous for his own good.

I could see that like me they didn't like political appointees who came out of cloak and suits shops to exert what little power they had.

He hung up the phone and turned to his partner with a cross look on his face 'We've been ordered to let her go, someone from the spook office is coming to pick her up' he said in Hindi

I stood up and said in Hindi 'Thank goodness that is over. Would someone get my Beretta please?'

It was like I poured egg on their face when they heard me.

From that moment on, the cops did everything they could to accommodate me. When the Peugeot arrived to convey me back to my hotel, they bided me a warm goodbye and then someone clipped me over the head as I was about to enter the vehicle.

I fell into a dark pool of unconsciousness.

## SIXTEEN

Thirteen minutes later, a circular motion and a thud made me wake up in start. The ache in my head was supplemented by the thud and bangs from the outside of the vehicle. I was lying in the rear of the car I was knocked unconscious into. Behind the wheel was the resilient missing eye biker who had escaped my grasp and whose name I now think was Veer. There was a swatch of bandage all-round the right side of his face. There were no binds on my ankles except my wrists which were secured by an old Hiatt "Darby" type circa 1950s handcuff. The handcuff wasn't tightened round my wrists meaning it was done in a hurry, it confirmed to me that it hadn't been long since I was knocked out because whoever secured me didn't have time to do it properly. That or there was some other unknown reason for the cause. I didn't dwell on it because I got my answer immediately, a hit from the side informed me that we were in a car chase.

The car was whining as it gathered speed, speed which I expected would radically curtail its movements, specifically my driver's life expectancy. The whizzing light cast from both vehicle's headlight illuminated the dusty path we were taking.

There was nothing impressionistic in the way Veer drove or the driver alongside did. A couple of thumps and side swipes as the pursuing vehicle tried to bypass us demonstrated his skills, cutting the following driver off and narrowly sending him into the roadside ditch. Veer was anxious to accomplish his orders, bring me back alive despite his own wellbeing or the pursuit of the car behind us.

To him I may be spoiled meat on a hoof, an angreji kutiya and his car may not be up to scrap and damaged, but he was more so. Desperate and frightened but determined to get me to Brahma as fast and as unencumbered as possible. Troublemaker that I was to him, I was here within his grasp and on my way to Brahma, there was no way he was going to give me up now.

Regardless of the condition we were in I was grateful that I now had an escort into Brahma's villa.

Veer and the driver behind the wheel of the pursuing vehicle.

Though I would prefer to be on my two feet and under my own steam when I entered Brahma's villa, I wondered who could be in the pursuing vehicle. Briggs or Anard?

I was betting on Briggs. He must have seen them abduct me at the police station and pursued the offending vehicle.

The driver behind us – Briggs presumably - tried to bypass us again but Veer again cut him off. The driver behind us took pains to avoid a direct head on collision and I didn't blame him. I didn't want him to lose control of his vehicle and slam into the roadside ditch, unable to continue his pursuit. Without actually side slamming into Veer, Briggs was still able to keep him in line, preventing him from escaping with me. I could have at any time have disabled Veer even with my wrists handcuffed, however I wanted to see how this played out and I was still hoping my escort was warranted, besides the pain in my head hadn't subsided yet. But it was not going well, so I decided to act. Leaning upward and forward, I balled my hands together and struck Veer on his right quadrangular space, that is the anatomic interval between his head and shoulder. The impact was like a well-aimed punch, knocking his breath away. He whirled sideways, drunk with pain unable to control his grip on the steering wheel. The vehicle ended up careering into the roadside ditch as intended. We both were jolted out of the vehicle, tumbling down a hillside made of rubbish and into a rolling valley of waste. The stink was overwhelming, in any case I tried to ignore it. I came to my limping feet without so much as a scratch, but grimy and so did he.

Fat, peppy bluebottle flies woke up and circled us trying to settle on us like shit in a bush.

Limping, I moved quickly. Getting to my feet I thought about letting Peko fall into the palm of my hand between the hole in the cuffs and then brandishing him in one outstretched hand to forestall any attack of his, I didn't. It would feel like overkill. There was no time to lose, for after I have dealt with Veer, I still had Brahma - Harsha Kannauj, one of the richest men in India - to contend with. A man whose snares I had eluded time and time again.

Veer was on his feet before I could reach him, he too was limping, a wad of bandage was wrapped round one of his ankles. He had snatched up two parts from a busted plastic chair from the refuse that he didn't know what to do with and merely threw them at me, one after the other. The plastic parts bounced off me just as he rushed me with my cuffed hands, crashing into me and I found myself on my back.

He pummelled me with both his fists against the refuse heap, Veer was no longer rational, bloodied matter still leaking from the swathed bandages across his face dripped across my body. His face was contorted into that of a mad man which peered down at me like that of a cycloptic monster. He chopped down at the inside of my left elbow and I flinched from the wound that was already there. My buffeted hands had no grip on him, loosening from the defensive posture I was in. I reached out blindly but he continued to thrash me, again and again.

He didn't know karate, however he obviously picked up pointers from movies and the like. He used his weight and whatever skills he possessed to try and get the best of me.

The vehicle behind us came to a slewing halt, casting its head light beam over our thrashing bodies. I heard a door open but knew that Briggs was barely in a position to help me. With Veer striking and whacking me repeatedly at my bad side and leg, our fight was not going to be quick and easy as I envisioned it. Panic and rage were firing him up, giving him added strength and determination. The man no longer saw me as a woman, he knew how formidable I was hence now he was fighting for his life.

And to a point, so was I.

I trust forward with both my palms and rolled to one side. He scrambled up on top of me, but I had managed to grab hold of one of the plastic parts he had thrown at me. There was a method I could use to make it a weapon and I sought my opportunity to apply it. His knee crashed into my side, followed by a kidney punch and again I grunted in agony. The night light danced up and down before my eyes and everything around me began to double or treble in size and amount. I was somehow finding it difficult to focus, everything was blurry, fading in and out of my vacillating vision.

Veer was blathering excitedly and incoherently, spitting out words in some unknown dialect. If I didn't know what he was saying, I surmised the message from the essence of his wild ranting discourse. It wasn't sanguine or sociable to put it gently.

My thigh was cramping, twisting up against his crushing weight and the kicks it had been subjected to. I turned my head to one side just as he reached for something across from me. It wasn't much but it was an opportunity.

At that moment, with the synthetic part in one of my hands I struck him and rolled away from him, trying to pull myself up to one knee. Veer wasn't about to let me get away that easily. Throwing himself forward he struck blindly using his fist to strike back and forth. I recoiled, pushing myself back, trying to maintain my balance. That was when I struck again. Despite my swimming vision which I now realised was from the refuse fumes, using the plastic I lashed out instinctively and struck his shoulder. Whether it hurt him or not, it didn't matter. The strike unsettled him, enough for me to pull a real uncompromising counterattack that ended with me wrapping the synthetic part around his thick neck.

This was how it all began, first, the attack in my hotel room, then with Imah at the café, the surprise ambush at the Shreyansh Fort, my clash with Sigrid and now with Veer, it was coming to a close. The curtain going down on another of Brahma's reprehensible cult of cutthroats.

With me on my knees, I gripped both sides of the plastic to the edge of my cuffed reach. It was secure as I twisted it around Veer's throat. He gave an astonishing, high pitched scream of terror just before he began to claw at my grip trying to get the plastic off his throat. The steel of my handcuffs prevented him from getting a grip on either the synthetic part or his neck.

Desperately, in a seated position he fought to save his life with whatever strength he had left. It wasn't nearly enough to do the trick. Maintaining my strangulating grip, I felt him gasp in shallow, asthmatic puffing breaths. Little or no air was entering his lungs.

Pulling the plastic part inwardly, tighter, there was no doubt as to who was now in control. Me, gimpy leg and all. He gurgled one final time and then it was as if his body gave up, no longer able to prevent the inevitable his head went limp in my grip. I wasn't taking any chances. I held onto the synthetic part till I was sure he was no longer breathing and, on his way, to meet his maker. The Daayan gods he so resolutely had faith in.

When I was sure there was no life left in him, I let his body tumble onto the refuse covered earth. Only an arm muscle twitched in him as I rolled him over. His mocha skin coloured face had turned purple and blue in response to my suffocation, his tongue was almost bitten off from between his gritted teeth which were contorted in a focus of trepidation.

'You were one tough bastard' I muttered to the dead Veer.

My remark, of course fell on deaf ears. I got slowly and exhaustedly on to my feet still keeping an eye on him. I was of the opinion that he not follow suit like a carpenter of old who beat back death. That surely would be a bummer. I needn't have worried, he was as dead as an axiomatic doornail.

'Is he dead memsahib?' called out a strange familiar Indian accentuated voice from above me. It definitely was not Briggs's.

'As a doornail. And whom might you be?'

'Anard! Anard Siddharth, Central Bureau of Security'

Ah the agent I had heard so much about but never seen. If surprise was the name of the game, then it was fair to say I was more surprised than anyone on the planet. Why was he here? If he was here, then it meant he wasn't one of Dass's stooges.

'Hello Anard. Nice to meet you at last' I greeted him as genially as I could muster as he made his way down to me.

'Same here memsahib, lucky I spotted your abduction huh?'

He was a tall, handsome, and hard-looking bald individual with a trimmed well-groomed beard.

'You took your time, didn't you?'

'Better late than never, my Ammi say, Bhee'

I couldn't agree with his mother more.

He had a forlorn look as he glanced at the dead body at my feet and then at me. There was something in his look saying I didn't deserve to be here, and that the kitchen was the right place for me. I had a feeling he was a middle-of-the-road conservative.

He inspected my cuffs on my wrists and without a word he reached into his pocket and produced a lockpick wallet. He opened it and handed me a shim type nail from it.

Reaching down I released the pawl of the cuff with the shim nail, then I literally broke free of the handcuffs by applying enough force from my forearms to loosen it enough to squeeze my hands through.

He took out a pack of cigarettes and offered me one. I shook my head. He lit up 'Let's get out of here' he said to me.

'Not yet. Do you have water or any alcohol with you?'

He had to think. 'I think so' he replied

'Well then help me take his clothes off'

He shot a questioning look my way. 'May I ask why?'

'I'm wounded'

He didn't question me further, not when the entirety of my left side was coated with seeping blood. He bent down not bothering to turn his head away and with his fingers grasping the bottom of Veer's kurta shirt and pulled it out from over him. Though it was bloody it was better than nothing. He began ripping the cloth into long strands avoiding the bloodied parts. He spared a minute to look down at Veer's body, without any sense of reticence or decorum showing on his face. I wouldn't have blamed him if he had any of the two considering the sight of the bulbous-gore-caked face and swollen flopped blue blacked tongue. The dull bloody ashen encrusted bandage surrounding his eye winked eerily back at us from the beam cast by the vehicle's glaring headlight above us. I wasn't sorry about Veer or the others who lay dead in Fatehbur alley. Not then and certainly not now. Victims not of my wrath or my determination to stay alive but their own inefficiency.

Anard helped me walk up the ridge to the car which had its engine idling over. The side of the Lada modelled vehicle was banged up in several different areas. Anard hurried to locate whatever liquid he had in the glovebox, which was a three-quarter full of bottled water and watched me as I worked.

Once I was able to peel off the bandages that the Police medic had placed on my thigh, I did my best to clean it with parts of the water and replaced it with strips of Veer's torn bloody kurta, Anard had handed me. I ceased the blood flow from the lateral wound along the left side of my torso. With that done, I hobbled around for a moment feeling the strain of what I had to cope with if I was going to move forward with my assignment-cum-revenge.

Assignment because it was what got me into this, revenge because a friend, well a potential friend of mine, was killed in front of me. That more than anything else was my reason for going onward at this point. Anard stepped back puffing on his cigarette. Thank god my wound didn't extend pass my bra or he would have had a tough time dealing with my feminity.

'So, what now memsahib?' he asked

'We get in the car and head to the villa' I replied

His face went gaunt.

'Harsha Kannauj sahib's villa?' he asked

'You've been briefed'

'I've been ordered to stay away Miss Dax'

'Let me guess, by Safi Dass?'

'Maybe, I'm not sure. My immediate superior did the instructing'

'I bet' I said 'Look I'm going to that villa, you either tag along or stay here'

'And what are you going to do when you get there?' he asked pointing to my bandaged leg.

Much of the pain in my leg had stopped, it was the pain in my left side that I was worried about

'Beats me, but I'll think of something' I said taking out Peko from his slim leather sheath on my forearm and replacing him back.

Sameer had said his uncle had eight men. I had killed six not including Jia. That left two or three besides Brahma and Kavin Chandra to contend with, that is if Kavin Chandra was a willing collaborator of his. I was not worried about his worshipers because I think most of them were in the hands of the authorities if Briggs and my belladonna toxin had done their jobs well enough.

It wasn't going to be easy confronting Brahma but then again, what about my trip has been easy.

*    *    *    *

We drove in silence. Anard kept both hands on the steering wheel of his small car. When Jaipur was far behind us in the dust and darkness, he turned his head toward and pointed to the glove box.

'I brought you a present' he said 'That is if you already have one'

I opened the glove compartment and reached in. I touched the butt end of a Sig Sauer Glock P385. I examined the pistol in the light of the dashboard. 2019 saw the rise of the P385 Glock, its slim polymer garnered a tremendous following, maybe because it was quite effective in close quarters. It may be small but it's impact was big, definitely an uncommon article for a young lady such as myself to be brandishing about, then again I wasn't the normal kind of lady to not have a gun in my handbag and a stiletto up my sleeve.

I checked the weapon, pleased to know that the 11+1 cartridge was full. 'When we get within sight of the house, slow down and pretend there's nothing wrong. You're just trying to get your bearing' I said to him as I slid off the seat to keep out of sight. It was a tight fit especially since my gimpy leg refused to cooperate. There was nothing to worry about except get an infection and then my leg would get gangrened, which I hoped wouldn't happen.

'You sure we shouldn't wait until you are much able. It seems risky to do this now. Me and you against his might and men, I mean'

'It's the only chance we might have' I told him filling him on what I had ascertained concerning his boss Safi Dass's allegiances. By the time I finished telling him about security leaks and Brahma's connection with Safi Dass he was ready to strangle everyone of his bosses. He didn't really fully believe me, but his own deductions and observations over the past weeks of the orders being given partially confirmed it for him.

I ducked down further as we came in view of the villa. He decelerated the car.

'What do you see?' I whispered

'Nothing'

'You sure?'

'Nothing yet'

I glanced up at him. He was sitting semi relaxed behind the wheel, his back lounged easily up against the front seat while his left-hand half propped on the door. His eyes taking in everything around him. He seemed to be a cool customer under pressure.

Suddenly he stamped on the brake. 'One guy!' he whispered 'He seems like a guard ... Down ...' he yelled.

The sound of sudden gunfire reached our ears just as I was thinking that this was our last stop, from here on I couldn't afford the luxury of making one single mistake.

He ducked down on the seat. A hailstorm of bullets was coming at us free and fast, shattering the windscreen, sending shards of broken glass showering down on us.

'There must be two guns to be that many bullets' I presupposed 'Hold still and sit tight. Wait until I give you the word' he warned me 'You have that backwards, mate' I said to him pushing down the latch of the door, shoving the side door open to crawl out onto the dusty path. The door was my shield, bullets ricocheted into and over my head. The ground vibrated beneath me with the sound of running footfalls. I raised the Glock, lifted my head just enough to spot any target and take aim.

I spotted the guard almost immediately. He went down like a broken glider when I fired. I'd caught him right in the chest and unlike his cohorts, his death was swift and relatively painless.

Everything was silent for a second. Then a continuation of fire aimed at us came at us again, ferociously. Someone from behind the gate was rooting for me. I squinted and peered from side to side and up to try and spot him and in case he outsmarted me and caught a bead on me, I'd be ready. But the hail of bullets prevented me from getting an exact lock on him.

'Stay down' I hissed at Anard who had withdrawn his gun and was trying to crawl off his seat to spot the second gunman. He stopped and did exactly as I had ordered.

Another fury of shots rang out, giving me a good idea where the unseen gunman was likely to be. The shots had come from the right behind a thick wall of yew and juniper hedges which camouflaged our opponent. He was dug in like a gnat in a horse's arse. If he moved beyond that position, beyond the position where we were protected by the vehicle, I wouldn't stand a chance and neither would he. I would have to lure him out and make a move fast enough in case he thought of changing his position before I did. A thought occurred to me, a spot of ventriloquism might just be the advantage we might need.

I once spent two months with a French hooker named Marie and her gigolo boyfriend called Javier. While she was teaching me the art of seduction, her boyfriend Javier taught me Ventroquilism and pickpocketing. *"Vous ne savez jamais quand vous pourriez en avoir besoin, mieux vaut avoir que de ne pas"* he once suggested.

I signalled Anard to get prepared and showing him where our gunman is likely to be.

Pursing my lips, keeping them slightly separated, I waited for another shot to be fired. When the shot rang out, I threw my voice out and screamed. The scream was such that no one who heard would think twice that the person whom it belonged to was hurt bad.

It wasn't sufficient to lure him out. Yet.

I threw my voice again. Another cry and it was enough.

'On count of two' I whispered to Anard

This seemed to be the last man between me and Brahma. We had to get rid of him fast.

The hedges parted and a wary figure stepped out onto the path. Too late, he realised there was no body writhing in pain or even hurt. He understood the scream was a lure to draw him out. Before he could duck back to his previous position I yelled 'Two'

Anard began shooting where I had signalled him to. Anard's first slug hit him high in the shoulder, it spun the guard around towards the hedges. He tried to claw frantically at it when the second bullet drilled a hole through the back of his head.

Not a sound escaped the man's lips as he made a two- step macabre dance. His body bounced on the earth as he collapsed on the dusty earth, managing to squeezing off several ineffective shots from his machine pistol.

The gunmen looked like marionette dolls whose strings had been suddenly cut as they lay there sprawled on the ground before the villa gates. Victims of their own folly and their belief in the mortal Brahma's divinity.

Anard got slowly out of the car as I got to my feet. 'That's a neat trick' he said to me as I stepped up from behind the car door riddled with bullet holes.

'A French madam's boyfriend taught it to me. He said you never know when you might need it'

'He was right' he replied, surveying the scene '… about Harsha Kannauj …' he started to say.

'He'll get his soon enough' I whispered

There was nothing phoney about "A-tome" and there was nothing funny about Brahma's plan to bring India under his egotistic heel. He had implied his hatred of the west but not his desire to feed or cloth his people. He was a tyrant, aiming for the dictatorship and the means to power were inhumane as were his methods be if he attained that power. Pol Pot, Hitler, Idi Amin all had that inhumane means of obtaining and keeping power when they had it.

I crouched down and hunched myself in a half-kneeling position, trying to keep my left thigh wound from cramping. Flexing my knee several times in quick succession, I got the blood flowing again.

I took a several steps towards the villa's gate that held a dusty portentous corrugated sign saying *Danger. No Trespassing"* in English and Hindi. I figured that the gunman's heavy calibre machine pistol had fewer bullets than the ones in my Glock, so I felt no need to exchange weapons.

The darkened row of hedges suddenly was illuminated as the buildings behind it in the compound were lit up with fog-type guard lights. A ring of powerful dimmable LED lamps lit up the villa making hundred of insects, moths and buzzing gnats get caught suspended in the beams of light. It was bright enough that I had to shield my eyes, I was sure Anard had to too. Flies danced a dizzy ballet, mingling in the dust and scent of death.

Despite the lateness, fat, lazy bluebottle flies circled the bodies of the guard like the vultures I had confronted two dawns ago. They settled like an ungodly buzz on the bodies. The droning sounds they made, prickled my skin.

'Dev!' A harsh metallic voice suddenly called out. 'Tash' cried out the voice again. A voice that wasn't imitating anybody but itself echoed through unseen speakers.

Anard glanced my way.

'It's him' I whispered 'Be careful from here on special agent from the bureau of security'

'Goddam you Dax, you filthy whore! Dev! Tash! Where, the fuck are you boys? Dax, what the fuck have you done?' Brahma called out again for his men. His voice floated back to me as if it were a recording from top of an old scratchy record.

# SEVENTEEN

My long-awaited confrontation was at last here.

The face-to-face meeting, I so long wanted to happen was finally within my grasp. I tightened my Tripmaster jacket around my shoulders, steeling myself for the encounter, motioning Anard to be careful as I walked through the high steel gates. Brahma had once again called me out. First call out was the lure from the café, this was his third enticement after the botched attempt to capture me earlier.

'I will kill you, you worthless bitch' the speakers screamed, his crackling voice betraying both wrath and outrage. 'Not for your stupidity Dax. Not for your presumption, no, I'll kill you just for the principle of it'

He made no move to step out into the open. Rather, a deadened silence descended upon me and except for the droning flies behind me the night held a heavy hush.

Once again, I could see the lush of the inner garden and the inner courtyard, I had escaped from two nights ago. Because of the lights the renovated lush that was surrounded by an arid plateau was much easier to see in a landscape of dense foliage. The array of peacock colours however was not. Why Brahma couldn't have found a better spot for his home was beyond me. As a billionaire he had seemingly unlimited funds, rupees to burn and dollars aplenty to lure the likes of Safi Dass and the local cops. As a staunch believer in the Daayan cult, recreating the glory of the cult of old and the dream of becoming the next Kali or Naga, Brahma seemed to be another homegrown fanatic. Whatever his motives, he was dangerous but not as dangerous as what he had in his possession. "The A-tome"

With the Glock at the ready, I pushed myself slowly into a dense row of hedges, hoping that the faint snap of a branch or rustle of the leaves would not betray my whereabouts.

'Dax?' the speakers called out to me. The voice was tainted with far more than just an insinuation of sarcasm. Brahma's voice was different, altered significantly. 'Is that you, the thorn in my side? Come to pay me a visit huh?'

His voice was calm now and maliciously poised. I wasn't in the mood for a conversation or snippy one-line clever repartees. I preferred to end the discussion with something drastically bloody note i.e. his death. Yet I could not see him. Approaching the main villa, I stopped and surveyed my surroundings. At the door where I hastily exited from seemingly weeks ago instead of hours before I saw what I never intended to see.

I blinked and stared again, not certain it was a trick or an optical illusion before my eyes. Could it be that my eyes were being deceptive? Yes, it was Brahma, full faced and nothing like I imagined from that brief time with him in the caves of the Aravalli mountain range. Now I understood why he stayed in the shadows and sheltered his right-side view.

He was more than I imagined he would be. His huge balding frame was almost majestic. His black turban held a coiled cobra with a fearless stance poised over his head. His coarse tunic was replaced with a black combat suit, but it was something else that held my attention and that was his right arm. It was missing, but in its place was an artificial limb. Not a conventional product or an ordinary artificial limb but a steel cobra prosthetic device. From the tips of his fingers to the edge of his shoulder the man called Brahma displayed a stainless-steel limb.

Like before, his whole persona evoked a strange nightmarish smallness that attacks the human spirit, the prosthetic limb made him look even more so. His tough, toned physique only added an air of cunning and consummate deceit.

The diabolical cleverness of Brahma knew no bounds. To say he was eccentric and far -fetched would be a crass and a giant underestimation. I kept blinking, but this was no mirage or hallucination. My eyes were not being deceptive. It was real, very and alarmingly real. The steel cobra limb was anatomically exact to his other arm, which was holding a .45 calibre Colt, down to the last detail. The hand part had a bell-shaped wedge-shaped hood and roguishly gaping jaws with fangs. The fangs I had no doubt contained hypodermic syringes filled with the toxin from a Cobra's venom.

Now that I could see all his face, I saw it was nothing like the pictures on the goggle page I had scanned earlier. Oh, there were similarities, in that both his arms were visible and he had less lines on his face than the pictures depicted, which was normal.

My chest felt tight, just as my mouth had a dry feeling when I pulled my eyes away from the menacing bizarre limb and focused on the huge man's face. His sloe coloured narrow eyes hooded by bushy but carefully trimmed eyebrows were set in a hewn carved brown granite that stared at the hedges around him, indiscriminately searching for me. It was a face from antiquity, brutal, sagacious and ancient. A cold, stone-like creature with a titanic presence. It was easy to fear him and difficult not to fear him.

He was not going to be an ordinary adversary but a man in the same league as Sigrid or my old friend and Seymour's stepson, Kane Zielinski whom I had bested in battle some time ago.

If the steel cobra prosthetic wasn't enough to serve Brahma's defensive and offensive need, I had no doubt the incredible efficient Colt handgun would make it up for him. He swung his prosthetic arm back and forth, alert to any sound or motion which might aid him in pinpointing my position amidst the overgrown hedges.

'Come out Dax, face me' he tauntingly called out to me 'I promise I won't shoot you. I promise not to kill you quick … but we must talk. Your conversation with Safi and Sigrid's death are one of several things we should talk about'

I didn't reply.

Instead I raised the Glock and took aim. It was cold-blooded, I know but I think in this circumstance it was worth it. Levelling the gun at him I took aim at his chest and squeezed the trigger, hoping that I would have heard the last from him or about him. But instead of seeing the man drop to his knees and hearing his last gurgling croaking moans before death, he just stood there. The slug bounced right off his chest like a splinter of wood from a strike of an axe. The slug ricocheted, striking a piece of statuary in the middle of the overgrown garden. There was no sign he was wearing a bulletproof vest beneath his black combat suit. If anything, his chest looked bare beneath the combat suit. I could almost make out the outline of his ribcage and his musculature.

'Hah … you thought it was going to be that easy huh?' he snickered, squeezing off a round from his Colt. His high penetrating slug whistled a few inches away from me.

I instinctively ducked down, still not believing what I had seen.

'So, there you are?' he said pinpointing my exact position and sending another shot my way.

Unless his chest was made of steel too, I had little chance of overcoming him. He couldn't be a superman, could he? Maybe he was a Robot or an immortal, were some of the wild theories rattling around in my head.

No, of course not. However, what was the adequate way I could explain what I had just seen? I took another aim, this time I aimed for his head and squeezed the trigger but just then he ducked back through the door and the bullet buried itself in the wooden door, narrowly missing him.

He was vulnerable. He was no mythical beast, he was a plain and simple man, though enhanced with superficial condiments. Uncertain of the number of slugs I had remaining in the Glock, I didn't wait for Brahma to take his time. It was a mistake I had warned myself about not making. I took off out from my cover and started to run, tearing myself from the thorny hedges, meandering my way towards the side of the house. I knew I would hear or feel the bark of his Colt any second, it was not a sound I intended to hear or feel but I took my chance anyway. Praying that he would keep out of sight until I made it to the side of the house.

'Going someplace?'

I spun around and jerked the trigger at the same time, then again, the Glock had had it. The hammer clicked uselessly. I threw the gun at Brahma's warped, sneering face. His steel cobra hand caught it midway in the air.

'Do not move Dax, not one inch' he snapped. He had his Colt aimed at the middle of my chest. The section of my chest I did not want to ever part with, at least not willingly or permanently.

'What are you waiting for?' I asked 'Shoot me and get it over with'

'Shooting you is too easy a death for you. That's not me. I need you to squirm in pain, have a death that will rival Reeven's after all my fanged beauties are still hungry. Reeven was not much of a waiter but his brother and my clan were sad to see him all chewed up' he clucked his tongue admonishingly, his gun never wavered from my breasts 'The remainder of my clan deserve to witness your death. He and Ranjit were one of their own' No wonder Ranjit had in for me, I had fed his relative to the snakes.

Behind me I heard someone moving cautiously towards me. I turned my head to see one of the men I had wounded outside the business centre the previous day. His bandaged arm was holding a revolver pointed at my back.

'Ah Vansh there you are' Brahma said with contemptuous joviality. He looked at me and winked conspiratorially 'I believe you two have met'

'Yes' I murmured 'Yesterday on Pratham street'

'Yes, I recall Vansh's tale of your last encounter. Quite efficient of you. One thing you didn't know'

'And what might that be?' I enquired

'Vansh was Abhiram's older brother'

I was assuming his use of the word "was" meant that he was no longer among the living.

'Who the hell was Abhiram?' I asked

'One of my people you killed in our temple'

I turned to Vansh 'Oh my bad' I quipped at him. 'Don't feel so bad, at least he died quick and with honour'

Vansh's brown face turned livid, he took a step towards me, but Brahma stopped him with a gesture.

'You really know how to rile someone up. Don't you think Vansh deserves his animosity towards you?'

'It was him or me. The law of the jungle' I replied 'You know that and if you don't, then you and him deserve more than psychiatric help'

Vansh didn't say a word, he didn't need to, his face did all the talking. He had no idea of Peko up my forearm and neither did Brahma, but with one gun aimed at my back, one at my breast, I had little chance to use him. I didn't dare make a move or they'd both pull their triggers. So, I stood there, trying to keep my weight off my wounded leg.

'May I ask you a question?' I enquired.

'Go ahead'

'Where are Sameer's parents. He told me you had them imprisoned, I really didn't believe it'

He raised his cropped eyebrows, a flicker of emotion registered in his sloe menacing eyes 'What does it matter to you, he's dead'

'Humour me'

The reverse psychology worked almost exactly as I hoped 'I rather not' he hissed 'The treacherous lying bastard services was not all that great lately, but I shall miss the little whores he procured for my men and me, not to mention those deluded worshippers of mine. They loved his playing' he licked his lips and grinned at me. 'As for his parents they're not far from here. You recently paid a visit to it, caused quite a scene. Too bad you didn't stay for a guided tour'

Was he talking about the slaughterhouse?

Now the words on Sameer's note saying his parents were at Vadh Dvaar, slaughterhouse gate made sense.

'So much for blood huh?' I queried

'Whatever, he doesn't matter now. My brother and his wife will not mourn his passing for too long'

'Such deviousness to hide your family tree. Is it worth it?'

'More than you know' With each passing second, I was learning how to hate this depraved man anew. 'We shall have much fun with you' he chuckled 'Such an amusing time we shall have with you' he added

'So, get on with it' I taunted.

'Oh you don't have to worry. We shall get our comforts worth out of your pain'

I just stood there, unable to make a move, unable to upset the current balance. I was being covered from the front and the rear, easily to be converted into corned beef in two seconds flat. It was the wrong time to try any of my favourite tricks, especially since Vansh was motivated by revenge, eager to get back at me for killing his brother, Abhiram.

The shot rang out quite suddenly taking all of us by surprise but quenching all Vansh's dreams of revenge. The slug came from the hedges behind me. The aim was faultless that I had no doubt who had fired the weapon. I jerked to the side, avoiding Brahma's shot, I saw Vansh from out the corner of my eye, an ugly scarlet stain spreading across the front of his cream cotton shirt. He dropped to his knee like a wicket bar, the impact of Anard's slug had sent him reeling against the ground.

I hoped to use Anard's surprise shot to turn the tables on Brahma and use it to my advantage. I jumped forward, chopping down on his gun hand, trying to get him to drop his Colt. He fired off another shot just as his steel Cobra hand slammed down hard across my right shoulder. His blow exasperated the already inflamed wound on my right arm, making me cry out in pain.

The dripping fangs were poised a mere inch from my neck, I slammed my fist into the man's side. I still didn't know what the man had beneath his combat suit and the last thing I wanted was to be hung by my wrists over his snake pit.

'You'll never win whore' he hissed even as I sent the edge of my hand against the bridge of his nose. The knife hand did the trick and his clawed hand loosened its grip of my shoulder, uncurling for an instant. A final chop to his hand sent the Colt flying from his fingers. I stepped back.

'Let's finish this, man to woman. One on one' I said to him letting Peko drop to my fingers.

He grinned wryly.

To come to hand to hand conflict with Brahma would be fatal for me. I knew it and so did he.

Was this confrontation going to be the end of me?

I thought not, the fat lady has yet to sing and she won't unless I find a different approach.

Brahma's sloe eyes narrowed until they were like serpent slits, making his appearance more reptilian than ever. Spotting the stiletto in my hand he saw it as a plaything he could easily overcome. He edged towards the door. Another shot rang out, however Anard's aim was not as accurate as before. His slug, like mine ricocheted off harmlessly into the dust and air.

'Isn't that cheating?'

'You are in no way liable to lecture me about cheating' I replied, keeping my distance from his Cobra arm. The prosthetic glittering fangs were a fierce reminder of Brahma's insanity and his sadistic methods.

'Bhee!' Anard cursed from behind me 'The ... *Lanat* gun is jammed'

'Back, back away Anard' I warned him. His damn gun was no use to me now.

I had to use Peko, either to stab Brahma's body or else to slice him six ways to Sunday. The difficulty would be getting close to him given the wounded pained inability of my body.

'You do know my babies ...' his eyes flicked to the fangs on his prosthetic arm '... are filled with the deadliest poisons known to man. Venom from a green mamba's, an Australian brown snake and my own personal favourite the King Cobra. Together Miss Dax I will make Reeven's death pale in the epitome of mercy and you know how much he suffered, don't you?' Was he really talking because he was a little bit afraid or was he stalling, in any case, I was measuring and calculating ways to come at him. I had a strategy in mind, but I never knew if I was going to last long enough to use it or even if it was going to work.

'Where's the A-tome, Mr Harsha?' I asked ignoring his tirade about poisons.

My use of his first name didn't seem to faze him one bit. His face twisted with a grin etched on his thin lips. 'Ah' he said, 'Is that what you want?'

'Probably'

'Alright let's make a trade?'

'A trade?'

'Yes, your life for Kavin's invention'

'How about your life for the box' I countered

'And what would my Chinese pals say about that?'

'Do you think I care?'

'Of course, y…'

He didn't finish his sentence, he suddenly came at me with such speed I almost didn't get out of reach in time. I moved suddenly taking one long sideways stride then changed direction with a quick almost floating movement then dropped. With my hands on the ground I shot out with my two booted heels. Brahma tried to move his leg fast, but my heel caught the knee of his left foot. Winching from the pain in my left leg I rolled away and came to my feet in the same movement. Out of distance of his prosthetic arm.

Brahma cursed.

Unlike Naveen, my kick had not landed with full force, but it was enough to make it startle him.

I circled Brahma warily, he was cautious now, waiting.

Talk and playtime was over.

I stopped and abruptly darted to him again. I began chopping at him with the edge of my hands, stabbing with the Peko and stiffened fingers, then as quickly as I began, I darted out of reach again with a grunt of pain.

There was a little cry of exultation from Brahma's grinning lips as I backed away.

In that flurry of movement that lasted less than six seconds, I did not dare to block the metal arm. I could only duck and sway and block against wrist and forearm, but he did not have time to really get a grip of me with his prosthetic arm, but then he could always get lucky.

My elbow had encountered his chest and I had felt something hard under his combat suit, it was not metallic, probably some space-age type of nano-knitted polymer.

'Ha! Another of Kavin's inventions' he gloated at my crouched form. What ego he had on him. Not able to shut his mouth without going through every detail. Just wished he'd say something useful for me to listen to.

I had backed away because he had caught me by the side of my head, making Peko fall from my hand. I crouched before him shaking my head to clear the spinning feeling I was undergoing. I put my hand to my face, I could feel a mottled welt down the side of my head, where his metal arm had caught me with a glazing blow.

He moved slowly towards me and in a flurry of fierce exchange of blows and chops, I broke free from his attempted hold onto me by a rolling somersault. He had little skill when it came to Karate, his advantage was his prosthetic limb and size. He didn't have to move much because he covered a lot of ground.

I had not been alone in the wounds instigated. Brahma was slightly limping, one of his eyes was half closed, they was blood trickling from his side, an effect caused by Peko no doubt and then there was the swelling on his chin.

Yes, I had done some damage, all the same, not enough. 'You're fast' he grunted

He stepped forward and this time I darted towards him trying to get in-between his arms before he could manoeuvre his hovering arm of steel for a deadly strike. The move required me to be a split second faster than necessary. I wasn't.

The instant I lunged at him the steel arm came down on me, pummelling me down to the earth. It was a good strike and I had a troubling time in getting away. Before I could crawl away his steel arm clamped down on my shoulder like before. The dripping fangs edged closer and closer towards my neck. Ramming him against the wall of the villa I grabbed the steel Cobra with both hands heaving it off me. Brahma gasped as he used his other hand to assist the venomous arm to clamp down harder onto me. I wondered if the limb had humeral joints or radial joints or transcarpal operated fangs. I didn't know how the steel limb worked and I wasn't exactly in a position to find out.

With mere inches from me I did the only thing I could, I used my teeth to bite down on the flesh of his left arm. He screeched loudly as I bit off a sizeable morsel of his flesh. Heaving his arm and his body off me, I spat out the flesh. I didn't give him time to recover from the bloody bite wound. I attacked again low, using my booted heel more than my hands. When I came away from that attack, I was breathing hard, my jacket was torn and my limp had gotten worse. Backing away I felt it was time to put my strategy into effect.

I reached for the tunic on my left shoulder and savagely jerked the whole length of the sleeve from my Tripmaster jacket. Still backing away, I gripped the cuff part of the sleeve in my hand and flicked it at him. Instinctively he backed away.

Brahma laughed abruptly as I snapped the sleeve again and again at him. All the while I was retreating still and out of his reach. I was like a schoolgirl playing flick the damp towel.

This was half my strategy and it seemed to be working. Brahma was getting his confidence back.

He increased his pace towards me with his prosthetic arm leading the way, he did see me swap the edges of the sleeve but paid no attention to the deed. I was now holding onto the ripped part of the sleeve.

When I knew he was in position and least expecting the effect of my sleeve, I snapped the cuff edge at his head. As expected, he didn't bother to shy away from it. The cuff hit his temple like the end of a whiplash and a grasping cry escaped his lips. He staggered away dazedly.

I knew why. Within the double thick cuffs Seymour had had a not so reputed tailor of mine sewn in a flexible band of lead. It was two and a half inches wide, eight inches long in its curve round the wrists and just over one fifteenth of an inch thick.

I had been squeezing the cuff end into a solid chunk while holding the cuff end and flicking the harmless part at Brahma. When I was done, I had almost a cubic inch of lead or half a pound in weight of lead which Brahma had felt.

He reeled away almost crumbling to the ground.

Again, I lashed out with the weighted sleeve, catching him on the top of his bald head. Twice more the lead struck home, not with full force for it was impossible to flick the lead ball with that much timing, accuracy and placing. All the same the big Indian man was staggering blindly before me, as expected. This strategy of mine had aided me several times over the years when I really needed it. The lead ball was a one-stopper and quite effective.

The defensively groping metal limb caught hold of the lead end and clung to it desperately. I let go and launched myself directly at him. Lunging between his arms. My arms flashed out wide, hands curving in. It wasn't long before he was now swaying, sagging barely able to stand on his feet, I caught his left wrist and heaved, swinging him in a circle. Then I jumped behind him with a hand hooking round his throat from behind, my legs drawn up with the flat of my boots against the small of his back. For a moment, all was still, it was then I heaved with my hands and thrust with all the strength my long steely muscles in my thighs could muster.

It was a reverse stomach throw made from the rear. Brahma whirled over me in a backward arc, landing almost six feet away from me. His prosthetic arm coming off loose from his shoulder. I got slowly to my feet and stood over him. Doubled over on the ground I watched him groaning.

My back was savagely bruised from the throw, one side of my face was in agony, as was my thigh, my right arm and my head, which throbbed with pain. Every muscle in me was slack from exhaustion.

Standing over him I rammed a foot into his groin, but he could barely react to the pain rooting up his midsection. I raised a foot, stepped on his cheat and taking hold of his prosthetic limb I wrenched it from his body then shoved the fanglike hypodermic needles down into his own shuddering flesh and buried them along the side of his thick ham-fisted neck.

Tossing the steel arm aside I watched as a look of astonishment followed by terror, consumed his features. Stepping back lest the steel arm was capable of a second strike, I stood over him watching Brahma gasp trying to catch his breath. He didn't lie. The venom was fast acting and seemingly amazingly effective. His breathing and his brown skin were starting to turn blotchy. Dark crimson splotches of a gory colour marked a rapid spread on internal haemorrhage.

'Da … Dax … ple … anti … antidote …' he pleaded at me with his sloe eyes.

He tried to get his legs to function, no doubt to get this antidote but his feet were already feeling the paralytic effect of his poison. He sank further into the ground twitching as a series of violent, convulsive shudders tore through his body. It wasn't a pleasant death to watch, then again Brahma was not a pleasant man who lived.

I shrugged internally figuring that was what he had intended for me. Seconds after he stopped moving Anard was by my side.

He stared down at the huge man 'You know the stock market will drop a few points when they learn of his death' he amusingly said

'Good thing I don't trade in stocks'

*　　*　　*　　*

I wish I could say that everything was finally wrapped up as neat as a bow with the death of Brahma, but it wasn't. In the aftermath of Brahma's death, only two men managed to escape the net which descended on the sect that had once called itself Daayan.

Sir C informed me that a reliable source had given him good reason to believe that Kavin Chandra had successfully made it to the Indian border where it was presumed, he was swallowed up by the sprawling hand of China. As had been the case with Brahma, Kavin was an enigma, a faceless threat whose scientific genius was already going to be put to use by the power-hungry men who ruled from Peking, but that did not concern me. At least for now.

As for Safi Dass he told his assistant he was going for lunch and simply disappeared. It took Sir C surveillance tech guys almost seven days to track and find him in Singapore. He disappeared again among the towns of the southern province but they successfully tracked and pinpointed his position again. I had plans for Safi Dass and informed Sir C that I would handle him if he could locate him. Safi Dass had betrayed me twice so it only fitting that I be the one responsible for his pains.

Five days earlier, I had other things on my mind. Namely Brahma and the "A-tome". Brahma was dead, the "A-tome" box Anard and I found in a safe. Once I liberated it from the locked safe, I promptly smashed to pieces. Sir C was later furious with me about that. In the villa were several children and women, parts of Brahma's harem. Most welcomed our liberation, some did not know what to make of us, while the others simply refused our assistant. Afterward Anard called in local cops from two districts away and assisted me in raiding the slaughterhouse gate. We found an elderly pair of couples and two dozen or so girls aged between six to fifteen years old who were being put through indoctrination for sex slave labour or the sex trafficking trade by use of beatings, starvation, LSD and *Psilocybin* hallucinogenic drugs. Four or five of them were to be the unseen, unheard and unknown of the Daayan Cult.

The three perpetrators surrendered after a brief gun fire exchange and were promptly arrested. Like the batch taken into custody at the temple, Naveen wasn't among them.

It wasn't hard to figure out which one of the elderly couples were Sameer's parents. Telling them of Sameer's death, I offered them my condolences and informed them that as Sameer considered Harsha Kannauj his uncle that made them entitled to his wealth and homes which I promised would be transferred over to them in due course. I doubt they believed me and thought of me as a crazy English lady, but I was sure as hell going to make sure it happened. I needn't have bothered. Anard said he'd take care of it. Two weeks later when I checked in on them, Anard had done what he had promise.

When Seymour arrived a couple hours later he promptly flew me out of the country after I sorted one or two things out, namely open a scholarship fund for Hameed the street urchin boy and Amira, Nadir's daughter. I also paid a visit to Mishka before he had me flown out of the country and had me checked into our nearest clinic in Paris and had me take a full medical work-up because he had heard of a new virus, from China that was heating up and may sweep the world. A virus which had been named Covid. He was afraid that due to the several injuries I had received, I might just catch one or two infections that might compromise my immunity making way for the virus to take hold. I took no heed to his over-exaggerated concerns but in the interest of peace and quiet I entertained his hypochondriac phobia.

During my check-up I laid out my plans for Safi Dass.

'Oh, the Ibru Gambit, you mean?' he mused when I was done.

'Not exactly, but close enough'

I convalesced at my mansion home, *"De Vaugrennier"* that stood right smack in the middle of a 200-acre landscape, restored living area in the south side of Paris's Buttes-Chaumont Arrondissements. During my recuperation I spoke to both my charges and received a call from Sir C informing me of Safi Dass's location as relayed to him by his savvy top-notch tech team. It took a day for me to convince Seymour that I needed to finish what was started and another day to finish with the arrangements I had already put in effect.

Two days later, a certain hotel clerk from Jaipur arrived at a four-class hotel in the Downtown Core district of Singapore to meet a person she had never met before.

'Good afternoon sahib Dass' said Mishka Sanjit to the seated man registered under the name Curzon Bangla she had come to see. The greeting of her host in Hindi surprised him. 'This is a nice hotel' she said of the Fullerton Bay Hotel

'Who are you and what are you doing here? How do you know my name?'

'I'm sorry sir, my name is Mishka Sanjit and I didn't want to come … she made me'

Safi Dass cocked his head to one side then to the other side searching the restaurant for another recognisable face among the numerous patrons. He didn't find any. A flutter of a smile touched his lips, but he did not say a further word.

He looked at the strange woman before him and sized her up.

I was glad to see Mishka no longer had red talons for fingernails. It had been a week since I had scared the wits out of Mishka Sanjit and twenty-four hours since I had called. She had listened while I talked and had asked me only one question. When I hung up, I bet she showered, changed, waited for the two packages I had sent her and started her journey.

After several phone calls, a bus ride, a three and a half hour flight from Chhatrapati, Mumbai to Changi International Airport in Singapore with a stop-over in Delhi and another rough two hour drive down to the coastal district of Downtown Core, I bet she was tired but exhilarated.

From across the marina I watched through a 680 telescopic lens the waiter Zeng Wei as he placed a Kopi-O coffee drink before the man I was targeting in the restaurant. I couldn't hear what he was saying however I assumed he was thanking the waiter I was paying $3,000 Singaporean dollars to spike his drink.

After two hours of waiting I finally saw Mishka Sanjit approach the Fullerton Bay Hotel of Downtown Core. She winced her nose as she took in the pleasant scenery of the restaurant. It was no surprise to me that this was her first trip abroad and the unfamiliar smells were giving her a slight bother.

The normal lean talon nailed Indian who had seen better days picked her way round the tables and chairs around her. One of her hands was in a sling. After her initial greeting, Dass gestured for her to sit down.

I listened to their conversation via the digital watch I had sent Mishka which housed a listening device.

Dass asked, 'How did you find me?' he asked. I had to say that this man Dass had as much sensitivity as a toilet seat.

'Sahib, I not think they ever lose you … at least she didn't'

'Who?'

'Madam Dax. It she who send me here'

'How did she know where I was … Mishka isn't it?'

'Yes sir … I not know'

'Why did she send you?'

'To deliver a message. She say for your own good you must listen'

'Does she?' Dass's face did not change, but his dark silent eyes shone with a smirk. For a long moment he was silent. His silence was excruciating to watch but his guest knew it was not a bothered silence just a reflective one.

After a while, Dass asked 'Would you like a drink?' he asked beckoning a waiter. Not Zeng Wei.

Mishka shook her head 'No'

'Tell me Mishka, what do you make of the woman who sent you?' he asked.
Mishka Sanjit did not hesitate 'She scare me plenty, sir'
'So, what do you make of this woman?' he asked
Mishka Sanjit did not hesitate 'She scares me plenty'
'So, what do you think I should do about her?'
'You … no, sahib I get no say in this. If I was you, I say do as she ask' Mishka Sanjit replied 'I sell her to some bad people but she pardoned me and now my life she owns"
'You are here to do her bidding like a *Dass*?' I detected a slight note of contempt in Dass's voice
'A slave for her, yes'
'And what is this message of hers'
'Surrender to the authorities before midnight tomorrow, disclose all your contacts, your links everything you know or else. She say I am to escort you myself if you desire and that if you do not wish to surrender say goodbye to your life as you know it'
A small smile appeared on Dass's face 'You joking with me huh?' his voice shaking with false amusement.
'No'
'You should get out of here Mishka if that is your name. I never want to see you again'
'It is her word, I swear by Shiva'
'You want me to take the word of a woman? An *angrejee inphidel*. Me?'
Mishka shivered, looking about her. 'Infidel she may be, but for what me and you did to her we should be in Jail or worse. She spared me, my life, so yes I take her word'
'I should take that life'
Mishka slowly got to her feet 'If you do then be it so' Mishka said pleasantly 'I die free and unashamed'
Two hundred and seventy yards away in a five feet dinghy by the marina, I shook my head in sorrowful contempt.
I made my way off the marina to the Fullerton Bay Hotel and checked myself in. I was handed my room key card and I went upstairs and continued to watch the video feed on my OnePlus8 Pro Phone from the miniature cameras one of Sir C's agent had placed inside the director-

cum-organiser's room two days previously when they finally got a lock on him.

12.03 am I left my room via patio doors and climbed down two floors towards room number eleven on the second floor.

Accessing the terrace, I slinked into the room through the closed patio doors. Using an app on my phone, I disabled all the hotels security systems in the room, especially the silent alarms in the living room and bedroom and collected all the miniature cameras in the suite.

The living room was devoid of life however the bedroom was not.

The man I had come to see lay in a large circuitously bed sleeping. Alongside of him was Tunku, the beautiful Singaporean male escort I had watched arriving earlier with him three hours ago through the miniature webcams. Close up I knew he was an awfully expensive hooker because his calves and face were smoother than a teenager's. A surgery that wasn't cheap to come by especially here in Singapore.

Sneaking over to the bedside, I headed straight for his pillow. I found the Colt I had watched him tuck under his pillow just that afternoon. Retrieving the pistol, I tucked it into the small of my hip before making my way over to the chair across from the bed, pulling out my Makarov as I sat in it.

So, this was the Deputy Director of India's Central Bureau of Security Safi Dass also known as Anurag Surte, riot coordinator extraordinaire. From the research the MI6 had conducted, I knew he was 55 years of age, a former British and Indian Army Sergeant. He had worked hard, paid his dues in getting to his former position, not bad for someone who joined the service as a reports officer. Since then he has consistently moved up the ranks.

Married once to a Navya Kapoor whom he was now divorced from. He had a son who was killed in a Sikh and Hindi clash five years ago and a daughter who lives in the United States and has rarely seen in the past ten years. Given his recent proclivities I don't think he has a religious demonym. He has one sibling, Rosa Dass a retailer in Mumbai with her own set of problems. While going over his resume, I saw that apart from receiving a Prime Minister Awards and an Intelligence Award, he has attracted one or two controversies. He was linked to a black site prison he supervised under the auspices of his government which was discovered to be torturing its prisoners some years ago and also when a cash for leniency operation was uncovered, his name was artfully mentioned and he came under what the Indian Parliament described as a "Precautionary scrutiny".

I made a subtle cough.

Mr Dass roused from his sleep. Alertly he glanced round, his hand darting under the pillow. He half jerked out of his skin when he saw me sitting in the chair across from the bed. His shudder alerted his companion who also lurched out of his sleep when he saw me.

Mr Dass glanced around the room again before settling his gaze on me, his hand still searching for his pistol.

'Who the fuck are you and how did you get in my room?' he asked, his Indian accent barely noticeable. 'What the hell are you doing here?'.

I winched at his questions. Instead of replying I ignored his query and addressed the man beside him.

'Tunku, you should make yourself scarce. You'll find enough cash in that drawer to start a new life. Take it and disappear?' I said politely, shifting my hand slightly for him to see the weapon in my hand.

The Makarov in my hand and my laid -back persona was enough for him to comprehend the fact that he ought to take my advice. He promptly threw off the beddings from his nude body, gathered up the pile of his clothes next to the bed and went diving into the drawer I had indicated. Dass was still searching with his hand under the pillow, I pulled out his Colt and showed it to him. His expression became crestfallen. We both watched as Dass's hard earned dosh was being bundled up by Tunku. I calculated that there was about 70,000 US dollars in the drawer. Where I hoped wherever Dass was going, he wasn't going to need it. When he was done, he went running towards the living room. Prior to him leaving the bedroom, I stopped him. 'Oh, and Tunku, I don't need to remind you that you didn't see anything here tonight?' He nodded, grinning with a lottery winners smile before tearing out of the room.

Turning my head to face my surprised host whose hand was already halfway towards the open drawer I said, 'So Mr Dass or would you prefer Mr Surte?'

'Who are you?'

I winced inwardly again at the question.

'Mr Dass it is then, shall we talk?' I asked, seeing him reach for the alarm button, I simply said 'Sorry, I've disabled that'
Concern covered his face 'You've got some nerve coming here …'
'Well they do tend to call me unpredictable. We spoke once if you recall'
'Ok you've got my attention … Miss Dax, nice to meet you at last'
'I can't say it's nice to meet you since you left me for dead twice' I replied trying to sound genial, but I ended up sounding a bit hoarse. 'Do you?'
He sat up a little straighter in the bed 'What is this … revenge?
Payback … what? … yes … I've heard of you and your reputation Miss Dax' He switched on the bedside lamp beside him.
'You have?'
'Come to put me on notice have you, bit petty of you don't you think?'
'Maybe, maybe not' I said grunting from the soreness of my body.
'Do you know what's in Dante's ninth level of hell?'
'Dante?' he asked looking at me sort of funny.
'Yes, Dante Alighieri' I told him.
'I-I know of Dante's Inferno' he replied
'Well?'
'What?'
'Dante's ninth level?' I asked again
'Liars' Safi answered
'And traitors stuck in ice'
'What the fuck you talking about?'
'You and the way you die'
He scoffed 'You think you are going to kill me?'
'Considering what you've done, yes but that question is mute, it's a pity I don't have ice, no … I killed you approximately thirteen hours ago I think …' I said glancing at my watch.
He stopped. For the first time there was a rise in his voice 'What … w-what did y-you d …?'
'Well not kill … kill kill you … half killed you, yes I think that's the right way to say this'
I saw puzzlement, then confusion cross his eyes which was followed by what I had said 'W-what … how … y-you've … half killed me?' I inclined my head but didn't speak.

I got up to leave. The soreness in my left thigh made me flinch for a second 'This get-together is ill-advised, I think?' I said 'Mishka said it all don't you think?'

'No no … no … Mish …' he snorted frantically 'Wait a minute … what do you mean you've half killed me? W-what do you mean …?'

He cried out to me as he got out of the bed, pulling on a plain coloured pyjama robe at his feet round his shoulders.

'Oh I can understand that' I sympathised 'Have you heard the term "Synergistic Effect"'

'N-no'

'It's when two nonlinear active ingredients come together to create a greater or lesser supplementary role. In this case two active poisons acting together to create a fatal effect i.e. your death'

'What?'

He followed me into the living room. I had to admire Dass's restraint and lack of imminent fear from the news I had given him. As a deputy head of a country's spy agency and perpetuator of an effective fake persona, I knew he was made of sterner stuff. I think I innately expected that as an ex-infantry soldier, uneasiness and distress was not a condition he would be terribly concerned about.

'You ingested a poison this afternoon' I saw the shocked look on his face 'Oh have no fear, it is one of two parts … harmless … at least for now, but it sits in the stomach for years on end doing nothing really … but if it comes in contact with a specific combination of drugs … which is in my possession … they'll meet and cause a calamitic effect within your stomach and before you know it …' I paused for dramatic effect; I clapped my hands 'Boom … you're dead from an indeterminate cause'

'What … w-what have you … what … done?'

'Nothing too taxing' I said stopping at the front door of his hotel suite.

'What …'

'Now listen carefully, you'll do everything Mishka advised you to do, otherwise one day very soon you'll be introduced to the other part'

'Wha …'

'Do you understand?'

He stood in the middle of the room not exactly sure what he ought to do. I opened the door.

'Do you understand me?' I asked again.

He unsteadily nodded his head.

'Good. See you in the funny papers Mr Dass' I said before closing the door behind me.

# EPILOGUE

Two days later a Saturday, in my London QCA penthouse, Seymour and I were in my indoor gym room. The indoor gym was more than sixty yards across with empty light high spaces between beige coloured walls and white square windows with orange lighting bathing us. There were several fitness mats, weight benches, a pommel and vaulting horse, parallel and horizontal ski bars. There was also a Nautilus S6.20 LC treadmill, Schwinn Cross Trainer, York Exercise bike, a Raleigh Lithium suspension bike, a bar counter with three rotating highchairs, a shower cubicle and two drinks vending machines.

In the middle of the wooden floorboards was a dojo, a twenty feet square of sponge rubber on top of a floor-protected canvas with the top end facing a 32-inch plasma TV set with soundbar and subwoofer accessories. Above the mat was a horizontal gymnasium bar, including the parallel bars and the vault horse across from it. To the right of it at the far end of the long room was a wall recesses for a target range, a tier rack of a dozen different weight class rubber hex dumbbell bars and a wooden-topped bench that ran from one end of the wall to the other. The gymnasium was divided into two. On one side was thirty-foot square runner while in the large part of the room was the exercise space. Across from me on the runner mat Seymour was dressed in a white wife beater T-shirt and jogging pants. I was in a red coloured sports bra and pants. This was my test, after more than a week of convalescing it was time to see if my form was up to speed from the last time we scuffled. The effect India had on my body had been stressful and now with most of my wounds almost healed it was necessary to test my effectiveness.

Too many injuries may have caused my muscles and mind to tighten too much. I had to limber up every strand of my muscle and mind to let Seymour know if I was healed and/or effective. The first step would be to test my vigilance and body, and to do that he would have to push me to the extreme.

I went round the room observing it in every detail. It was the perfect gym for a gymnast, and thanks to an old friend Mikhail and my early days on the road, I was a passable gymnast.

Just then Nadia came into the room.

My fourteen-year-old adopted daughter with brunette hair and hazel eyes walked lazily into the gym room with a hand-held games console in her hand.

'Oh, not this again' she whined with her Belarusian/Slovakian accent when she saw me moving towards the parallel bars.

'No complaining, child. You either stay or leave' I said to her

'We have a visitor *Mlada Mati* … Mr Conrad' she said. Mlada Mati was one of her Slovenian, Belarusian or Polish, I could never tell, nickname for me. "*Matka*" was also a polish nickname she had for me, while I fondly called her "*Nadya*". Essentially, they all represent the same thing. "*Mother or Young Mother*".

'Ask him to come on down'

'Galahad tell him to come down please' Nadia said

'*Yes Miss Nadia*' Galahad replied through the speakers.

'Talk to Sir C while I limber up, Seymour'

'Okay milady. Pity I haven't got much to talk to him about'

'You'll think of something, oh and please keep your anger on the side-lines please' I said to him

Seymour eyed the door at the end of the room behind which were an array of weapons.

I turned to Nadia. 'Daughter, be a good girl and stand back'

Nadia stepped away, parking herself next to one of the revolving highchairs, her digits still tapping on the Nintendo handheld between her fingers.

I made my way over to the pommel horse and wrapped each handle with my fingers. Getting a good grip of the handles I leapt.

I made a well composed start on the horse, swinging from one handle to the other in less moves than needed. I started slowly, moving forward and back. Two minutes after I got a regular methodical movement going, I flipped my hold on the handles and started swivelling side to side using all the rhythmic skill of an acrobat. During my routine, Sir Steele had entered the room and along with Seymour who was watching me intently.

I would wince at a mistake or a sudden pain on my left side but continued on. Despite that, I felt my body still retained the inherent grace it had before my injuries.

A glance at Seymour conversing with Sir C and I knew that despite their tête-à-tête, he was watching me with his icy blue eyes, like a lynx and the critical eyes of a perfectionist.

After I expeditiously made several Russian combinations of a *Stocklis*, I orbited the handles before making a left somersault dismount off the horse.

Landing perfectly on the mat to the single sound of applause from Sir Steele was enough to pull Nadia's attention from her console to smile at me before returning her thoughts back to her handheld video game.

Seymour approached me and took his time to feel the muscles on my upper torso and calves. After examining my body in silence, he was done. He only had one word for me.

'Again'

That simple one word moved me deeply, but I did not show it. There was no need to protest but simply to do as I was told. Better for me to make my mistakes now than make them while I was in another life or death situation.

Sir Steele in one of the highchairs by the bar looked on as I jumped up again and repeated my previous moves. This time I speeded up my arabesque moves to a fantastic degree. Faster than I thought I was capable of. Whirling, twisting repeatedly, steeling myself against any interference I coiled, straightened and battled against my own strength and supplety. I was alone in my own strange world of intense mental and physical focus. This time I hoped Seymour was entranced. When I was done, I stepped back breathing a little quick, waiting for his verdict. He walked over behind me and slowly began to massage my shoulders and my calves with his big powerful hands.

For five minutes he kneaded my body until stopping at last he looked at me and giving me a sudden grin, he said with much emphasis 'Much better ma'am'

'Yes, that was superb' Sir Steele interjected.

'It was not her best but good' Seymour added

'Sir C, why're you here?' I asked going over to the vault

'Came to see how you were, see if things were good with you. Update you with some news'
'You mean like a progress report? Do we need or give progress reports Sey?' I asked
Seymour looked at me and nodded 'Sometimes'
'Ok do you want to know what's up with me. Well I'm a little concerned about this coronavirus'
'I shouldn't worry, my intelligence suggest it wouldn't leave China'
'I wouldn't count on that' I turned to Seymour 'Perhaps we should get our people on it?'
'You're making a habit of this' Sir Steele said beaming with pleasure.
'What …?'
'Sticking your nose where it doesn't belong. Not that I don't like that aspect of your nature, but I would be happier if you curbed your desires occasionally'
Standing next to the balancing beam and using just the balls of my feet, I jumped onto the beam. 'Now you sound like Seymour. By the way, what's life if not indulging in a bit of whimsy. However, for now I think I might need a large amount of coddling' I said
'I should imagine' said Steele grinning and watching me 'Any candidates lined up?'
I glanced at Nadia before replying 'Not yet' I whispered, straining on the balancing beam.
It took me more than a few seconds to balance myself on the beam.
'Oh by the way Mahatma sends his love' Sir Steele informed me.
It was a few seconds before I was able to recall who Mahatma was.
'Does he?' I asked
'Yep'
'Well right back at him. Hope his governing practices are much more amicable now'
'Not my expertise'
'Mine neither' I said as I started into my routine. With my two hands I made a few handsprings before coming to rest on the beam with my feet. Twisting twice and flipping up and down the balance beam, I felt myself limber up. I was no Simone Biles, but I was supple and strong enough despite being slow when it came to precision. I moved with

fluency and purpose, but for a second, during my sobering exercise drill I was interrupted as my thought recalled part of the fight, I had with the Sin Eater. I had no idea why I would recall it at that exact moment, but I did. I could not help myself. It was so unnerving that I prematurely dismounted off the beam with a single backward twist in one fluidic movement.

With my kinks and ticks now loosened, Seymour went over to the steel cabinet underneath the window on one side of the room and retrieved a pair of MMA gloves. Seymour sometimes had a forced disadvantage when we fight each other, partly because he weighed heavier than me. Tugging them onto his hands, he joined me as I appraised the thickness of the dojo. 'You should know Mr Dass turned himself in last night. I guess your bluff worked' Sir Steele said

I didn't answer him, I was preparing my mind and body for the next phase.

I winched as I felt the pinch of pain from under the gauze on my left side.

Nadia looking up from her games console stood up suddenly when he saw us and became agitated 'Oh no … Mr Conrad we need to step back, this sometimes get ugly' she said taking his arm and pulling him back.

Seymour and I stood diagonally from each other on the opposite sides of the mat watching each other. There was a slight pause before we bowed in respect of each other then started to advance on one another. This was the time my body and mind will either make me proud or disappoint me. I prepared my mind by excluding everything else but the task at hand. And that was to make sure I was up to par with Seymour. We circled each other cautiously as we drew slowly closer to each other, before I reached him, I swayed, swung my body and our bodies locked briefly into one. He spun me over his back and my feet hit the mat as I twisted out of his reach. Seymour had known battle and danger even before we met hence, I never knew what he would be throwing at me. Which was fine by me, I needed to be tested to the extreme. He scrutinised me as I stalked him again. We clashed again in a sudden flurry of movement. A feinted here and a swerve there, lashing a kick at him from my bare feet. He launched a kick at my chest but pulled back at the last moment as he aimed for my head. I deftly evaded it. There was

an arabesque of movement between us, speeding up as our two bodies
whirled, fell and rose, separating for brief instances then joining again
We pirouetted with each other for a full three minutes not actually
making contact but testing each other's defence. Seymour pounced back
and forth giving short evaluating looks at me. After a while he grinned
and nodded.

'All right milady' he said

It was time to show him what I was capable of. This was what it was
about. Him and me. No more pulling punches. Him testing me and me
testing myself against him as we combated each other in a combinational
fight.

I led with my left hand, but Seymour swayed sideways, staggered in one
direction then changed abruptly sweeping my left hand aside while his
gloved hand came down on in a chop like strike towards my shoulder.
I turned instinctively flanking him as his hand came down. There was a
smack of my flesh against the side of the glove as my arm came upward
to block his chop. It wasn't an offensive block because he of course was
heavier than me. I blocked in the most defensive way that a fighter could
choose. The outer side of my lower arm but it wasn't good enough. A
fact that Seymour also knew. He backed off and looked me in the face
cocking his head. I stood looking at him panting. The preventive block
stung more than a little.

'Susan perhaps we …?'

'Stop speaking' I hissed at him.

He took the hint.

This time I approached him from the side knocking his arm away as he
leaned into me. There were no illusions this time, he knew that I was going
to pounce with whatever I felt necessary. I made my hand into a conk as I
coiled my right hand then lunged at him. I knew he had seen me bunch my
hand, so he knew at least partly what to expect but he was caught unawares
when I dropped. With my hands on the ground, I shot out my feet. He
moved his leg fast but not fast enough. My foot hit the side of his left knee.
It was not powerful to do damage but enough to put him on guard. I rolled
away and came to my feet as he abruptly darted towards me. I remembered
using this move on Brahma and Naveen. The next thing I knew was that
there was a blur of blows and chops between us. Me chopping fiercely

with the edge of my hands and stabbing with conked fingers. At one point we each evaded the punches we shot at each other, but I had the advantage because I was smaller even if he did have the longer reach. Quiet suddenly he took a long swerving stride and his leg swung with the body of his whole impetus behind him. He hit me hard in my side, I tried to move out of his way but before I could he hit me coldly with his elbow solidly high on the side of the neck, a little below the ear.

I flew through the air partly by the impact and partly by my own effort to avoid and ride the blow. I smacked the dojo like a salami. I was dimly aware that my lungs and body aching with a fiery pain.

I heard a cry of protest from Sir Steele but we both ignored him.

Seymour had me but it wasn't over, I rolled fast away from him as he came in fast. I approached him almost as if there was a race that I had to win. I attacked low going for his mid- section using my feet. I couldn't see my face but if I were, there would be a cold impassiveness on it.

At this point I didn't feel the needy facts of my fighting skills. My mind was far away from me. I presumed that this was how some men had seen me in the last moments of their lives.

As I drew ever closer to him weaving and dodging, several blows glanced off me, but I was determined to get to him and when I knew was close enough, I flicked my fist at the right spot. There are certain points on the body where if you hit hard enough on an artery against the bone, it could inhibit movement. A fact I learned first from Laminachi and one of my *Taekwondo* sensei's. I aimed for one such point, the *Kote*, just above his inner arm joint and punched. His arm recoiled from the pain I inflicted on it and he jumped back almost cat-like. Recoiling from the shock his left arm twitching, I went in pursuit of him.

I saw him sway sideways, change direction abruptly and sweep my on-coming hand strike aside while he chopped down towards my shoulder. I anticipated that move because he had already used it on me. I turned in a blur of speed, moving sideways towards him flanking forward as flesh smacked on flesh. I anticipated the next chop but blocked with the inner side of the wrist instead of the dangerous edge of his hand. I felt the pain and recoiled, grunting badly.

Coiling my arm, I straightened it and flicked it out like a whip again. Stabbing at a pressure point using my knuckles, my opponent cat-footed backward his arm hanging limp, working his fingers slowly trying to bring life into the nerves. I didn't wait, I went in fast.

By this time, I had no idea of how or who I was fighting. All I knew was I was fighting someone, someone who I needed to defeat. The man opposite me was backing away trying desperately to get his good side towards me. He was a good fighter and when good fighters are handicapped, they go small and act defensively seeking an opportunity to expand and lash out. In his case, he presented me with two small targets his broad shoulder and his right side. Why? Well his shoulder had no disenabled pressure points for maximum injury and his good right arm was his most powerful weapon. On some level, I knew this but did not care. An exceedingly small percentage of my awareness was visible as I went all-out on the man before me. My thoughts and emotions about everything else had been stripped away, all I was aware now was the fury of winning the battle before me.

My opponent still backing up kept his good side towards me, presenting me with a small target, suddenly he faltered. His knees collapsing slightly under him. I was beside him, slightly above him and much too close for comfort when I struck with my lead fist. My blow missed by fractions, grazing his shoulder. Suddenly his left arm still hanging limply in partial paralysis came alive. His elbow hit me solidly, high again on the side of my neck, just below my earlobe.

Fling myself sideways partly by the force of the blow and partly by my own effort to ride the blow I crashed into the dojo. For an instant I lay crumbled almost boneless, then rolling fast I rose to my feet.

I was facing him again as before slightly crouched in a ready position stepping lightly on the balls of my feet, when I heard a voice. A voice of someone calling my name. I ignored it and continued circling, my hands poised to strike, edging closer to him. I heard my name being repeated and shook my head.

Who was calling me? Why was someone calling me? My eyes darted left and right searching before awareness, faintly came to me.

I blinked twice and saw Seymour snapping his fingers, standing far back in a defensive position ready to defend himself against me. I didn't know how it happened, but I instant broke out of the trance I was under and recognised the target in front of me again. Seymour was still poised to act defensively and was speaking.

He was calling my name telling me to snap out of it He wasn't the only one. Nadia was yelling that I stop and wake up.
I stopped and took a long look at him.
'Seymour?'
'Yes, yes it's me and Nadia' he announced letting out a sigh of relaxed tension.
I turned to look at Nadia. She was breathing a sigh of relief at my actions. Sir Steele beside her had a strange look on his face. A face that seemed to be saying it was seeing something spectacular for the first time.
The power and energy I felt bubbling to the surface at once escaped through all my pores and I felt my body go limp. I swayed slightly, my legs buckling under my own weight as I fell to my knees 'Seymour?' I whispered again. I repeated his name again softly looking about me. At first not recognising where I was.
He came forward and put his arm around me 'Yes mistress, you're ok'
With my head falling sideways on his shoulder, comprehension came to me. 'How'd I do?' I asked
'Fine Susan just fine'
'Good. So, I'm good?' I asked weakly
'No' he said working the nerves of fingers on his left hand
That's what I liked about having Seymour's undiluted assessment, his complete honesty.
'No?'
'No, but Kiyitsu will be proud'
I grinned as he escorted me towards the changing cubicle.
Twenty minutes later I joined Sir Steele and Nadia on the veranda of my penthouse wearing black slacks and shirt and slippers. My hair was flowing loose down my shoulders.
Nadia continued playing on her console, while Sir C was reading the Times newspaper.
When I neared them Sir Steele looked up at me 'That was truly unreal. Hugely impressive'
'Glad you appreciate it' said Seymour as he stepped down into the room carrying a tray. On it was a bowl of cereal, a saucer of toasts with a butter cup, a pitcher of pulp orange juice and a cup of coffee. Seymour's

tone suggested he was to a certain degree displeased that Sir C saw that display of ours. He placed the tray beside me on the lounge chair.

'How far do you both go?' the Intelligence Chief asked both of us.

A glanced passed between me and Seymour, our communication over the years was such that it was finely honed to understand each other's intention or reactions.

'We have to make it as real as it can be because in the field there are no second chances, but we don't let it get that far' I said buttering a toast and pouring some juice in a glass.

'It looked pretty far'

'Maybe, but we have failsafe's Seymour said to Sir Steele who was beaming ear to ear.

Seymour straightened up and faced Sir Steele 'You look pleased with yourself'

'Yes, well apart from having minor cardiac events just now, I can now see how she bested the greatest combat fighter in the world' he said like a proud uncle.

'I had a bit of luck' I contended

'Nevertheless you defeated the Sin Eater, a task not one person could claim they have done'

'Should I take a bow?' I asked

'No, because my guys are still furious you destroyed a certain "The A-tome" gadget. Though, you wouldn't believe the report I received this morning about a certain Kavin Chandra'

'And that would be?'

'He has an offer for us'

'What kind of offer and why you? Any good tech company could offer him more' Seymour said

'I don't know but he won't be enticed by anybody but the woman who brought down the criminal Brahma' Sir Steele said.

'Come again?' Seymour solicited.

'Nadya, get your head out of that game and come eat something' I said to Nadia interrupting both men.

She looked up at me 'I'm not hungry'

'Of course, you're not hungry, you've been playing all morning'

She groaned and buried her head back into the game console. I started buttering another toast. When I was done, I poured some juice into a glass, walked up to her, relieved her of her games console and shoved both items in-between her fingers. She groaned once then took a bite from the toast and then a sip from the glass.

'Eat' I said to her 'And don't forget to take your medications' I reminded her. She grumbled a yes reply as both men continued to argue 'Galahad remind her to take her medicine, at ten-minute intervals' I requested of my Interactive smart house.

'*Yes miss*' responded the automated voice of Galahad.

'Why does he want to meet her?'

'A condition to negotiate a deal with us, I suppose'

'And you're asking her that now? I'm sometimes baffled by your tact and timing'

'Oh, please Mr Krakauer don't be like that, I still resent you for not backing her up'

'Sorry Sir C but we have work stuff to take care of' I said taking the glass and pills Seymour was handing me. 'I can't go rushing off to China just …'

'No no that's a misinformation … he's in Switzerland'

'Switzerland huh'

'Yes'

'Well forget it. She's not fit yet to go running around in Switzerland after some Indian scientist who thinks he's a special kind of genius'

'Huzzah' I yelled complimenting Seymour

'Susan please' pleaded Sir C.

'Remember you saying you wished I curb some of my desires. Well this is me curbing one of them'

'Damn me and my b…' Just then his mobile phone began to ring 'Yes … what … confirmed … yes … when … alright … normal protocols to be applied' he said into his mobile before hanging up.

'It's a moot point now. Kavin Chandra was involved in a traffic accident a couple of hours ago. He died from some serious blunt force trauma'

'Sorry to hear that' I said

Seymour also made his apologies to him.

Sir Steele turned to me and said 'Anyway I'm very relieved, we don't think much about consequences, I'm sure that recreating that box would have created more problems than required' he paused in-between his sip of coffee to gaze upon me 'I'm glad it doesn't exist but it's only a matter of time before someone somewhere recreates it. But for the moment I'm simply happy you're all right Susan'
'Ah look Seymour, Sir C is concerned about me' I said smiling at him. I was genuinely pleased to feel such nervousness from him spouted in my direction.
'Well … em …' he seemed uncomfortable.
'How sweet' Seymour said ironically
'There was one thing I would wish I had seen' Sir C pondered.
'You don't need to say it' Seymour said disenchantedly.
'Yes. Her confrontation with Sigrid'
Sir C said, turning to Seymour he asked, 'Don't you wish you would have seen that?'
'Yes but …' he left the sentence unfinished glancing at me. 'It would have been a sight to behold' he added.
'The way Mahatma describes it … I would say it was more and going from what I just witnessed, he wasn't exaggerating'
I interrupted their thoughts, changing the subject 'About Briggs, make sure he is compensated well Sir C'
Steele glanced at Seymour before addressing me 'You don't have to worry about him'
'If that's settled Sir C, you staying for lunch? I'm cooking'
'Now who could say no to that' replied the Intelligence Chief smiling.

**The End.**

# ABOUT THE AUTHOR

Stevenson Mukoro was born in Lewisham, London, on June 26, and grew up in the middle -class suburb of Ughelli. The son of Samuel and Rose Mukoro grew up with two older siblings Macdonald and Regina and five younger siblings, Ovie Freeborn, Susan, Tina, Gloria and Kingsley. From an early age, he wanted to be a professional pilot because he often envisioned the beautiness of the world from the air.

In high school, however, he developed two other passions that would define his career: A chance encounter with Peter O'Donnell and a prank, resulting in crashing the principal's car. Crashing the car resulted in an injury that put paid to his piloting career. That and the death of three of his siblings -Gloria, Ovie and Susan – has inspired him to write stories with a host of characters and long tenses.

Stevenson first came to the attention of British readers when he won two consecutive young poetry awards for excellence. Today he is slowly becoming one of England's acclaimed vivid adventure writers, and communicates to his readers a deep interest in back stage criminal theories. Disagreeing with the established order that espionage anecdotes are on a decline, he believes that the spying game has become too established or commercialised to be over and that there is "much more to spying than is normally acknowledged".

He has degrees in Business Computing and Administration but prefers the task of writing instead of a demanding mundane 9 to 5 business office hours. After the July 07 bombings in London, Stevenson wrote many articles about war, terrorism, and the clash of democratic western societies with fundamentalist Muslim ones.

A reporter once wrote, "His clarity of vision on the local impact of terrorist threat is alarming". He adds, "Terrorism is terrible business and at times it could rejuvenate a society, but more often than not, it destroys".

Stevenson is avid enthusiast of unknown heroes whose contributions are hidden in the annals of secret documents or power hungry officials. He believes his heroes should have Communion with tea in the morning, shoot a villain in the head during lunch, and still be able to read a bedtime story in the evening to a loved one. Similar views which one of his fictional heroines, Susan Dax expresses.

His fictional books are expressively imaginative. Stevenson says, "I've always been a big fan of Lara Croft and Jane Doe depictions. I figured it was time for a new heroine to take the stage and convey our minds off the near ugliness of the world. Enter Susan Dax, a girl lacking nothing, needing nothing, but doing her utmost to do anything in order to create the peace and punish the evil doers. Such passion is hard to come by"

He writes his bestselling adventure tales in a cottage overlooking the foothills of Bridlington, Yorkshire.

Steven is the 2010 recipient of The Book Foundation Medal for Distinguished Letters.

For more information about his books, visit Xlibris.co.uk / com or Amazon.com